THE SHINING CITY

By
RENA M. VALE

ARMCHAIR FICTION
PO Box 4369, Medford, Oregon   97501-0168

A DEADLY CONFLICT BETWEEN SCIENCE AND NATURE...

Thor Larsen was an outsider—a "Northerner." But he had left the wilds of the northern wilderness for a life dedicated to the greatest engineering feat of the modern age—the building of The Shining City, which was now a super-metropolis ruled by a cold scientific government. However, in spite of his staggering successes, Thor Larsen's heart was heavy with the suspicion that his own son was a traitor to the city—but heavier still was the feeling that Thor himself had betrayed something even greater!
Soon a war was brewing between the raw forces of nature and the technological power of hard, emotionless science.

FOR A COMPLETE SECOND NOVEL, TURN TO PAGE 75

CAST OF CHARACTERS

THOR LARSEN
The genius from the outside—the man behind the construction of the Shining City. But he was both genius and tortured soul.

MARSHAL ZACHARY
He could deal out ruthless executions when necessary, yet this smooth-talking head of the Police was the only friend Thor had.

DR. GNURIN
The leading scientist of the Shining City. He looked like a walking skeleton, was shrill as a banshee, and hated by all.

LEONARD LARSEN
As the son of the Shining City's most famous citizen, much was expected of him—until accusations of treachery fell upon him.

ANISSE LARSEN
Beauty is a wonderful thing, but even a cold statue can be beautiful—and this beautiful woman was very, very cold.

CAPTAIN SEARS
He had the grim task of hunting down a fugitive he had once called friend. Could his loyalty be trusted to get the job done?

IRENKA
Thor's former wife was a "Northerner." She was a woman of the forest—and as free as the wind.

CHAPTER ONE

"LEONARD is gone."

Thor Larsen did not turn from the tele-screen, on which a depiction of a javelin-throwing contest between two teams of Northerners was in progress in a field near the Argonne Pit. The challenging team was from Superior City, and Thor strained to see if any members were familiar to him. Then he noticed the faint image of Anisse behind him reflecting off the screen, and the Northerners were forgotten. It was the year all women of official rank had been ordered to wear red, and her costume was the same shade as that of the flames that stained the sky above the Pit—women called it "Exciting Red." Thor found himself reacting in the manner the Social Engineers had planned, though he hesitated a few centi-seconds before acknowledging the presence of the woman. She tossed her head in impatience, and the artificial yellow of her hair swirled above the flame of her dress as though her image-fire had been freshly fed. It was then that Thor became aware of the fact that she had said something about his son.

"Leonard?" he asked without turning.

The yellow cascade quieted as she stepped into the room. "Leonard is not in his quarters; his belongings are gone." She flung the words like a handful of hailstones at the hunched figure on the bench.

Thor cut the control of the screen and turned to face the woman. He was a large man of fifty or more, and he moved with sure deliberation. "Why should that alarm you, my cherished one?" He spoke with soothing tenderness. "Perhaps there is some reason why he should be in Paris ahead of us."

Anisse strode quickly across the room and seated herself on the bench beside Thor. It was the only seat in the room; in fact, the bench was the only piece of furniture in the room, though the walls were lined with communication cabinets, control boards, screens, charts and other apparatus necessary for the executive work of the President of the City Board. She tilted her face up to Thor's and forced a smile. "I thought it best that you hear it from me before the Eye Squad issues a call. I'm afraid—"

Thor embraced the woman clumsily. "There is nothing to fear, my little Anisse, my lovely Anisse. Leonard is capable of looking after himself."

She drew away from him, a look of mingled perplexity and cruelty written in the wrinkles around her eyes and mouth. She was a small, spare woman, about forty, with lingering traces of a beauty that had been hard and glittering. However, the adoration in Thor's face showed that he saw in her only the reflection of his desire. "They were here looking for him."

Thor waved her statement aside. "Leonard has an important part in the celebration tomorrow; he is to receive the scepter of Honored Scientist for his accomplishments in research on ancient chemical processes. Gnurin himself recommended it to the Board."

"Leonard cared nothing about the scepter."

"Cared nothing about the scepter?" Thor stared at his mate in astonishment. "Why, he will be the only scientist born outside the Band ever to receive it—the only one from the Shining City to get it tomorrow. It's an honor second only to the one they will bestow on me! Whatever gave you the impression he doesn't care about it?"

"Something he said yesterday."

"Oh, Leonard is a little obscure at times—he's been so much engrossed in matters of the past. You know you've never understood the boy."

"I couldn't fail to understand him this time. I met him in the corridor when I was on my way to the reconditioning salon, and, being pleasant, I asked him if he was excited about the Paris celebration. He said, in that way he has of tipping his head and looking way off into another time, 'Celebrations and honors are falsifications for future history.'"

THOR LAUGHED, an easy, fun laugh. "He was only trying to hide his eagerness. He'll be there tomorrow, and excited as any of us. There has undoubtedly been a change in his travel plans. So many are going from the Shining City, it's easy to understand how confusion can develop. It's to be expected." He rose and paced the great width of the room. As he spoke, his tone deepened and the blue of his eyes became darker with intensity. "You must realize, my dearest one, that ours is a time of flux—everything is changing with great rapidity. Why, twenty years ago—when I gave my allegiance to the world of science—Sun Conversion was not even used for travel. A heavy load of fuel was needed to propel a sky car from one city of the Band to another. Tomorrow we will go forth from the Shining City in a car that is propelled through space by an envelope of magnetic fog, and in two turns of the telechron we'll be in Paris!" He looked at the woman as though surprised to find an audience of only one. The realization brought him back to the subject they had been discussing. "Probably Leonard is already there."

"Your son is not in Paris, Thor of the genetic rating Two-Two."

The voice came from the tri-dimensional communication cabinet, and Thor whirled to face the smile of Doctor Gnurin, One-One-Seven. The head appeared to be little more than a skull.

"Gnurin!" Thor exclaimed. "I didn't hear your signal."

"I bypassed the signal in order to have an informal chat with you. I believe you will agree with me that it is better for our conversation not to be recorded by an Eye Squad spool."

"What is this about Leonard?" The muscles of Thor's face tightened, and it was an expressionless mask he presented to Gnurin.

"A little irregularity."

"Perhaps Marshal Zachary changed his transportation plans. Our official sky car will be fairly well filled—all the Board members are taking their mates, you know, and there are the heads of delegations…"

Gnurin cut into Thor's speech. "'Marshal Zachary is with me. He changed no plans."

"Then perhaps—" Thor groped for words. He looked helplessly at Anisse, but she supplied nothing.

The skull continued speaking, "Leonard One-Two-Two was to have reported to me at the hour of thirteen today, and when he had not appeared by another turn of the telechron I called on the Eye Squad to investigate. He was not in his laboratory; he was not in his quarters. In fact, he was not in the City. The Eye Squad captain reported that he had taken all the charts on sulfuric acid as well as many other secret documents from the laboratory files last night. This morning—and this is even more grave—he requested a hovering car from the transportation office; he has used it frequently on journeys to excavations, and in the present confusion the transportation office failed to check his authority. It appears that his plan was well thought out."

"Oh, I'm sure—" Thor fumbled, and, catching a look from Gnurin, changed his approach. "How did he set the gear lock?"

"He didn't use the gear lock, which means he didn't set out for a locked destination. All that is known is that he went in a westerly direction."

"Westerly?" Thor repeated in an effort to gather his faculties.

"The Argonne Pit!" Anisse exclaimed.

Thor shot a reproving glance at her. "I can't regard this as serious—a research problem that absorbed him, made him careless about formalities… Perhaps we had better discuss this in private, Gnurin."

Anisse rose from the bench and swayed toward the entrance, her short belted garment cupping to the curves of her body. "I must prepare for my stay in Paris."

"There may be a change in plans." Thor's eyes followed her hungrily.

"If the official sky car goes to Paris, I go. It has been overlong since I visited my home, and I'm looking forward to it." The door slid shut behind her.

"But," Thor stammered, speaking to her retreating figure, "if I don't go to Paris there'll be no celebration!"

Gnurin laughed, a harsh and grating sound that was almost metallic. "The ceremonies in Paris are being held for the purpose of celebrating the success of the experimental Unvalator and Invalator. That you employed those devices in constructing the City doesn't necessarily mean the honors go to you! Great scientists of the Band do not confuse deeds and personalities, Thor."

"I understand, Gnurin. It was just that I thought it might take a little time to change program plans. However, if they can be changed as easily as you imply, the celebration can proceed without Leonard, if need be."

"It will." A smile that was like the gash of a saber cut across the face in the cabinet. "However, there are matters for the Board to act upon."

"I will come at once to your laboratory." Thor closed the control of the cabinet and watched Doctor Gnurin's features fade.

*   *   *

HE PAUSED at the door to Anisse's room but did not enter. She had never liked Leonard, and Thor assumed it was because his son represented a link to the life she had not shared with him. For that reason he had not consulted her on matters pertaining to Leonard. As his mate she had counseled him on every other decision he had made for the past fifteen years; often she had prepared the speeches he had made in meetings. He was only a superintendent of construction—a mere overseer of denizen laborers—when he met her in a relaxing parlor in Paris, where he had gone to attend a conference on scientific city construction. She poured wine for him and told him he could be "ruler of the world." He had returned to the Shining City with a new, mate and a new ambition. Anisse had pushed him upward to the highest position in the Shining City, that of President of the City Board.

Without her—

He could not bring himself to finish the thought, and his hand trembled as he passed it through the beam that controlled the outer door to his apartment.

It was spring and he felt the need for outdoor air. He took a sun mask from a wall niche beside his door and swung it in his hand as he strode down the long, gleaming corridor.

Glasteel.

Proudly he thumped the wall. Every building in the Shining City was constructed throughout of glasteel, a product he had helped to develop. Doctor Gnurin One-One-Seven spoke of the silicones of the ancients, of polymerization, isomerization and ion exchange; but Thor, the builder, made no effort to understand these technicalities. He asked only for a material that could be molded to shape, that had high tensile strength, resiliency, and, for the purpose of Sun Conversion, high reflective qualities. Glasteel was the answer, and Thor had driven the swarms of denizens in his building crews to construct a city of the gleaming alloy. All other cities in the scientific Band had adopted it, and two continents were now dotted with shimmering citadels. The Siberian Outpost, Moscow, Prague, Paris, London, New York, Cleveland, Chicago, Kansas City and Los Angeles—all were phoenix-cities that had risen from the ashes of a ruined world and banded together to share their scientific knowledge. Now they were all monuments to Thor Larsen, the builder, who had been born a Northerner. To-morrow in Paris— But first he must clear up the difficulty about his son.

Thor slipped the sun mask over his face and emerged into the dazzling brilliance of the Boulevard. The rays of the sun were multiplied a thousand fold by the reflective surfaces of the hundred-story buildings that lined the west side of the

Boulevard; they splintered upward from the Boulevard floor into the graduated discs of the Sun Converters. Heat was intense along the buildings, but Thor didn't mind it. A refreshing wind blew off the lake, to the east, and he filled his lungs with the moisture-laden air. He gripped the rail of the walk for guidance and glanced up at the tiers of Sun Converters. It reassured him to see those slowly turning discs drawing the magnified sunlight into power-shafts. Power was feeding into the dynamos of the Shining City, and so long as that power continued to feed in and flow out to the apparatus of Science, the Shining City would stand.

Yet the counter-current in Thor's mind ran toward a lake of fear. Was it possible that his son—the son who had grown up under his guidance and whose thoughts he believed he had shared—had not completely accepted the authority of the Band? Did he retain a secret allegiance to the backward-looking people of the Northland? Thor knew that Leonard had never given up the hope of reuniting his parents, although he knew that his mother would never leave Superior City.

She, who had been Thor's mate, loved the customs of the Northland—the forests and the freedom of them—too much. One of Thor's clearest memories was that of Irenka standing on a mountaintop above an iron ore pit, hair flying loose in the wind and muscular arms folded across the lacing of her tight leather bodice. Her eyes, as purple as the wood violets at her feet, pulled to slits and her strong chin lifted as she looked out over the forest that stretched like green fur into the northern horizon. "My home," she said, speaking as much to the wind as to the man at her side. "It is part of me, and I am part of it. My son, who will be born in the deep of winter, will be a man of the forest."

That was the first that Thor had known of Leonard's coming. Once life had taken root inside her, Irenka had no further need for him until after the period of the infant's suckling, when the ice in her veins had again turned to steam.

The oldest had been a girl, somewhat of a disappointment to Thor; the second, Irenka pronounced, would be a boy. It was, and they named him Leonard. The birth of his son gave him new hope, and he built more sawmills and more houses from the product of the mills. There were other children, six more girls, but it was the boy in whom he centered his parental pride.

THOR HAD contributed much toward progress in Superior City. The dream of building had come to him when he was twelve. One winter day, while he fished through a hole in the ice of the lake, he looked at the helter-skelter of mud-smeared log huts in which his people had lived ever since the destruction of the Great Civilization over two hundred years before. He thought of the tales he had heard of the great city to the south where men of science were unlocking the secrets of the past. The big city needed food for the many thousands of people who were flocking there to work. The Northerners, spread out over forest clearings and valleys and prairies around the lakes, could produce food in abundance. They had boats that could sail the lakes. Why could not the Northerners exchange their surplus food for big saws and tools like those that were found in the mounds of ruined cities? The scientific city could produce such things with ease.

He got people to listen to him and to help him; and even though he was not grown to the size of a man, he went on the first trading boat to Chicago. He talked to men in laboratories, showed them the rusted and broken things from the ruined world. At length his plan was accepted by the men in the laboratories. The home that Thor built for Irenka before they took their wedding vows was made of lumber from the first sawmill in the Northland for over two hundred years. With that thought Thor wanted to forge ahead; but Irenka clung to the old ways, the superstitions and the ceremonies that had held the Northerners to primitive existence. Too many people agreed with her, and Thor found himself pulling against her influence. He began to prolong his stays in Chicago when he went there on trading trips. Frequently he took Leonard with him, and when the boy was ten Thor arranged to place him in school there.

Since all trade was carried on by barter, the transaction was involved; Thor had never thought it wise to inform Leonard of the price of the schooling. The majority of outlanders who presented themselves to the city entered a life of virtual slavery. They agreed to perform tasks assigned to them in return for food, raiment, shelter and "planned recreation." They were trained only for the menial tasks and driven until they fell from illness or fatigue. But the lot of the "denizens" was preferable to the sketchy, animal-like existence in the camps of the Wanderers, from whence most of them came. The Northerners seldom surrendered to this slavery. However, the Social Engineers of the city desired the more robust and healthy-minded Northerners to the weak-willed, unreliable and disease-ridden types that came from the Wanderers.

Thor agreed to supply Northerner labor for gigantic construction projects under way in the city in return for his son's education.

Two years later the Scientists requested him to oversee this crew, and he accepted. Irenka had refused to come with him; when he insisted on going ahead with his plan, she declared their union at an end. At that time Leonard had chosen to remain with his father—not because he was fonder of Thor than his mother, but with the apparent hope of bringing his mother to the city.

At the entrance to the building that housed the laboratory of Doctor Gnurin One-One-Seven, Thor paused and looked out over the sun-sparkled blue of Lake Michigan. Twenty years he had been away from the Northland, and each year the social gap between the city dwellers and the Northerners had become wider. His former people had remained much as they were when he was a boy—worshipping idols, tilting with javelins, even though they lived in houses of sawed lumber. And in that twenty years, Chicago had become the Shining City of sun conversion. Thor had risen to President or the City Board, and Leonard had become an Honored Scientist—that is, he would be an Honored Scientist if his difficulty could be straightened out in time for him to go to Paris to accept the scepter. They had chosen well, Thor decided.

Or had Leonard really chosen the Shining City? At thirty-three he was still adolescent in many ways. Thor realized that in spite of scientific training, his son was emotionally undeveloped. For one thing, he was a perfectionist—an idealist who was intolerant of reality.

Gray-garbed dial operators in the control room of the Citadel of Science glanced up with furtive adoration as Thor strode through on his way to the private elevator. He was the only member of the Board who had come from the world outside the Band; the denizens regarded him as their representative in the ruling body. He curried that favor, and never forgot to bestow a nod or a smile on those he recognized. Even now, with worries pressing him, he paused several times to call out the greeting, "Fair day," to the ones who looked up expectantly.

CHAPTER TWO

IN THE glittering vault that was the private laboratory of Gnurin One-One-Seven Thor found the diminutive scientist and Marshal Romain Zachary of the Band Police, their heads almost touching over a black light tank.

"We have been waiting for you." Gnurin's voice reminded Thor of metal grating on metal; the little scientist stood drawn almost backward in straight erectness, and his chin was thrust upward so that his back-heavy cranium rested on the collar of his smock. "Why didn't you come on the belt?"

Quickly Thor snatched off the sun mask he had forgotten to remove when he entered the building; he twisted it nervously in his hands as he approached the two waiting men.

"The mask is not what informed us that you were walking in the sun," Marshal Zachary said with a toothy smile. He, too, was a man of small stature, though the line of his graying blue-black hair was a little higher than the top of Doctor Gnurin's sparsely covered skull. Beside the other man's skeleton-like ugliness, the marshal of the Band Police was plumply pleasing to the eye. He filled his bright blue uniform with a bulge here and there, but he moved with a fluid grace and there was warmth in his wide smile and mischief without malice in his dark, flashing eyes.

"We watched you in the tank," Gnurin put ill. "It is a new police invention. Operates radionically. Can tune in and watch anyone whose vibratory pattern is known. See, here is Elmer One-Eight-One. He was in the shower stall a few centi-minutes ago; now he is plucking hairs out of his nose."

Zachary's laugh rippled out and he cut the control. "It would be much more interesting to watch a charming woman in her bath. We must have some vibratory charts made of the ladies!"

"You are not serious, Marshal!" The metallic rasp of Gnurin's voice made Thor shudder.

"Never more serious." The Marshal winked at Thor.

"Now to the business at hand." Gnurin sank nimbly to the floor and sat cross-legged. He would not permit benches to be installed in his laboratory, and commanded everyone who came into his presence to sit on the floor.

With some difficulty Thor seated himself on the floor and sat with his knees thrust outward like great knobs. Zachary remained standing.

"Now about Leonard One-Two-Two," Gnurin began.

"Nothing of intent is established yet," Zachary cut in. "We of the Eye Squad do not regard his actions as anything serious, and we feel certain, my dear Thor, that you can save the situation. It is only that—"

"He has disobeyed the rules of the Band. The City Board must denounce him as a traitor. That is the only possible interpretation."

"It is not up to you to interpret anyone's actions, my dear Doctor Gnurin," Zachary purred. "As head of the Research Coordinating Board you will concern yourself with research."

"I am responsible for the behavior of research scientists, and Leonard One-Two-Two has far exceeded mere willful disobedience."

"Very well, that is your report, and the City Board must reach its own decision. Leonard Larsen—I cannot get used to these genetic rating names—has taken leave without obtaining permission; and certain formulas, and other files, are missing. It is our assumption—based on the findings of the Eye Squad—that he has taken them to the Argonne Pit to turn over to the Northerners. According to our present intelligence, this group of Northerners may be able to use the information to some advantage."

"I do not understand why this encampment of pariahs has been allowed to remain at the Pit, or what they are doing there," Doctor Gnurin said.

"It's a kind of religious rite," Thor explained. "They think the Pit is the door to Hell, and they make pilgrimages of penance to it."

GNURIN snorted. "Humph! There might be other activity there! We must not forget that ten years ago the glasteel plant at Gary was destroyed by guided bombs of a crude design, though most of them didn't get through."

"You don't have to go back to ten year-old bombings at Gary, Doctor. We had explosions in Paris ten days ago; only last year, one-third of London was wrecked. Prague has been blown out of the Band, twice, in the past twenty-five years. So long as information on the Old World's explosives is available, people will use it. What is more, they will use it against the Band, because the Band rules all the world that is worth ruling."

He smiled broadly and gestured with both hands as much as to say, *That is what makes life exciting.*

"But this is not information of a military nature that Leonard has apparently taken." Thor's mind had wrapped itself around a thought and he could not leave it.

"*Any* scientific knowledge is military information," Gnurin snapped.

"We are not at war with the Northerners," Thor continued. "I don't see how—"

"You are not supposed to 'see how', Thor of the genetic rating Two-Two. Even though you are President of the City Board, you are merely Coordinator of Construction. You're not called on to exercise powers of scientific, social or political deduction!" Gnurin quivered with rising anger.

Thor prepared to defend himself, but before he could speak, Marshal Zachary cut in. "Recrimination does not settle an argument, Doctor Gnurin, and argument does not solve a problem." His eyes flashed a warning, and the little man withdrew into a sulky silence. "Before we call a meeting of the City Board," he went on, speaking to Thor, "I think you should know of some of the Eye Squad findings."

A frown of apprehension formed on Thor's face, but he erased it quickly. "If there are Eye Squad reports on my son, why hasn't Elmer informed me? He is Coordinator of Eye Squad work for the Shining City."

Zachary framed his reply carefully. "On occasions, Thor, when affairs of the Band are involved, a few formalities of procedure are dispensed with. Since I happened to be on the scene, it was only natural that the local Eye Squad Officers in possession of highly confidential information should give it to a marshal of the Band Police."

"They knew that Elmer One-Eight-One is on Thor's belt," Gnurin snapped. "They knew the traitor would not be exposed if those two handled the matter in secret."

"Let us remain objective." Zachary's warning to Gnurin was more emphatic than the last. "Only a few centi-minutes ago—

when I was on my way to Doctor Gnurin's laboratory to be exact—a Captain of the Eye Squad handed me a spool which was made by our counter-espionage agent in the encampment of the Northerners at the Argonne Pit." He opened a portfolio and took out the small cylinder. "I have not yet had an opportunity to play it, and therefore I do not know if it incriminates or clears Leonard."

Gnurin bounced on his haunches. "If you had informed me you had it, we could have played it while we were waiting for Thor instead of dallying with this police toy!"

Zachary grinned broadly and gestured with his outspread hands. "What do our Social Engineers say about pleasurable dalliance?" He slipped the spool on a spindle on the wall and opened the control. "Our agent was able to get only part of the speeches, but I believe the meaning is clear. That is what the Eye Squad Captain informed me."

A MAN'S VOICE, which was not Leonard's, came forth. *"What did we gain by dealing with the Shining City? We trade the summer's toil to a whole village for a circular saw, and many times in the bargain we give our women—our fairest women—to those sterile creatures who call themselves scientists..."*

"Sterile?" Zachary arched an eyebrow. "My wife is giving birth to our tenth child!"

"I say," the recorded speech continued, *"let's do without saws and live in log houses, like our fathers did, and their fathers before them!"*

"And keep our women for ourselves!" another man shouted.

"Let's have none of this science stuff. I'm not saying that Leonard Larsen don't mean well by us; but we been tricked so many times. We ought to be leery. How do we know this isn't just another trick aimed to do us in, or to sell us into slavery? Our spies report that Leonard is supposed to go to Paris tomorrow to get some kind of honors..."

Another voice, a resonant voice with laughter in it, cut in at this point. *"Honors within the Band are but the corn on which we are fattened for the moral slaughter!"*

"Leonard!" Thor exclaimed, the grayness of sorrow spreading over his face.

Zachary cut the control. "I believe our case is clear."

"Quite clear." Thor's eyes were curtained with sagging flesh and his mouth was a straight, hard line.

Gnurin bounded to his feet. "We can send out a hovering car carrying the Unvalator to wipe out the entire camp at the Pit."

"And when the word of this wanton destruction reaches your denizens, who will be left to perform your menial tasks?" Zachary asked. "Experience has shown we only create difficulties when we use the methods of the ancients; somebody always escapes, then we have vengeance to deal with. Most troublesome."

"Who are you to moralize?" Gnurin demanded. "You, who have incinerated whole towns as a disciplinary measure! You, who had liquid fire poured on fleeing mobs. You put poison in rivers, sowed disease germs over two continents! And you tell us to spare a handful of enemies at our gate!"

"What better way to learn?" Zachary spread his hands, palms upward.

Thor shuddered. He had heard rumors of warfare, more hideous than that of the ancients, which had raged among cities of science before he came to the Shining City; but nothing concerning it had been recorded on history spools.

"Furthermore," Zachary picked up the thread of his argument, "the Unvalator is a device designed for construction. If we use it as a weapon of warfare, is it not possible that denizens in the construction crews might not revolt, seize it and turn it against us? Let us put not the means of our own destruction in the hands of possible enemies, or we ourselves may be reduced to cosmic ash."

"The denizens have a deep sense of justice," Thor added.

"Ah, I have it!" Gnurin rocked on the balls of his feet. "Thor will volunteer to find his son and bring him back for trial!"

"Is that not the duty of the Eye Squad?"

Zachary placed a hand on Thor's shoulder. "I believe the doctor has a point there. We must deal with these matters legally—give Leonard an opportunity to defend his actions before the Board."

"If such a trial should take place," Gnurin smacked his lipless mouth, "Thor would have to yield his seat—temporarily, of course."

"Of course." Zachary's sarcasm was lost on the other.

Thor strode to a cabinet and pushed three buttons simultaneously to call other members of the Board to the meeting room.

IN ADDITION to the Building and Research seats on the Board, there were Security, filled by Elmer One-Eight-One; Social, by Juno Sixty-Seven, a tall, angular woman of unfeminine appearance, and Economic, by a round, bald little man who wore correction lenses over his eyeballs. For a reason no one could ascertain he had chosen the name of Doctor Vivian, and he refused to allow use of his genetic rating in connection with his name. It was his duty to supervise the production and acquisition of foodstuffs for the city; he maintained laboratories that were separate from those of Gnurin.

As they filed into the Board Room, the members—other than Thor and Gnurin—were under the impression the meeting had been called for the purpose of making last minute preparations for the journey to Paris; for a few centi-minutes, while Thor prepared his announcement, Zachary answered questions about transportation arrangements.

In accordance with custom, the Board meeting was to be carried on a "compulsion" channel; that is, it would appear on all tele-screens in the City, and all denizens not engaged in the operation of vital public utility dials were compelled to watch them. It was taught in all schools—from kindergartens to Specialty Colleges—that the governments of all cities within the

Band were "democratic" since it was forbidden to argue the meaning or words everyone accepted this myth.

Thor caught sight of his reflection in the testing mirror beside the reception disc. His face was ashen, and a wisp of graying blond hair stood out like a horn over one ear. He smoothed his hair, and on the pretext of clearing his throat behind his hand, he moistened his lips and bit some color back into them. Whenever he stood before a reception disc, he appeared to grow in stature and his voice took on a resonance that was almost musical. He spoke caressingly, even if a little condescendingly, and his enunciation was careful so that the newest denizen might understand his words.

"The meeting will come to order," he announced. It was a command to all those who gathered before the tele-screens as much as to those in the BoardRoom. His eyes traveled from one face to another. Elmer resented Zachary's presence and he slouched in a sulky pout; Juno was preoccupied with the social theories she hoped to have an opportunity to propound in Paris the next day. As Thor's glance fell on Doctor Vivian he recalled something Leonard had said about him: "A mass of yeast; if you'd stir him, he'd bubble." Gnurin licked his lipless mouth in anticipation.

"A very serious matter has come up, and at a most inopportune time," Thor began. "I know all of you of the Board are occupied with preparations for tomorrow's celebration; but I will have to ask you to give undivided attention to the problem before us. And let us approach it with complete objectivity, as true scientists. I well remember that statement of my esteemed predecessor with which he opened all Board meetings: *The Old World was wrecked by ten parts subjectivity and one part fissionable material.'* "

He paused dramatically, then with an apprehensive glance at Gnurin, he called on Zachary to give the security report.

The Marshal rose, bowed to Elmer and mumbled, "With your permission, sir." He then gave the facts as he had previously outlined them.

A stunned hush fell over the room, and Thor again took the disc. His voice was grave, though he showed no signs of emotion in his bearing. "Fellow Board Members, I regret to say that, because of this unfortunate occurrence, I cannot accompany you to Paris tomorrow; but I want the celebration to proceed as though nothing had happened. The honors I was to accept are, in fact, honors for the Building Department and the Shining City as a whole; the next in rank on the Board will accept them in my stead."

Doctor Gnurin made no effort to conceal his pleasure, but Thor held up his hand for silence. "I feel I can best serve my City and the Band by bringing this errant scientist, who happens to be my son, back to face trial. If Science is to triumph over superstition, ignorance and disorder, we must allow none of our cherished secrets to fall into the hands of people who do not accept our plan of life. Our justice must prevail; if my son has committed a crime against our society, he must be punished. It is my duty as a scientist of the Band and as a parent to bring him back to the Shining City. That is my proposal, is there any discussion?"

All members of the Board were on their feet, but Elmer was the first to reach the reception disc. "This is a simple matter for the Eye Squad, Mister President. I do not feel that Leonard's defection calls for more special attention than any other case. We have able counter-espionage agents among the Northerners, and it will be a simple matter to locate and apprehend the culprit."

"I disagree!" Juno bounded to the disc as though propelled by a spring mechanism. "We have here an example of parental subjectivity against which I have long campaigned. If we are to progress as a scientific nation we must put an end to family ties! Leonard One-Two-Two would not be a fugitive and a suspected traitor today if he had been trained scientifically. Our President's nobility comes a little late; punishment should be inflicted on father and son alike, for one is as guilty as the other..."

"Are we not being over-dramatic?" Doctor Vivian pushed up beside Juno. "The difference between our scientific civilization and others that have perished ignobly is that we can profit by our mistakes. Let us not waste time on recrimination or costly trials and executions, but let us go forward in a truly scientific manner. Our Eye Squad has certain lethal equipment with which to deal with traitors. Send a good man, or two, after this criminal, deal with him on the spot and end the matter there."

"You forget one thing!" It was Gnurin who spoke. "Research scientists and apprentices must be taught the sanctity of secrecy. If making an example of Leonard One-Two-Two seems costly from a purely economic standpoint, we must realize that the eventual social gains will more than justify the time and effort spent on a trial. I propose that Thor Two-Two's plan be accepted."

Thor's face was a mask as he called for a vote on the proposal.

"Concur!" All were in agreement.

"So ordered. Meeting adjourned." Thor closed the connection on the reception disc and walked rapidly from the room. He was not sure how much longer he could retain his composure.

CHAPTER THREE

MARSHAL Zachary overtook him in the corridor. "Splendid, my dear President, splendid!" he panted. "You were magnificent! Objective to the last!" Then, in answer to a sidelong glance of suspicion from Thor, he added, "I will go with you to your quarters to assist you in preparing for the expedition."

Thor wanted to be alone, but he realized that, under the circumstances, it was impossible. Not until he delivered his son for trial—or resolved the matter in some other manner—would he be free from Eye Squad surveillance.

He and Zachary rode a low-level belt through a strip that was called The Park, which was bright and fragrant with blooming fruit trees. Here the artificial spring sun shone warmly, and plants sprang to life in the prepared soil. Much of the food for the City was raised in the Parks, above which towered the glasteel buildings. Doctor Vivian continually harangued the agronomists and food chemists to speed up their food production experiments to a point where it would no longer be necessary for the Shining City to trade with outlanders for food-stuffs; so far, the goal had not been reached.

Thor was not thinking of food production, however. A shower of peach bloom petals from an overhanging branch fell on the belt, and the sight brought back to his mind another such ride through an indoor Park in spring—his first trip though the City with Leonard. The boy was only ten, and had just been accepted for schooling in the city that was then called Chicago. They clung together, each trying to conceal his fright, and gazed in wonder at blooming trees that were not native to the Northland. At length the boy had spoken. "Father, there are no birds."

"I guess there is no need for birds, my son," Thor remembered saying.

Whereupon the boy had added thoughtfully, "Perhaps the birds do not choose to live in this great cage."

Marshal Zachary spoke, bringing Thor back to the present. "You may rely on me to look after your charming Anisse in Paris."

"She will not go without me!" Thor blurted out.

"Oh, but she will, my dear Thor; arrangements have already been made to welcome her."

"They were also made to welcome me; the plans will have to be changed."

"It has been a long time since Anisse was in Paris. Surely you would not want to deprive her of the visit to her home city."

"It's hardly proper," Thor parried, remembering her last words to him.

"As you should well know by this time, my dear Thor, the world of Science does not adhere to the rigid standards of your Northland."

Thor decided there was a secret understanding of some sort between Zachary and Anisse, as he watched them during the Social Hour. It did not come out in anything they said, but in the glances they exchanged as they talked of the Cultural Decline in the Twentieth Century. That was the topic of the day chosen by the Social Engineer, whose discourse had already begun when Thor and Zachary reached the apartment. Thor had difficulty concentrating on "the manifestation of mechanical prisms in musical scores," and he was relieved when the ordeal came to an end.

ANISSE rose as soon as the tele-screen went blank. "I may not see you in the morning, Thor," she said, brushing her cheek against his in perfunctory caress. Her eyes evaded his. "Good rest, my dear."

He waited hungrily for a word of encouragement or sympathy on the expedition, but she spoke none. Instead she turned to Zachary with a smile that was warm and full of meaning. "I will see you in the official car, if not at the sky station, Marshal. Good rest."

Zachary bowed from the waist. "Good rest, Madame the President, and may health be yours on the morrow." When she had gone he turned to Thor. "I hope it won't disturb you if I remain with you tonight. Mere formality, you know."

"A pleasure, indeed," Thor responded coolly. "You may take Leonard's room; or, if you prefer, we will bring his pallet into my study."

"I'm afraid regulations require me to share your sleeping room with you."

Thor smiled at the marshal's tact in permitting himself to be watched.

"Women!" Zachary made conversation as he dialed Eye Squad headquarters. "We are drawn to them as a sky car to a gear lock, and yet it is good to be away from them at times. As soon as the Paris celebration is over tomorrow, so is my vacation from my wife. She has given birth again, as I believe I told you, and she will make life difficult for me if I do not attend the christening ceremony. A true daughter of old Syeria, my wife—fat, shrill-voiced, a tyrant in the harem, as ugly as all the sins of the world. You would be fascinated by her ugliness, Thor—one side of her face covered by a purple birth-blotch. But feminine, ah, how beautifully feminine! Soft limbs and yielding lips—what a woman, my wife!"

He completed the sentence after the face of the Control Guard appeared on the screen. The guard tried to suppress a smile, but Zachary winked at him mischievously. "At sixty-two I should settle down—no?"

The guard's stern face crackled with lines of laughter. "You called, Sir?" Any lingering loyalty to Thor that might have slowed the guard's hand at the controls was overcome by the marshal's ebullience.

"First, and most important, send my dinner...to Thor's apartment. Then, get me Transportation—and don't go away, I'll be wanting a lot of things."

Several times Thor felt that his dam of self-control would give way as he and Zachary worked out the details of his trip. He could not eat the food sticks that were delivered to his wall slot, and watched Zachary bite into them, feeling a touch of revulsion.

"What the Shining City needs is an expert on flavor," the marshal commented as he picked crumbs from a wrapper. "In Prague we have paprika; in Paris they use too much garlic flavor; London has its leeks; but the Shining City has nothing—nothing but tasteless and slimy gook."

"I believe Doctor Vivian is experimenting with flavors," Thor responded absently.

"So long as Vivian stays on the food vats, you'll have nothing but gook. A most unimaginative creature, but that is the curse of our scientific world—too little imagination, too little laughter! Why, stars above me, I seldom have anything to laugh at but my own jokes, and that gets tiresome."

Captain Renlow Sears was assigned to go with Thor on the search for Leonard, and Sears agreed to select an assistant. Elmer said that Sears had volunteered because he knew something of Leonard's habits. "Also," Elmer added in a tone he hoped would not carry to Thor, "Sears won't stand so much in awe of the President as other officers would. He had accompanied Leonard to his apartment on occasions and has seen the President in informal attire."

"Very good," Zachary pronounced, and directed his next call to the sky station storage room.

Thor would travel in a sun-battery-powered hovering car, similar to the one Leonard had taken. These cars were used for research expeditions outside the Band since they were small, light, and could execute landings and takeoffs on any terrain— although they were incapable of rising above the atmosphere or traveling faster than two hundred kilometers in a telechron turn. The only weapons requisitioned for the trip were small carbon ray guns with a few rounds of reload capsules.

"Squad regulations" Zachary explained as Thor protested. "Leonard will obey my command." Thor did not expect the marshal to believe him, in fact he did not believe it himself. But he could not let himself regard Leonard as hostile to the authority of the Band. "There must be some explanation," he went on, hardly aware that he had spoken.

Zachary smiled at him with something akin to sympathy. "We must get some sleep," he said, cutting all controls.

THOR'S CAR was scheduled to launch ahead of the official car for Paris, but when he and Zachary reached the sky station it was ablaze with red-gowned women. They all looked much alike as they fluttered around, talking in knots of three and four;

their combined voices reminded Thor of the cawing of crows in a field of freshly planted corn. Eagerly he looked for Anisse—there were twenty women who were stick-slender with a billow of artificial yellow hair falling over their shoulders. A profile that was like hers turned out to belong on another face; another woman moved with her quick grace, and a third affected the same nervous toss of the head. At last he saw her on the other side of the great room, but by the time he reached the spot she was gone.

"Captain Sears and his assistant have your car loaded," Zachary announced as he caught a signal from the station guard.

Thor turned with some relief to follow the marshal. Elmer One-Eight-One stood beside the car speaking to the Eye Squad Captain.

"You will not leave the car unguarded at any time. If the Northerners attempt to seize it, destroy it and make your way back as best you can. Remember, Captain Scars, you are in charge of the expedition." The marshal's eyes avoided Thor's.

Sears touched his cap in a salute and assisted Thor into the cabin. The assistant followed and took the seat beside Thor. Thor's eyes sought Zachary's for an explanation of the Captain's unprecedented authority, but already the rotor was whirring. As the hovering car rose upward on the launching platform Thor fancied he saw Zachary's smile following them. It followed them into the air and stretched across the entire sky above the Shining City. It was a smile without the malice of Gnurin's fleshless grin, or the chill of Anisse's smirk; Thor had a feeling that Zachary was the only person in the Band who wished him to return. This slight reassurance kindled a warmth in him for the city that was diminishing below the car. It appeared a fragile thing, that glasteel band that clung to the curving shore of Lake Michigan, a glittering toy resting on a pad of earth brown and water blue.

Thor watched the toy city grow smaller until the car passed over the Argonne Pit, when the view was obscured by flames and curling smoke. He shuddered slightly, thinking of the scenes of horrible destruction that had taken place in the great wars that had left such scars as the volcanic crevice below them. He could evoke no feeling for the folly-ridden humans who had invited their own incineration; he cared nothing about the demolition of the ancient stone and rubbish piles that were the city; but he resented the red-raw wounds in the earth's surface, such as the Argonne Pit and others he had seen in the European continent.

Captain Sears, who operated the car, circled the Pit several times in order to get an opportunity to search all the surrounding fields for the hovering car Leonard had taken.

"He is not there," Thor pronounced after the fourth turn.

"Evidently he has gone—but where?" The captain held the car in a hovering position awaiting Thor's suggestion as to course.

"He has done considerable work at the site of the old Colorado shale plant. Perhaps he has gone there."

Thor endeavored to convince himself that Leonard's departure from the Shining City was along the line of duty.

Captain Sears, a tight-lipped, square-jawed veteran of the Eye Squad, turned to fix Thor with a dispassionate stare. "Would it not be your suggestion, sir, that we search the site of the shale plant *after* we have exhausted other possibilities?"

"I suppose so." Thor settled back in his seat. "Your guess is as good as mine, Captain."

"Headquarters may have a suggestion." Sears cut in the outlet grille in the ceiling of the cabin and adjusted the dial to the Eye Squad wave band.

THE CABIN of the car was somewhat crowded with the three men, their food supplies, medical aid equipment, heavy coats for the Northern cold and their weapons. They carried food for ten days, since they did not know how far they would have to go in search of Leonard. Thor and the assistant, Erik Forty-Four sat behind Captain Sears, who handled all the controls alone. Erik was a youth of not more than twenty-one or twenty-two. Thor guessed from the reddish-blond hair that was visible below the band of his uniform cap that he was a descendant of some branch of Northerners. He sat stiffly erect in his seat, apparently uncertain how to conduct himself in the presence of the President of the Shining City Board.

Thor, in turn, was ill at ease, knowing that he was virtually a prisoner. It was an Eye Squad axiom that until he had proven himself innocent each suspect or associate with a suspect was to be regarded as guilty. One of the refinements that Elmer One-Eight-One of the Board had added to Eye Squad investigation procedure was the plan for providing suspects with *"tasks of test."* Now that Thor had time to reflect on the matter, he realized that he had been maneuvered into a task of test. He sought escape from the unpleasant thoughts that continued to boil in his mind, and turned his attention to his companions.

"Headquarters reports that Leonard left the Pit yesterday afternoon; he loaded Northerners into his car and they traveled in a northeasterly direction from the Pit. They are twenty turns of the telechron ahead of us, but it is suggested we try the Ten Cities on the eastern shore of the lake."

It was no use; he could not escape. Thor remained silent. Once they were over the blue monotony of the lake the silence in the cabin became oppressive. Sears tuned in the celebration in Paris, but shut it off before long. The broadcast was the formal greetings of arrivals at the Paris sky station. Genetic rating numbers were used instead of surnames, and Thor caught himself smiling at what Leonard would probably say: *"Sounds like a kindergarten counting lesson!"*

Leonard had left the Ten Cities by the time they arrived. Reports to the Shining City Eye Squad headquarters from espionage agents in that area were to the effect that he had landed, dropped the men he carried with him and picked up three "agitators" of that region. The agents making the report from the Ten Cities were more thorough than those stationed at the Argonne Pit, and the report was detailed and exact—although it had not been possible to make a sound recording of everything that had taken place. The men Leonard left at the Ten Cities were expert javelin throwers as well as competent organizers. Apparently, the report went on, it was his aim to coordinate forces of various settlements around the lake that were antagonistic to the Shining City. This was the only explanation the Eye Squad could offer for the exchange of leaders.

"People from a kilometer in every direction ran to the hovering car when it landed," the agent reported. "Some thought It was a kind of heavenly body come to earth; others thought it was an invasion from the Shining City, and they were about to attack when Leonard halted them by shouting through an amplifier: *'I am Leonard Larsen, a Northerner. I have come to bring you a plan to get some of the good things from the Shining City without selling your sons and your daughters into slavery!'* "

The report ended with that quotation and Sears cut the control. "If I may comment, sir," the captain laid, "that speech attributed to Leonard is not characteristic of him. I have accompanied him on many expeditions and I have never heard him say anything that was not—how shall I put it?—kind of pointed with bitter humor. He didn't make declarations straight out that way."

Thor regarded the Eye Squad captain in a new light, and he let down some of the barriers of his reserve. "No, it doesn't sound like anything Leonard would say," he agreed; "Leonard's wit was somewhat mordant; he was frequently accused of 'spouting epigrams'."

"That's it, sir," Sears responded warmly.

"I never heard him say anything," Erik put in, speaking for the first time on the journey; "but one time I was on duty in the sky station when he came in from someplace. I seen him make a face at the outlet grille when Doctor Gnurin was speaking. It was so funny I had to laugh, but of course I hid my face and pretended I did not see him."

"He meant nothing disrespectful, I'm sure," Sears added quickly.

"Of course not," Thor agreed with a relieved sigh. "Just boyish. I guess I forced him to study too hard when he was young and his playfulness came out later."

EYE SQUAD headquarters decided Leonard's next destination was Superior City, and without making a landing at the Ten Cities Sears set his direction to the northwest. Again they were over the monotony of water, and Thor suggested that Sears tune in the Paris celebration.

The roar of applause came through the grille before an image appeared on the screen and a voice was saying, *"...calls for a report from you, Doctor One-One-Seven, on the Invalator and the Unvalator."*

Erik groaned. "Gnurin again!"

"A correction, if you please!" The image of Gnurin appeared, standing stiffly erect. "The *Unvalator* should always be mentioned first, since it was the first to be invented. Also, this device must complete certain operations before the Invalator can function.

"I suppose by this time," his tone indicated that he had launched into his prepared speech, "that everyone within the Band knows that my Department of Research in the Shining City developed these scientific marvels. Now a word about the principles on which they operate—and who is better qualified than I, who have spent years in consultation with my inventors, poring over these charts."

He waved a sheaf of parchments. "First, the Unvalator. It operates like this: These multiple sonic drums—" He held a chart before the reception disc and pointed with a bony finger. "—record the vibratory pattern of any mass to which the reception slate is exposed—buildings or other installations, an earth formation—anything, and in less than one-tenth of a centi-second counter-vibrations are set up in these drums here..." He traced his finger down the chart. "These counter-vibrations will instantly disintegrate everything to which the slate has been exposed. An Unvalator the size of the experimental model in the Shining City could be mounted in a large hovering car and transported to a field of battle, if need be, and in the time it would require for the car to pass over the area, everything within a radius of a kilometer square would be reduced to cosmic ash!" He lowered the chart exposing a ghoulish grin to the disc.

Applause again swelled and he acknowledged it by bowing first to the right then to the left; then he stepped to one side and bowed to someone apparently in the wings of the Coliseum stage. Thor was familiar with the building in which the ceremonies were to take place and his imagination filled in details that were not recorded in the reception disc.

The doctor's grin faded and he held up his hand for silence. "Warfare is costly," he announced in round, oratorical tones. "I repeat, warfare is costly, and we scientists of the Band hope to avoid it forevermore. And we will, so long as we keep all science within the Band. We must ruthlessly put down all attempts to pass the smallest secret of our science to the primitive hordes that swarm at our gates. Science is for the scientists and those who accept our leadership!" He barked these words defiantly, as though challenging an enemy.

"Enough!" Sears cut the control and Gnurin's livid face sputtered to grayness.

"Quite enough!" Thor was grave. "He said many things that should not have been said."

"He usually does," Erik said solemnly, apparently unaware that criticism of a Board member by one of the lower rank was forbidden.

Sears shot a warning glance over his shoulder, but Thor laughed. "You're very right, Erik!" The tension was relieved, and the two Eye Squad officers laughed with Thor.

DESPITE the grimness of their errand, Thor was deriving considerable pleasure from the company of these men. While the grille was silent they talked as men who are equals, and Thor told them something of life in the Northland, of the industry and simple pleasures of people who lived without benefit of science.

Erik revealed that he had come from the region of the Ten Cities. Like Thor, he had brought a crew of denizens to the Shining City, had been rewarded with a position on the Eye Squad. He, too, had fished through a hole in the ice when he was a boy, had danced square dances and played a catgut fiddle.

At length Sears interrupted. "The public ceremony in Paris will soon come to an end," he said, consulting the telechron on his arm. "Should we tune in for the last of It?"

"By all means..." Thor straightened, suddenly remembering his position.

The figure of a Master of Ceremonies appeared on the screen. "And now, men and women of Science, we have a still greater treat in store for us. Never before in the history of the Band have so many of our great gathered together, and never before has the world of Science enjoyed such an intellectual feast. We have heard from Doctor One-One-Seven of the Shining City of our greatest scientific achievement—the invention of the all-devouring Unvalator and of the miniature Sun Converter, the Invalator, while other inventions described here today are noteworthy, these twin building apparati far overshadow everything else. Now to make the summation on these inventions, I want to present a scientist to whom the Band owes everything. Without him there would have been no Band of scientific cities, there probably would have been no Science, as we know it today. It was his great foresight, his organizational genius, his tireless effort at the time when the cities of science were contending bitterly one against the other, that made it possible for us to meet here today in peace. But he has worked so unobtrusively that few of us have heard his name, and none but his intimates have seen his face. His modesty exceeds his genius, yet because of the great significance of this occasion, he has consented to come forth. He will speak to you now from behind a shielding screen. May I present— Doctor Eli Julian of Prague!"

The applause that followed lasted during the time the fleur-de-lis shielding screen was moved close to the reception disc. There was a moment of confusion and the tele-screen was cluttered with attendants of the great man, among whom was a woman who apparently had been speaking with him. Her dress was the official red, and her hair the color of a flame-tip. Though her face was on the screen but a centi-second, it remained long enough for Thor to recognize Anisse.

At first he tried to tell himself he had been mistaken, but he knew he was not. Anisse was among the "intimates" permitted to see the face of this mysterious manipulator of Band affairs. *How intimate?* Thor asked himself. A parade of long-suppressed thoughts flashed through his mind; the way her eye slid aside when she responded to his caresses, an impatient toss of her head while he was talking, a suggestion about City policy that was given with the ring of an ultimatum. Was it possible that Anisse had been in league with Doctor Julian all the time he had shared her pallet? An observation of Leonard's came to his mind. *"Women of the Band are motivated either by passion or politics—generally politics."*

Doctor Julian spoke in a deep, though somewhat nasal voice. It was a well-modulated voice, trained for public speaking, and it had the resonance of great energy in it. No accent of colloquial expression gave a hint of the man's geographical origin; Thor wondered about his physical appearance, whether he was tall and fair, round and ruddy or squat and dark. Thor tried to picture him, but his thoughts were colored by jealousy. Whether the speech was poetic or prosaic he would never know. Julian said something about the Unvalator and the Invalator and the Shining City, and vaguely Thor realized that the great man had paid tribute to the work he had done, though he was sure the name of Thor Two-Two had not been mentioned. *Perhaps,* he thought bitterly, *Julian implies praise for Anisse's accomplishment.*

"We are coming to Superior City, sir." Captain Sears spoke and Thor became aware that Doctor Julian's speech had ended; the blare of martial music came through the grille.

CHAPTER FOUR

IT WAS growing dark, and the lights of the town twinkled like a small constellation at the edge of the steely gray of the lake below them. "I think you'll find a suitable landing spot near the south edge of town," Thor said.

Gone was the sense of camaraderie that had developed among the three men in the cabin, and Thor felt sure that the others had noticed his reaction to the appearance of Anisse. Had Sears recognized her? Thor fervently hoped not. Although Leonard's behavior had grieved him deeply, he was more chagrined over his discovery of Anisse's betrayal. At the moment he was almost glad he had a sorrow on which to concentrate.

Sears maneuvered the hovering car down in a small, freshly-plowed field; as soon as the door was opened Thor examined the ground to see if they had broken the young sprouts of plants. Sears laughed. "Leonard used to say it was better to risk the wrath of the gods by landing on a rough spot, rather than the wrath of a farmer by landing in his field!"

"Leonard loves growing things, and people who tend them," Thor sighed. A sadness had settled over him, a sadness he could not analyze.

After they had stretched and made themselves comfortable, they opened packages of food and ate in silence. All around lay the forest, great trees that sheltered the small, cultivated plots and the scattered buildings. In the twilight, low mountains looked like the furred backs of sleeping green cats. Thor's mind went back to his boyhood fancies about those mountains and the lake that was always cold. He had imagined the mountains were enormous cat-creatures that had slept for over two hundred years, and that chill-blooded reptilian monsters slumbered in the lake. He had believed that the destruction at the end of the Twentieth Century had been the work of these terrifying creatures, that they would again rouse to spread death and horror if human beings tampered too much with Nature. Even now, though he accepted Science's interpretations of the wars that had wiped out the old world, he found himself trembling at the thought of bringing a sun-powered car into the presence of those sleeping monsters.

Erik, too, appeared to be wrapped in strange thought, and listening for something. Sears shot a questioning glance at the boy, who grinned apologetically. "Can't help it; when I get out in the country this time of year I always listen for cicadas."

"It isn't time for cicadas." Sears frowned sternly, and it occurred to Thor that it was strange an Eye Squad officer from the Shining City would know about things of the country. He concluded that Sears had learned much from Leonard on their trips together.

Sears gave Erik instructions about guarding the car. Handing the youth a carbon ray gun, he said, "Don't shoot except to protect your life. If Northerners try to attack you, take the car off the ground and hover around the location. Flash the blue signal light so we can find you. Remember, it will be better to run some risk rather than to antagonize these people; we are far outnumbered, and there may have been some weapons in the car Leonard took."

Erik's "Yes, sir," was not very forceful, and Thor felt a sudden wave of pity for the young officer on his first important assignment. "There won't be any trouble," he assured the boy. "This is my home; these are my people. They will not harm you."

"You should go, sir. It's growing dark very rapidly."

Sears, too, showed signs of uneasiness, though he was more adept at concealing it.

THEY STEPPED out of the car, put on their uniform greatcoats and set out for the town, half a kilometer distant. Sears walked cautiously on the balls of his feet, and glanced with apprehension at the shrubbery, which was just taking leaf.

It passed through Thor's mind that their energy guns, intended for use at close range within the City, could not protect them against a shower of javelins hurled from ambush. If they were attacked they could not hope to escape; however, the excitement that pounded in his veins was not altogether that of fear.

The ozone of evergreens was in the crisp, cool air, and as they came nearer to the cluster of whitewashed houses the smell of wood smoke and frying fish came out to greet them, and off in the distance they could hear the shouts of children at play. They were healthy, happy sounds, unlike the machined rumble of the Shining City.

Thor felt a well of pride as they trod on the plank walks that led into the little city. His effort in getting saws for the Northerners had made those walks possible, as well as the trim frame buildings along the streets. Something akin to a sense of guilt crept into his thoughts as he dwelt on this past, but quickly his gyroscopic rationalization righted his ego. He had done the only thing possible by going to the Shining City and taking Leonard with him. Had not the great Doctor Julian—and here another thought rankled—recognized his work, if not him, when he praised accomplishments with the Unvalator and Invalator?

His reverie was interrupted when a door of a nearby cottage flew open and a yellow light streaked out across the walk. A woman threw out a pan of slop and a dog ran out, barking. They were discovered.

The Eye Squad Captain stiffened and made ready his weapon.

"Let me do the talking," Thor said.

Before he could speak, however, the woman called out to the dog. "What is it, Pete? Who's there?" She was a young woman, ample of figure with strong, round arms and a determined chin that thrust out as she turned her profile to call to someone indoors. "Come here, Axel. It's strangers."

The dog continued to bark, though he made no attempt to attack. Thor pushed aside the gun that Sears leveled at the animal. "Which is the home of Irenka Larsen?" he called to the young woman.

She raised her hand to her brow and peered into the darkness. "Hush, Pete, be quiet!" The dog ceased barking. "Who wants my mother?"

A huge man towered beside her in the doorway. "Get inside, Helga." Roughly he pushed her back into the room, then he took three great strides out to where Thor and the captain stood. "I never seen you before; who are you? What do you want?"

"We're from—from—" So that was Helga, the youngest, the little girl with hair like spun moonbeams and eyes the color of deep ice. A lump swelled in Thor's throat, choking off his voice; he forgot he was President of the Board of the Shining City. He wanted to rush past the glowering man and sweep the woman into an embrace, but a warning from the Eye Squad captain restrained him. "We've come to see Irenka Larsen on business," he added weakly.

"Two squares down, turn left one square. You can't miss it, a two-story white house on the corner. With six sons-in-law to support her, the old woman gets the best!"

The dog barked again and other dogs took up the barking; then doors and window shutters along the street opened and the openings filled with the curious faces of men and women and the tousled white hair of fair children. They were not unfriendly faces, but Thor became conscious of the uniforms he and Captain Sears wore. By now, people along the street knew that two men from the Shining City were on their way to Irenka Larsen's house. Shadowy figures darted across garden plots, and Thor imagined he saw them come from the large house that stood out white against the backdrop of mountain darkness.

"We'll either be welcomed, or—" Thor did not finish the sentence because a woman running toward them blocked their way.

SHE WAS dressed in the black clothes of mourning, with a black head-shawl fastened tightly at her throat so that her long and rather homely face appeared to swim bodiless in the gloom. Thor's first thought was that he was staring at his own reflection.

The woman scrutinized him closely, her eyes burning with emotion. "Father!" It was an announcement, not a cry.

Thor fumbled in his memory, trying to recall the faces of his daughter...

"It's Irenie," she went on. "A widow, thanks to the sawmills you brought to Superior City. It's no use seeing Mother; she knows nothing about Leonard—and that's who you came to see, I know. Go back to the Shining City, Father, back to that harlot in the red dress. We don't want you here!" Her voice rose to a shrill that was almost hysterical.

"Irenie..." Thor reached out to touch her but she evaded him. "I must talk to Leonard; it's the only way."

"Talk to the wind!" she spat. "You won't find Leonard!"

"Come, Captain." Thor stepped off the walk and waded through the rutted mud of the street toward the tall house.

Light streaked through the shutters of the house that was Irenka's. As Thor approached it he remembered the cottage he had built for her on that site. Leonard and the seven girls had been born in it. He remembered the smell of the sweet peas that had been planted in neat rows beside the walk, the violets that had bloomed in the shelter of the garden wall, the first onions of spring, the water, cool and fresh from the well back of the house, and the shouts of laughter of his children at play. He stumbled on the steps and Captain Sears caught his arm.

"I'll wait for you at the car, sir." The Eye Squad Captain saluted and turned away, leaving Thor to enter the house alone.

He pushed open the door that stood ajar. It creaked on crude hinges, and he noted that the construction was not so good as in the tidy cottage he had built to Irenka. The odor of cabbage soup was strong in the cavernous hallway, and it guided him to a lighted room in the back of the house.

"Is that you, Irenie? Supper's ready." A large fair-skinned woman stood over the brick stove in the corner of the kitchen holding a wooden ladle. As she turned, Thor saw that his former wife's face and figure were more rounded and her eyes were less blue than when he had last seen her; but there was little gray in the pale gold of her hair, and she still radiated the same vibrant strength that had first attracted him.

She stared, eyes wide, and the ladle fell from her hand.

Thor felt his knees grow weak, but he fought for self-control. He picked up the ladle, wiped it on the skirt of his coat and dipped into the steaming soup pot. "What we need in the Shining City, Irenka," he said putting the ladle to his lips, "is an expert on flavor. All we get to eat is gook, tasteless and slimy gook." He blew on the soup, then sipped it from the ladle. "This tastes like food."

Irenka backed away from him, still staring in disbelief. "You wouldn't dare, Thor Larsen! You wouldn't dare come home after all these years, and walk right into my kitchen! Why, your sons-in-law will thrash you, take you out to the whipping post and thrash you with leather lashes, like they do the men that desert their families!"

THOUGH he was trembling with excitement, Thor cast aside his coat and lifted the lid of another pot that simmered on the stove. "Ah, burnt wheat-coffee! It's been years since I've had a cup of coffee, Irenka."

"You're the President of the Shining City, and you just walk into my kitchen and start talking to me about soup and coffee!" She lifted her apron to wipe away tears that ran down her cheeks.

"I'm hungry, Irenka; let's eat supper."

"Irenie isn't home yet. She lives with me now—since her man was killed—she and Jamie, but he's out on a fishing boat." Irenka turned to a cupboard and took down three pottery bowls and put them on the table that stood in the center of the room. "I've got a tablecloth for company, but it's dirty."

"You've had company?" He got wooden spoons from the cupboard and laid them beside the bowls.

"There's cups in the dishpan; I'll dry them. I can't imagine what's keeping Irenie. She knew supper was ready."

"Leonard's been here, drinking coffee." He took the towel from her hand, wiped the cups and set them on the table.

Irenka's shoulders tensed and she busied herself at the stove, ladling soup into the bowls. "He was here and gone. Just for dinner he stayed, then coffee in the afternoon. He had one of them little talking things that he wore like a belt around his waist, and kept listening to it. A little while ago he got some kind of warning on it. He kissed me and said he couldn't stay for supper. Irenie went with him, but she wouldn't go in that flying car with him. Maybe I ought not to tell you this, but it's kind of good having somebody to talk to. Leonard didn't talk much to me—only to Irenie and to some of the young men Jamie knows. They were in the sitting-room while I was out here in the back." She broke chunks from a loaf of bread and laid them on the table.

Thoughtfully, Thor crumbled bread into a bowl of soup. "Leonard is gone? Where?"

Before Irenka replied she bowed her head and mumbled a short prayer of grace. "I don't know, Thor. I was so excited, him coming home after all these years, and I was hurrying around trying to make things nice for him. I was in there changing the blankets on Jamie's bed when he said he had to go. He's not in trouble in the Shining City is he, Thor?"

"Jamie?" Thor sipped the black brew that was called coffee, and pretended not to hear Irenka's question. "Why he wasn't born yet when I—when I went to Shining City." He wondered what Anisse would have said had she known that he had a grown grandson.

Irenka studied his face for twenty heartbeats before she spoke. "You have ways of staying young in the Shining City?"

Thor knew that Leonard had told her of Anisse. The vision of the woman in red beside Doctor Julian's screen rose up in his mind, and his appetite left him. He laid down his spoon. "There are things, Irenka, that make one grow old very fast in the cities of the Band."

"What's the 'Band?' "

Thor did not have the opportunity to reply to her question. There was a commotion in the hallway—a barking dog, a shriek that was Irenie's, and heavy footsteps. Captain Sears, followed by Irenie burst into the kitchen. "The car, sir! It's been stolen! And Erik with it, abducted! There was a struggle...I came right back here, sir."

"He's lying!" Irenie cried. "It's a made up story to blacken Leonard!"

"The woman's insane!" Sears' eyes flashed anger. "You must come with me sir, immediately!" He took up Thor's coat and held it for him.

"They *traded* flying cars! I heard the whole thing; Leonard didn't do anything wrong!" Irenie went on.

"Where is Leonard now?" Thor demanded.

"He flew away."

"He's gone, sir. I got there too late to stop him!"

"You liar!" Irenie cried.

"Come, sir. He left the other car in the field. It may be destroyed if we don't hurry!" Sears laid hold of Thor's arm and pulled him toward the doorway.

Thor glanced back at Irenka. She had detached herself from the scene and was calmly refilling the coffeepot. She did not look up as he left.

ON THE WAY back to the field Thor endeavored to find out what had taken place, but Sears replied only, "We must hurry, sir!" and set the pace so fast that talk was impossible.

A group of twenty or more youths surrounded the hovering car that stood on the field near where the other car had been; but they fell away as Captain Sears drew his gun and waved it threateningly. Some of them called out mild insults, but compared to Irenie's vehemence the demonstration was dispirited. Recalling it later, Thor was somewhat puzzled, but decided that the group had been drawn to the scene by curiosity only. The other car had disappeared.

Sears pulled Thor into the car, slammed the door and lifted it immediately. It had been stripped of all communication devices, the extra sun-battery and all weapons. Thor made several attempts to learn exactly what had taken place on the field, but Sears was uncommunicative; he had reached the scene too late to assist Erik, he insisted. The car was already in the air, he said, and he had not used his gun on the crowd for fear the Northerners would destroy the car Leonard had left—which would leave them at the mercy of the Northerners. Instead, he ran back to get Thor, and Irenie had followed him.

He showed signs of considerable strain and Thor did not press him further. For one thing, in order to find their way back to the Shining City it was necessary to follow the shoreline of the lakes, but not to allow the car to drift over water because the battery might become exhausted at any time. When Thor came to a full realization of their predicament he relieved Sears at the controls; but due to his lack of skill, the car drifted, rocked and oscillated.

In less than a turn of the telechron, Sears rose impatiently from his improvised pallet of coats and took the controls from Thor. "We'll probably drift down into the Argonne Pit," he said sourly.

"The hot air will cause us to drift in the opposite direction," Thor pointed out.

"We'll drown in the lake, then."

"Not necessarily." Thor did not feel the cheer he tried to put into his voice. "These cars are buoyant; we'd float for days if we kept the cabin sealed."

"What would we breathe? Air conditioning stops when the battery goes out."

"A searching party would undoubtedly find us before anything happened."

"Without a broadcast from us how would they know where to search—even if anyone wanted to look for us?"

"The Eye Squad—the Board. They always send out searching cars when a scientist gets lost, and we are a little more important…"

"To whom?" Sears refused to shake his morose mood. "As Leonard used to say, *'The more important you are, the more people want your ash in an oven.'* "

"I suppose that's true," Thor sighed. The reference to Leonard plunged him into gloom deeper than that of Sears. He was now convinced that his son had deserted the Shining City; the evidence was overwhelmingly strong that Leonard had stolen valuable secrets, as well as property from the Shining City, for use by the Northerners—a capital crime. Also, abduction of an Eye Squad officer—if such it was—would call for the death penalty. By now Thor realized that he could not excuse Leonard's acts as boyish pranks or even as temporary unbalance. His son was motivated by lofty ideals—of that Thor was certain—but exactly what were these ideals that caused him to risk his reputation, his life, his father's position and the lives of his people in the Northland? Perhaps he wanted to put over some scientific point, some theory Gnurin would not accept, and had taken this means to bring the matter before the Board in a dramatic manner. This might account for his theft of communication equipment. He had to take the other car in order to obtain the fresh batteries and additional supplies. And he had to take Erik with the car. Or, perhaps he had abducted the Eye Squad officer in order to gain a bargaining point. Thor was not satisfied with his attempts to rationalize Leonard's actions, but he could not bring himself to regard his son as a willful wrongdoer.

What could he say to the Board in his report? How could he present the facts in a light that would not be too unfavorable to Leonard? Most important, there must be no conflict between his presentation of facts and that of Sears. Sears' testimony would clear Thor of all blame in the matter, and his in turn would clear Sears. That is, if he did not mention Irenie's hysterical outburst. He tried to find a way to bring up the subject of testimony to Sears, but the officer's clamped jaws and taciturn frown discouraged conversation. They rode in silence for almost a turn of the telechron.

CHAPTER FIVE

WHEN THEY came in view of the sky glow over the Shining City, which rose like a huge and misty moon before them, Sears, relaxed somewhat, but not until they were on the landing platform did he unclamp his set jaws. "The worst is ahead of us." A new anxiety furrowed his brow, and there was something of a plea in his eyes as he turned to Thor. "Explanations will be—most difficult, sir, but for your protection I am going to report that we were together the entire time in Superior City."

"I believe that is right, Captain." Thor chose to manipulate his memory rather than his veracity. "We landed in a field near town, went to the home of my former wife, where Leonard was most apt to be, leaving Erik Four-Four to guard the car. Leonard was not in the house; we heard a commotion in the direction of the field and we ran back, only to see our car in the air. How many men would you say we could see in the car through the viewing windows, Captain?"

"Five or six," Sears replied in a matter-of-fact tone; "among them Leonard and Erik. This stripped car was in the field nearby; we made a run for it and got in before the Northerners attacked—didn't use our guns on them for fear they would destroy the car."

"We came direct to the Shining City by the shortest possible route because we had only the battery that powered the car and we didn't know how nearly exhausted it was."

While they rehearsed their recital, the landing platform descended into the sky station. Thor had barely finished speaking when the car door was pulled open violently from the outside and the nozzle of a gun appeared in the opening.

"Unscheduled flight, unannounced landing!" a voice behind the gun barked. "Alight and give an accounting."

It was a full turn of the telechron before the Eye Squad officers at the sky station released them. It was apparent from the type of questions asked that they had been specially alerted to watch for Sears and Thor. Apparently, espionage reports on the incident at Superior City had come in. Thor was sure the reports did not agree exactly with his and Sears' story, but it was also apparent the discrepancy was not great enough to cause particular concern at Eye Squad headquarters; the lieutenant in charge authorized the dismissal of Sears and Thor without consulting Elmer One-Eight-One.

Although Thor was numb with fatigue when he and Sears passed through the sky station, he noticed that the official car from Paris was in its stall. Had Anisse returned with the others? His heart beat with wild hope, even though he knew that she planned a stay in Paris.

At the station entrance Sears saluted wearily. "I assume my assignment to guard you is at an end, sir. Good rest."

Thor made his way through the sleeping city, the only passenger on belt cars and elevators. His footsteps echoed in the long, silent corridors; his own distorted reflection in glasteel was his only companion in the waiting room of the third level Ten North transfer station where he changed to the local stop belt car that served his apartment building. His apartment was tomb-silent. Leonard was gone; Anisse was gone. He wandered through the bare, cold rooms that he had shared with them searching for something either of them might have left behind—a memento, a discarded garment or even a crumpled container. There was nothing; the cleaning attendant had removed everything that was reminiscent of both of them— even the fragrance of bath oil Thor had often noticed on

Anisse's sleeping pallet. The pain of loneliness pressed in on him but he could find no relief. At length he bathed, put on his night robe and lay down on his pallet. The empty dark pressed in on him and a dull pain thudded in his chest. It was as though a band had been drawn tightly around it, compressing his lungs; he was not sure whether or not he slept.

"Awaken, men of Science." A strange voice filled the room, a woman's voice, rather pleasant, but too calculatingly cheerful. Frightened, Thor sat up on his pallet and looked around expecting to find a new companion. The voice continued, and he ascertained that it came through the outlet grille. *"It is the hour of seven, sun time, and the day dawns, this one hundred thirty-sixth day of the first glorious year of Science. You of the Shining City are being awakened to your tasks by the means that is used in the mother city of Prague..."*

Thor scrambled off his pallet and went into the shower stall to shut out the forced cheer of the female voice.

"...mother city of Prague..." The phrase brought to his mind a fleur-de-lis pattern and a flash of red beside it—Doctor Julian. *So, Doctor Julian's city becomes 'the mother city' of the Band!* he thought bitterly. The dull pain in his chest sharpened.

WHEN HE emerged from the shower his communication cabinet was buzzing insistently. He opened the control and the frightened face of Elmer One-Eight-One sprang to life in front of him. "Something terrible has happened, Thor! The third level, ten north transfer station, blown up, shattered! Two guards on duty were killed, as well as a hundred, maybe two hundred denizens, on their way to work!"

"Why," Thor stammered, trying to collect his thoughts. "I came through there not more than two turns ago! It was deserted, not even a guard!"

Doctor Gnurin's angry face filled another segment of the screen. "Why didn't you report to One-Eight-One upon your arrival, Thor? Where is Captain Sears? Why did you dismiss him? How do you explain the fact that it was your transfer

48

station that was wrecked?" He directed the next question to Elmer's image. "Why did you call Thor before you called me, the President of the Board?"

"I was so excited I guess I forgot," Elmer answered contritely.

"A few denizens more important than *procedure?* You heard what Doctor Julian said yesterday about the importance of correct procedure if we're to synchronize in the Band!"

"The Band isn't going to mop up that mess on the third level, Gnurin," Elmer retorted with sullen resentment. "The Building Coordinator's got to get an emergency crew there with the Unvalator to clear out the wreckage, and the Invalator to rebuild it. I've got an investigation to conduct, traffic to reroute..."

"Not until we've had a meeting, One-Eight-One! The Board has to find out why Leonard One-Two-Two was not brought back to the Shining City, and why—"

"That's got nothing to do with the emergency!" Elmer's face was redder than Gnurin's now. "It's up to the Police Coordinator and the Building Coordinator—me and Thor. Hold your meeting with Juno and Vivian; we've got work to do. Meet me at the scene of the accident, Thor." With that Elmer cut out.

"Accident it is now!" Gnurin shrieked. "Don't cut me out until you've answered a few questions, Thor Two-Two."

"Ask Juno and Vivian; I've got bodies to remove." Thor closed the control and turned away.

"I can bypass your cutout! Come back here!" Gnurin shouted from the screen.

"Talk to the walls, doctor," Thor shot back as he hurried from the room.

Thor had seen the aftermath of many construction accidents—some in which entire crews of denizens had been mangled—but he had never beheld such gruesome carnage as confronted him at the wrecked belt station. Torn parts of human beings and oozing black blood lay scattered thickly over all the floor that remained in the station, some of them straggling into the great hole in the center of the room. Groans and cries came up through the opening; here and there a living person made an animal effort to extricate himself from the mass of death. No rescue operations had been undertaken because of the unsafe condition of the structure. Supporting pillars had been broken, and the ceiling sagged threateningly, while the entire floor was mottled with cracks.

Thor grew faint and he took hold of Elmer's arm to steady himself, then found he had to support Elmer. The Coordinator of Security had fainted.

IN LESS than a turn of the telechron Thor had the Unvalator and the Invalator as well as an emergency construction crew on the job. He ordered everything cleared, the dying as well as the dead, because salvage of any kind was impossible. In a few centi-seconds all human flesh was rendered into cosmic ash for the Invalator's digestors. Reconstruction was slower, but in ten turns it was well under way.

Elmer took charge personally of the Eye Squad Control Board. For ten turns his orders crackled steadily through the compulsion channel to the entire City. First it was necessary to reroute traffic and call up emergency crews. Denizens who were to have been relieved by those who were killed in the blast remained at their posts until replacements were recruited, and some of them required resuscitation. Doctor Vivian had to be instructed to supply rations of hot food and stimulants to the emergency crews, then before long it was discovered that Social Engineers were needed to provide emotional anodynes to those incapacitated by terror, thus Juno was drawn into the disaster work.

There was nothing for Gnurin to do, however. For most of the emergency period he screamed at Elmer demanding a channel to call a Board meeting, or so Elmer reported to Thor when Thor entered Eye Squad headquarters after he had reconstruction work in progress. He was numb with fatigue, but dreaded to return to his tomb-like apartment.

Elmer turned from the Control Board. "It's terrible, Thor!" He threw up his hands in a gesture of despair. "I'd rather handle a hundred disasters than another day of Gnurin! If there was only some way. He keeps bypassing…"

At that moment a skull-like head popped out in a segment of the wall screen and Thor moved out of range. "I'll call in Band Police!" Gnurin shouted hysterically. "I've got to have discipline! Give me a channel to call a Board meeting or I'll notify Prague!"

"What's Prague got to do with us?" Elmer demanded sullenly.

"What does Prague have to do with us? It's just the mother city of Science, that's all! All cities of the Band must obey the wishes of Prague—and Prague would not tolerate laxity. What have you done to establish the blame for the explosion? What have you done to prevent recurrences of sabotage?"

"I've got my best man on the job," Elmer replied with frayed patience. "I called Captain Sears off his pallet to take charge of investigation."

"And *who* has investigated Sears? What assurance do we have that he is not in league with the saboteurs? After all, he was an associate of Leonard One-Two-Two, and he spent all day yesterday with the former President—who was, by the way, the last person known to have been in the third level transfer station before the explosion! Have you had an accounting from him? And what of the Eye Squad officer whom Leonard abducted? Have you sent out a searching party to locate him?"

"I'm doing all that is humanly possible." Elmer motioned to an Eye Squad Lieutenant in an anteroom and turned the Control Board over to him. "I'm going to get some rest—somewhere where there are no communication cabinets," he said to the Lieutenant. "Don't call me for six turns, even if the city blows up!" He motioned to Thor and led the way into an Eye Squad officers' lounge.

Gnurin's scream followed them. "I'll have you brought up on charges!"

THE LOUNGE was quiet and dark, except for a night-glow light. Several Eye Squad Officers were asleep on bunk-shelves protruding from the wall. Elmer and Thor tiptoed into the room, found empty bunks and lay down without removing their clothing. Thor slept the sound sleep of complete exhaustion; he was not sure how long he slept, but a brilliant light shining in his eyes awakened him.

The room was in confusion. Eye Squad officers who had been asleep were dressing hurriedly; others lined up before a weapon storage vault door, waiting for guns and reload capsules. Elmer, his hair uncombed and his blouse unbuttoned and his eyes puffed from sleep, stood in the vault dispensing the arms.

"What's wrong?" Thor asked as soon as he could gather his faculties.

Elmer did not hear the question. An officer in the line answered, "Emergency—the whole ground-level belt of eighteen, west."

"Explosion?" Thor guessed.

"Several explosions; denizens in a panic fleeing the city. We've got to stop them."

"*Try* to stop them, you mean," the man in front of him said with a cynical grimace.

"From what Sears says, they're so panicky they'll run right into our death rays."

"No telling what a denizen'll do. They're primitives—act like animals when they're scared."

Thor reeled under the impact of the news, and it was not until the fourth man had spoken that he realized the gravity of the situation. "I'll go out on the emergency belt car with the officers," he called to Elmer.

"Better not, Thor," Elmer advised him. "Gnurin's been howling all night. Zachary's on his way in a special car—may be at the sky station now. We'll have to have a Board meeting."

"But the emergency," Thor argued.

"Send an assistant. Renlow Sears is out there; he can coordinate emergency work."

The Eye Squad officers piled into a waiting belt car and it shot through the archway and quickly disappeared. Elmer closed the vault door, smoothed his hair and buttoned his blouse. "Breakfast is on the way, but we'd better not wait for it. Gnurin and the others are in the Board Room."

They paused in the Control room to give orders to assistants, and while they were in communication cabinets an attendant brought a jug of hot stimulant and poured it into containers. Thor sipped the warming brew while he spoke to Cliff Davis, his first assistant. The stimulant revived him somewhat, though it increased his heart action, which brought back the dull pain of compression in his chest. However, he had no time to dwell on his own pains.

Elmer emerged from the cabinet where he had been talking, his face ashen. "An unexploded bomb was found in the sky station some time last night. The guard took it to the laboratory for analysis. First I've heard of it; communications have been jammed."

"It appears to be organized sabotage," Thor pronounced gravely.

"Looks that way."

They stepped into the elevator for the BoardRoom. "I called Sears in to make a report to the Board," Elmer went on. "He's leaving Captain Seventy in charge at the disaster scene; main thing is to halt the denizens."

"Remember what Zachary told us? This sort of thing has happened frequently in other cities," Thor offered in an endeavor to rationalize the situation. "Probably timed for the Paris celebration; the plotters thought all important officials would be out of the City."

"That's not what Sears thinks."

Thor's heart skipped a beat. He didn't want to connect Leonard to the plot, but he thought he read the implication in Elmer's remark. "What does Sears think?" he asked at length.

The elevator door opened and they stepped out into the corridor that led to the BoardRoom. Zachary approached them.

"Later," Elmer whispered in answer to Thor's question.

"Gentlemen, gentlemen!" The marshal of the Band Police held out both hands in greeting. "Could you not hold up your emergency until my tenth son is christened with his genetic rating number?"

"Ten sons!" Elmer exclaimed. "You have an Eye Squad of your own!"

"The three eldest are Social Engineers," Zachary's lips curled with scorn. He turned to Thor. "It is good to see you back safely from your expedition, my dear Thor, but I was indeed sorry to hear that it was a failure. Too bad about the Eye Squad novice. Risky business, this police work."

CHAPTER SIX

THEY STEPPED into the BoardRoom to be greeted by a blast from Gnurin. The diminutive scientist appeared more mummified than ever, and the gash of his mouth opened wider as he spoke. "You are tardy, Elmer One-Eight-One and Thor Two-Two—twenty turns tardy! The City has been blown up, the denizens are fleeing in terrified droves, but do you come to a Board meeting? No, you go chasing around doing the tasks of menials while strategy planning goes to—goes to—" He choked in anger, unable to finish the sentence.

"Goes to Hell," Zachary supplied.

"Hell!" Gnurin shrieked, "there's no such place!"

The marshal shrugged. "Opinions differ."

Gnurin fixed the marshal with an angry glare, then as if he remembered something important, he changed his expression to a grin that was almost ghoulish. "Thank you, Marshal Zachary for responding to my call; it is always a pleasure to welcome a representative of the Band." He moved to the reception disc and opened the control. "The meeting will come to order. Thor of the genetic rating Two-Two will be allowed to sit in as Coordinator of Construction until such time as his status is definitely established. Now, if you will all be so good as to give your undivided attention I will proceed with my report. Elmer One-Eight-One, the Board Room is *not* a sleeping chamber!"

Elmer sat up and blinked the sleep from his eyes. "Sorry, sir."

"My report is of an exceedingly grave nature," Gnurin went on as he drew a thick sheaf of parchment sheets from a portfolio.

Zachary rose. "Might it not be better, Mister President Pro-Tem, to hold an executive session in order to evaluate the material in the reports? I assume there are others beside yours. We must remember that many operations in the City are on an emergency basis and it might seriously disrupt vital work if we keep the compulsion channel open for long."

"His point is well taken!" Juno added quickly.

"Zachary is right," Vivian put in.

"Let's have it that way." Elmer was awake now.

Thor said nothing.

Gnurin's face grew livid. "Every word of *my* report is important to every scientist and every denizen in the Shining City!"

Zachary held the floor. "I must beg your pardon, Mister President Pro-Tem, but the Band frowns on undigested reports. I am sure you do not wish to arouse the displeasure of leaders of the Band."

Gnurin deflated. "Our procedure will be altered to suit the pleasure of the Band representative; a digested report will be given later over the compulsion channel." He cut the reception disc control and seated himself at the conference table. "Now, with your permission, Marshal Zachary, I will proceed with my detailed report."

The marshal nodded solemnly, and Thor smiled to himself. *The cat toys with the squealing mouse,* he thought.

Gnurin's report was detailed indeed. It began with a listing of all missing scientific data that he implied had been taken by Leonard. "It might be asked at this point," he interjected, fixing Thor with an insinuating stare, *"where* the suspect stored the stolen data before he disappeared with it. About the only possible answer is that he stored it in his quarters, which he shared with his father. Since the father was a Board member, these quarters were not subject to routine inspection by the Eye Squad. And it might be asked what form of eye disorder afflicted the father to make him blind to the suspicious behavior on the part of his son!"

"I object!" Elmer bellowed.

"And well you might object to these exposures!" Gnurin snorted. "One of *your* men, your most trusted Captain of the Eye Squad, Renlow Sears, whose genetic rating has never been tabulated, was a frequent caller at the quarters of the suspect. May I ask why, in view of this fact, Captain Sears was put in charge of the expedition to apprehend Leonard One-Two-Two? Might *that* not answer the question of *why* the mission failed so miserably?"

"Is this a trial?" Elmer demanded. "And if so, *who* is on trial?"

"It is a report on the sabotage of the Shining City," Gnurin retorted blandly. "The chemical analysis of the unexploded bomb taken from the sky station was manufactured from sulfuric and nitric acids, the data files on which were taken by Leonard One-Two-Two."

"That proves nothing whatsoever!" Thor exploded. "It has never been established that my son took those files. I never saw anything suspicious in his room; he never carried portfolios or packages of any description. It's true he stole a hovering car— two hovering cars—and certain equipment; but as to his stealing research formulas, and especially formulas that have to do with the current bombings, that is pure guesswork, an accusation which is apt to be proven false! Isn't it more reasonable to assume that someone else who had access to those research files took them and is now using the information in them to manufacture the bombs right here in the City?"

"What is this?" Elmer shouted. "A guessing game? I suggest we get a few facts in front of us before we arrive at any conclusion!"

ZACHARY clapped his hands. "Bravo, Elmer! Spoken like a true police officer! Doctor Gnurin, may I suggest that you take your bombast back to the laboratory and analyze it for factual content…"

"Concur!" Elmer shouted.

Gnurin puffed up for a blast, but before he could speak Captain Sears burst into the room. "I have information of great importance," he announced. He showed considerable agitation and glanced nervously from Gnurin to Elmer.

"As Coordinator of Security I will take your report at Eye Squad headquarters, Captain Sears." Elmer rose and moved to the captain's side.

"Not so fast, Elmer One-Eight-One. I insist that the officer's report be given to the assembled Board."

"Concur!" Vivian had vacillated toward agreement with Gnurin.

"One moment," Zachary interrupted. "A Board meeting at this time is not in order. I have come here, at great expense to the Band, to assist in solving a police problem in your City; I did not come to listen to opinions or to give lectures on procedure. I operate by Band rules. If I'm not permitted to follow them, I'll return to Prague at once."

"And your rule is—?" Juno asked the question.

"That all evidence pertaining to the security of a City of the Band be gathered and summarized by the Eye Squad. The Board may evaluate it at such time as the Eye Squad submits a report."

"Meeting adjourned!" Gnurin tossed the parchment sheets into the air and stalked angrily from the room.

Captain Sears had remained standing beside the door. As soon as it slid shut behind Gnurin he spoke. "Use the rear elevators! A bomb has been placed in the Boulevard elevators. It may explode at any centi-second!"

"Stop Gnurin!" Juno shouted.

Sears did not move. "He will not endanger *himself*."

Stunned, everyone in the room stared at the captain, who waved his hand to open the door. Zachary, nearest the door, rushed out into the corridor, then turned back to announce, "He is taking a *rear elevator!*"

"But he always—" Doctor Vivian began.

Sears interrupted him. "Where is his laboratory?"

"No! Not Gnurin!" Vivian covered his face with his hands.

Juno shrugged. "I thought all along he acted guilty."

"Let's not jump to any false conclusions," Elmer warned. He turned to Sears and asked, "Have you apprehended any suspected saboteurs, Captain?"

"More than a hundred are in the Compound and more coming in. I've assigned five men to question them; can't spare more."

"Good work!" Elmer returned.

They were all in the corridor walking toward the rear elevator bank. Marshal Zachary, ahead of the rest, had summoned a car. Thor's mind was a-whirl but he had not found voice for any opinions, however, he noticed that the compression in his chest had eased and his step was lighter. *Gnurin, after all!*

AT THAT moment there was a dull thud somewhere below them in the direction of the Boulevard. The floor swayed, and a splintering crash followed. Everyone staggered, and Juno screamed.

"The explosion!" Sears announced calmly. "On the ground level; those who planted the bomb couldn't reach the Sun Converters."

Cries and screams came from the corridor behind them as doors flew open and white-clad research scientists ran out. Sears turned and raised a hand authoritatively. "There is no danger!" he shouted. "Merely a drill. Go back to your work, but use the rear elevators when you leave the building. The Eye Squad has taken over the others."

Slowly, and with some grumbles of suspicion, the scientists returned to their work.

When the corridor was cleared, Zachary opened the elevator door. "Do you have the guilty ones?" he asked Sears when they were inside.

"All in the Compound; some have confessed. We will soon have the situation under control."

"Are you going to arrest Gnurin?" Doctor Velvet asked.

With a glance at Elmer, Sears shrugged.

"When guilt is established we will arrest the conspirators, no matter what their position," Elmer replied; "right now we will proceed to question the suspects."

"A suggestion," the marshal offered; "all Board members should remain in quarters and direct their activities by communication cabinet for the time being. You will be called when the Eye Squad has prepared a report."

"What about Gnurin?" Velvet asked.

"None of you should contact him." Zachary turned to Sears, "I assume that certain—necessary alterations—have been made at the controls to his communication cabinets."

Sears smiled. "We are leaving nothing to chance."

On Zachary's advice, Thor went first to Eye Squad headquarters where he dictated to a spool a full account of the expedition into the Northland in search of Leonard. He paused at several points, not sure just what he had told the Eye Squad at the sky station. "We made our way to the home of Leonard's mother, after asking directions from some townspeople," he dictated carefully. "The front door was open and we went through the house, finding—finding—" He realized the repetition would sound suspicious, and he stammered over the next words, "—my former mate, Leonard's mother was in the kitchen. She informed us that Leonard had gone..."

Thor's heart pounded heavily; the pain in his chest was severe and perspiration dripped from his forehead. He remembered too late that, while they were being questioned at the sky station, Sears had stated they had searched Irenka's house; also he had later given the information that there were two stories to the house. Neither had mentioned seeing anyone in the house, leaving the impression that their conclusion about Leonard being gone was the result of their search.

He wanted to re-dictate the spool, but he had been given only one. The discrepancy was nothing serious, he told himself; they always showed up in several truthful versions of an incident. Besides, the emphasis was not on his expedition to locate Leonard, but on finding the persons guilty of sabotaging the Shining City. In spite of his rationalization he fretted, an inner, physical fretting that affected all his organs and aged him years in a day.

Gnurin is guilty, Thor told himself over and over as he sat in his apartment impatiently waiting for a summons to the communication cabinet. Gnurin craved the adulation of underlings; he wanted power and prestige, and he had plotted a disaster in order to get them. Undoubtedly his madness had been the cause of Leonard's behavior. Probably, Leonard would return to the City after the doctor's execution. These thoughts with which he sought to console himself did not dispel the pain in his chest.

THERE WERE twenty more explosions in the next four days, and one of them disabled a Sun Converter. The use of power and light was curtailed severely, and the dim light aided the saboteurs. By now, the denizens were in complete panic; their bodies piled high at all the City outlets where Eye Squad officers had stopped them. Yet many escaped. They dived into the lake; some drowned and some managed to swim far enough south to reach safety. They crawled through holes blasted by bombs in the City's outer wall. They stole guns and left the corpses of Eye Squad guards atop of the denizen dead.

The City was almost paralyzed. Elmer remained at the Control Board fifty turns of the telechron—two days—without relief other than for a few centi-minutes at a time. He closed the research laboratories and the Specialty College and put scientists and students at the dials. He directed the Unvalator crew to clear away wreckage and carnage, but the Unvalator had to move too rapidly to permit rebuilding with the Invalator. The released cosmic ash from the Unvalator blackened the bright buildings and clogged air vents. Columns of smoke rose up and mingled with the steam from the Argonne Pit, and a cloud, like a pall of black gloom, hung over the Shining City.

Suspects arrested by the Eye Squad overflowed the Compound, and Elmer ordered the empty laboratories and schoolrooms, converted into jails. Most of the suspects were research scientists, though some were denizens, and a few were Eye Squad guards. Not all the research scientists who were suspects came from the department under the supervision of Gnurin; some were food chemists, and this gave rise to a new wave of fear. However, Doctor Vivian remained on duty to inspect each batch of food, and no casualties resulted from poisoning.

Zachary and Sears supervised the questioning of the suspects, and they obtained a mountain of confession spools, many of them conflicting. Some claimed to have made the bombs themselves, though none knew the exact formula. Most of them said they had gotten the explosives from "a stranger." None had a very well defined reason for participation in the sabotage. A plot there was; of that the marshal was sure; but he could not pull out the threads of it.

"I'm completely baffled," he told Thor in a cabinet conversation. "We have plotters but no evidence of a plot."

"Have you a complete check on all of Gnurin's contacts?" Thor asked. "He uses the bypass more than the Control Board, you know."

"Every hole is plugged," Zachary assured. "He's hermetically sealed in his apartment—and screaming his head off. If he's the brain behind this thing, he must have had it all laid but in advance. But why? There is no why! If he were guilty he would be making demands by now."

Thor pondered a moment. "What's he screaming about?"

Zachary threw up his hands in a gesture of disgust. "Meeting, meeting, meeting! Just wants a sounding board!"

"Maybe he intends to spring his coup in a meeting."

"My dear Thor..." Zachary rolled his eyes thoughtfully and his image faded.

THOR WAS asleep when the compulsion channel signal buzzed. His first thought was that the Board had assembled for a meeting without him. He rose from his pallet and stumbled into his study. The screen was already glowing; he seated himself on the bench and waited for the intensity to increase. He waited twenty, thirty, fifty centi-seconds, but still the screen continued to glow only faintly and no voice came through the grille. His mild alarm heightened into terror. Was the City's power supply so low that communication equipment could not operate? If so, belt cars and elevators wouldn't run, doors wouldn't open, the air circulation system would fail. He felt as though the walls were pressing on him, and an animal cry rose in his throat.

Then a voice came through the grille. It was clear, though faint. Thor had heard it before, but he was unable to recall where, or under what circumstances, and no image came on the screen to identify the speaker.

"Are you tired of bombs, Shining City?" the voice asked. *"If not, we have plenty more which can be delivered to you by means you can never detect. If so, flash the blue signal light on top of your Sun Converter— while you have Sun Converters!"*

There was no more. The glow faded from the screen and Thor sat very still in the thick dark, not sure whether the buzzing in his ears was a signal or an echo of blood rushing to his brain.

The buzz came from the communication cabinet. Thor opened the control and looked into Elmer's blanched face. "You heard?"

"Of course."

"How did *he* get the compulsion channel number?"

"I've no idea, in fact, I can't quite place the voice. It's one I heard—recently, I think."

"Is that the truth, Thor?"

"Of course; why should I tell you anything else?"

"You'll have to come to Eye Squad headquarters immediately, Thor. I'm summoning Zachary."

"Very well, but I don't see why—"

Elmer had cut out.

While he dressed Thor fumbled In his memory for the identity of the voice. *"Flash the blue signal light."* He had heard that instruction recently. It was—It was—Sears' instructions to Erik...Erik Forty-Four! The voice was that of Erik!

By the time he reached Eye Squad headquarters, he had answered one of Elmer's questions. There was but one source from which Erik could have gotten the compulsion channel number—from Leonard. His mind rebelled against further deductions, and when he presented himself before Elmer his clothes were damp with cold perspiration.

Marshal Zachary was already at headquarters and he beckoned Thor into a questioning booth. He held four spools in his hand and he did not smile as he greeted Thor. "There are a few discrepancies," he began.

"Yes, I know," Thor hastened to say. His mouth was dry and his voice sounded strange to his own ears. "I can explain."

"Please do; the future of the Shining City may depend on your explanations."

"Naturally I didn't know at the time I made the statements that the matter would be so important, but you see—" He moistened his lips. "You see, it was dark on the field. There was considerable excitement, and I was—well, I was frightened. And surprised, I think—yes, surprised. Terribly hurt, too, over what Leonard had done. Perhaps I didn't see clearly, and later when Captain Sears said—I felt his vision would be more accurate than mine. Trained man, you know."

The next question came like a blow to the face. "Did Sears coach you on what to say?"

"No... Well, not exactly. We talked it over, but my statements were based on my own observation, perhaps clarified a little, so that I understood my fleeting impressions."

"That is all for now, Thor." The marshal rose and smiled down on Thor. "This has been very difficult for all of us—you most of all. Have pity for me, Thor; I have ten sons to worry about."

Thor sighed with great relief. "It is good to know someone like you, Zachary."

CHAPTER SEVEN

WHEN HE reached his apartment he tumbled onto his pallet and slept more soundly than he had for several nights.

"Awaken, men of Science. It is the hour of seven..." Thor roused, angry at first at the sickish-sweet voice that poured through the grille, then relieved. It was the first time in four mornings that the record had been played, and it indicated that the City was getting back to normal. *Soon,* Thor thought as he stretched on his pallet, *everything will be cleared up.*

"Yes, awaken men of Science! It is time you awakened!" Startled, Thor sat up. Another voice cut in over that of the morning greeter. Leonard's! His words were clear, easily sorted but from those of the young woman's, and they continued sharp crackling over the background of music that completed the greeter's spool.

"The dribble to which you have just listened will soon be stilled. Men of vigor and men of vision will not long follow the foolish patterns laid down for you by the intellectual dwarves who seek power for the sake of power alone! Arise, men of Science! Arise, men! Shake off the shackles that bind you to your narrow bands of glasteel, to your vats of tasteless yeast-food, your communication cabinets and your barren pleasure women! I speak to you from the wide prairies where freedom still exists and men stand tall with pride. This freedom is yours, if you will but take it! If you will but rise and stretch and feel your strength, men—men, not political cuckolds betrayed by depraved weaklings who seek to enslave you!

"Arise and listen to the strong voice of free wind, the snap and roar of thunder over the plains! Lift your faces to the cooling rain and drink with the trees and grass. Throw open the doors of your prisons, men of Science, and let all the world share your secrets. Let your neighbors build houses not just of sawed lumber, but of glasteel! Let us sit down with you around your conference tables and exchange evenly—our wheat and berries and fruit, our corn and cheese and animal meat—the products of our toil for the products of your toil!

"We have demonstrated to you that we are strong. We have demonstrated to you that our ways can win. Think well, men of Science. Will you die in the shambles of your artificial world, or will you throw open your gates and live in the freedom we offer you in exchange for some of your science?"

Thor was trembling violently when Leonard ceased speaking. Pride swelled in him, yet fear gripped him. That was the son born of Irenka, the strong—his son! And *there* was the plot against the Shining City. For a fleeting moment, he wished that it were he who was in league with Leonard. If he were, he would answer that call by flashing the blue light on the signal towers above the Sun Converters.

At any moment Elmer or Zachary will summon me, he thought. He waited in his night robe beside the communication cabinet. The telechron dial turned slowly—ten centi-minutes, twenty, thirty. Perhaps only underlings were on duty at the Control Board and Elmer would have to be summoned. A turn was completed, still no signal. Perhaps Elmer and Zachary were so exhausted that they had left word they must not be disturbed.

Thor dared not go into his shower stall for fear he would not hear the signal. He shaved and dressed—he'd have to be ready when the summons came. His breakfast lay in the slot. It was cold now. The sight of the slimy yeast mass and the scum-covered greenish liquid nauseated him. Quickly he stuffed everything into the discard chute; if only he had a cup of burnt - wheat coffee!

His thoughts were only of the immediate. No reflection or contemplation was possible, and as the centi-minutes turned off the telechron dial his anxiety grew. When two turns were completed, he realized that the silence was something more them mere routine delay. Undoubtedly by now he was "hermetically scaled" in his apartment. In that case his innocence would be established. Here a thought sent the blood pounding to his head. Would Leonard try to contact him? He would have to face his son, guilty of treason, while the Eye Squad observed, made records and depictions for future analysis. If he revealed the slightest hint of sympathy they would—

No! Leonard was an adult. He had chosen to betray his City as well as his father; he deserved no pity. He must be destroyed like any other enemy of Science! Thor paced and prepared his speech of denunciation to Leonard, mumbling some phrases aloud. Then he stopped himself. If there were listening devices in the walls the Eye Squad would think he had some secret means of communication with Leonard! Perspiration poured off his face, soaked his clothing. He loosened his collar, removed his jacket. Had the air cooling system failed? Was he sealed in a death chamber? The walls pressed in on him, the silence rang in his ears and he gasped for breath.

Then the signal buzzed. Trembling seized him as he opened the control. Did it mean the reduction oven?

It was Gnurin, grave and calm: "Report at once to the BoardRoom, Thor." That was all he said.

The BoardRoom—only the BoardRoom! Thor laughed hysterically. Of course they knew he was guilty of nothing! He would speak to them, tell them how much he revered the Shining City, and he would denounce the traitor who was his son. Soon everything would be cleared up.

WHEN HE entered the BoardRoom, Thor was in a state of elation that was almost hysteria, but his spirits were soon depressed when he saw the faces around the conference table. All were grave. Gnurin sat quietly on the President's bench, a very deflated and composed Gnurin. Vivian's face was puckered with perplexity, and Juno appeared bewildered. Sitting at the foot of the table, between Elmer and Zachary, was a stranger, a swarthy man with iron gray hair, heavy overhanging eyebrows, and a long, thin face with a straight line of a mouth. He and Zachary were studying a sheaf of parchment charts. No one spoke for several centi-seconds. Gnurin glanced questioningly at the stranger when Thor entered, and at length the stranger rose.

Thor noticed that he walked with a decided limp; his left leg was several centimeters shorter than his right, and he grimaced as though each step caused him pain. Yet there was a strange fascination about the pain-twisted face. His eyes were large and expressive, brown, flecked with gold lights, almost feminine in their beauty. *Here is a man who has thought deeply, seen far,* Thor thought.

He stood beside the President's bench and placed a hand on Gnurin's shoulder as if to steady himself. "We will dispense with formalities and with preliminaries," he said, speaking with slow emphasis. His was a deep, though somewhat nasal voice, well modulated, trained for public speaking.

Thor closed his eyes and saw in his memory a fleur-de-lis pattern.

Doctor Julian!

"The reports that Marshal Romain Zachary have given me about members of this Board are indeed alarming. We have handled together many serious situations in cities of the Band, Romain and I, faced many a crisis. But we still have a Band, and it is my hope that the Shining City will remain in it. In the first place, there must be some replacements on this Board. Romain knows better than I who is capable of filling these important positions, and I will rely on his judgment in the matter. But I sincerely trust that those of you who remain will alter your attitude toward security. Faith is a beautiful attribute of character—in literature—but it has no place in the emotional makeup of one who occupies a position of responsibility in a city of the Band. We all love a trusting child, but if that person remains trusting after he has attained the stature of man, then he remains a child.

"The Band needs adults, men and women capable of objective thinking, capable of detachment, capable of exercising judgment which is uncolored by emotion of any kind.

"In the first place, your President Pro-Tem, Doctor Gnurin One-One-Seven, throughout this entire crisis has shown an admirable amount of healthy suspicion. But perhaps the reason he did not convince the rest of you was that he erred by presenting his suspicions in a highly emotional manner. I sincerely trust that he has learned the lesson that will henceforth make him a useful Board member.

"The report that Romain has given us on the Eye Squad of the Shining City is most shocking indeed, and the condition was brought about by the mental attitude of the Coordinator, Elmer One-Eight-One. This plot against the City, and the wave of destruction that resulted, would never have gotten beyond the initial stages if One-Eight-One had properly distrusted the men in his department. He should have turned a critical eye on Captain Renlow Sears when he offered to assist in the capture of a man with whom he had been closely associated. *Never accept the help of volunteers*—isn't that a rule of the Band police, Romain?"

Zachary nodded affirmatively. "One moment, Julian. Thor Larsen came in late and does not know that Captain Sears has been executed as the coordinator of the sabotage plot."

He turned to Thor, who was reeling under the impact. "His full confession enables us—shall I say—to close the case."

THOR FELT faint and clung to the table to hold himself erect. He was unable to speak.

"At this point," Doctor Julian continued, "I want to touch upon the case of your former President, Thor Two-Two. The relationship that was allowed to exist between Two-Two and his son invited trouble; the social scientists of the Band insist upon separation of parents from their children. The emotional fixations that are inevitable where sons or daughters remain with their parents are always detrimental to the community as a whole. The Social Coordinator, Juno Sixty-Seven is solely at fault for allowing this condition to exist. As it developed, that was the crux of the whole problem in the Shining City. I had had some reports on this matter, but I was loath to interfere in the affairs of any city of the Band. I felt sure—and I blame myself for this inexcusable faith—that things would eventually right themselves."

Anisse did report to Julian! Thor found breathing even more difficult.

"Now I come to Doctor Vivian, the Economic Coordinator. I have eaten some of the food prepared under the direction of this worthy scientist—"

Vivian puffed with pride.

"—and I find it the worst offense of all!"

Vivian slumped and dropped his head.

"We all heard the brazen plea of the traitor, Leonard Larsen. On what did he base his plea to the scientists and denizens of the Shining City? Food! *We'll give you corn and berries and animal meat,'* he said. What healthy individual, be he ever so loyal to Science, could fail to heed such a plea if he had been eating three meals a day from Doctor Vivian's yeast vats? Why, if I had eaten Vivian's gook for long I, myself, would have been willing to take up a javelin with the Northerners!

"Seriously, my fellow scientists, if we are to have loyalty to our cities, we must have proper food, not just nourishment with the correct molecular vibrations to sustain our bodies, but food with flavor—flavor that will stimulate our imaginations, give us the zest for living!

"As Romain knows—and I believe I mentioned it to Gnurin in Paris the other day—it has long been a dream of mine to *seal* our cities—build walls around them so high and so thick that no enemy can penetrate them, and cover them with a roof to protect our scientific world from the vagaries of climate, from the harmful airborne bacteria which now causes us needless suffering and brings untimely death to our scientists.

"The invention of the Unvalator and the Invalator brings this dream closer to realization. Within sealed cities, Science can control our entire environment; we can control population. It's still a dream, but as Romain knows, I am one to implement my dreams. Sun conversion, photosynthesis, the Unvalator and the Invalator—all these are steps on the way, and soon, within a few years, the Band will become the Sealed Civilization of Science."

All sat agape with wonder...all but Thor. He passed a hand over his brow. *No more sunlight on the water...No trees bending in the wind...no blaze of stars overhead at night, no summer storms with lightning darting out of the blackness...a tomb for the living—the Sealed Civilization!*

JULIAN continued. "And now for more practical matters. Your first problem in the Shining City, now that the conspirators within have been dealt with properly, is to discourage this clamoring horde at your gates. Drive them away or wipe them out. You have the means; Doctor Gnurin gave us an outline of possibilities in his speech in Paris.

"I propose that Thor Two-Two, the father of the ringleader of this band, take the disc and speak on the compulsion channel so that all the City as well as the ingenious ringleader may hear, and make the proposal." He turned to Thor. "You understand, of course, what is required." Julian limped back to his seat.

Thor rose and steadied himself by placing his hands on the table, and Gnurin opened the reception disc control.

"I propose at this time…" Thor moistened his dry lips, "that the Eye Squad equip a large hovering car with the Unvalator…and proceed to wipe out the nest of conspirators…at the Argonne Pit! I believe…that is all."

He sat, heavily, and Gnurin rose. "You have heard the proposal of Thor Two-Two; what is your pleasure?"

"Concur!"

"It is so ordered. The Eye Squad Coordinator will proceed to carry out the instructions of the Board. The meeting is adjourned." Gnurin cut the control.

Thor stood. The room whirled around his head and his knees crumpled. As he sank down he caught sight of the doctor's skeletal grin. There was mockery and triumph in it, and Thor knew that he had been replaced as President of the Board of the Shining City.

"Perhaps the birds do not choose to live in this great cage…" Thor was not sure that he had spoken. He opened his eyes and saw that he was lying on a pallet in a questioning booth at Eye Squad headquarters.

Zachary bent over him. "You were saying, Thor—?"

"I don't know what I said." He sat up and looked into the face of the only friend he felt he had left. "I did my best, Zachary; it was a matter of honor."

"An obsolete word, 'honor'; the world of Science never uses it."

"I see. It's the reduction oven now, I suppose."

"Patience, my dear Thor, patience; at the moment the ovens are terribly overcrowded."

"May I go to my apartment?" *Perhaps Anisse has come back to the City with Julian.*

"Sorry. Rules."

"Then where—"

Zachary shrugged. "We are very busy, Thor. By the way, I have some news about your wife…"

"Yes," Thor replied.

Zachary stared haltingly before continuing. "She was seriously injured on her return trip from Paris." Thor looked up in an expression of dull shock as Zachary went on, "Yes…it seems a robotic device in the official sky car ran amok and injured her—practically pulled one of her arms off. It's under investigation. I'm very sorry to give you this news. I don't have all the details just yet, but I'll give you a full update when I find out more. At any rate, you must find ways to busy yourself until we are ready to go further into your case. Perhaps you would be so good as to look over the reconstruction project at the western wall? The work there is behind schedule." With that he hurried from the room.

THOR LEFT his uniform jacket on the pallet and walked out of the room, stunned by the news. He went down the corridor and took an elevator to the transfer station for the westbound belt cars. An emergency construction crew was loading into one, and as he had so often done, he climbed in and sat amidst the construction tools that smelled of raw earth.

The car stopped at the project and the men took their tools and filed out. Cliff Davis, the overseer, came up to Thor. "We're almost through with this job, sir."

"Take your time, Cliff." Thor walked through the hole in the wall, past the Eye Squad guard who had seen him with the overseer, and took a path that led through the shrubbery.

The path, which apparently had been beaten by fleeing denizens—or by the saboteurs—went straight into the bronze glow of sunset, which lingered over the blood-red glare of the Argonne Pit. The pain in Thor's chest was intense, but he continued to walk westward.

Dusk had settled down when he came to a stockade around a cluster of tents. Here and there among the tents a dying campfire flared feeble competition to the glowing pit. The encampment was breaking up. Men scurried to and fro loading rolls of bedding and bundles of supplies into horse drawn wagons, some of which were already on the move.

"Leave the rest for the Unvalator!" The voice was Leonard's.

A dog barked and a sentry ran back to the open gateway of the stockade. "Who goes there?"

Thor gathered his strength and answered, "Thor Larsen!"

"Thor Larsen!" The name echoed through the camp, and several other sentries appeared.

"The President of the Shining City?"

"Ya! I have come to my son, Leonard."

"Leonard Larsen!" Again the echo. Several dogs were barking now, and one ran out, snarling. The sentries closed ranks and Thor saw a row of javelins outlined like sharp pickets of a fence against the glare of the Pit. Then a man broke through the line, javelin poised. He hurled it, and Thor felt the point drive into his chest. The pain expanded, like a bud bursting into flower, and petals of red spread over the white front of his blouse.

A flare from the Pit threw a harsh light over the scene, and Thor saw a man taller than himself with hair like moonbeams and eyes the color of wood violets. The man smiled grimly and spoke to the sentries. "Leave that, too, for the Unvalator!"

As Thor crumpled around the flower of pain, he gasped to the retreating figure—"Leonard!"

THE END

If you've enjoyed this book, you will not want to miss these terrific titles...

REVENGE IN AN ALIEN WORLD

When Gail Loring chose Bill Drake to be her husband—in name only—for the duration of the flight to Mars, she didn't know that she had just signed his death warrant.
Jealous Dr. Spartan, the leader of the expedition, swore to get revenge and force Gail to share his maniacal plan for power.
Bound together in space, five men and a woman strained against the powerful tug of twisted emotions and secret ambitions.

But all plans were forgotten when they landed on the Red Planet and encountered the Martians—half animal, half vegetable— with acid for blood and radar for sight.
When the Martians launched an assault against the spaceship, linking their electrical energy in an awesome display of power, Spartan realized that this was the perfect moment for personal revenge—and touched off his own diabolical plan of destruction against his fellow crewmen.

CAST OF CHARACTERS

BILL DRAKE
Married in name only for this expedition to Mars, it soon became apparent he was the target of an assassin plot because of it!

AXEL LUDSON
Spending two years in space with people he didn't really know was quite a problem—especially when one of them was a killer!

DR. WARNER JOEL
A mousey brownnoser at heart, it was a wonder he even had a part in this grand expedition into space.

DR. LEWIS SPARTAN
Curt, pompous, and the genius that had planned everything for the expedition to Mars, he hadn't figured on love—or had he?

GAIL LORING
Already having been to the moon, she was quite qualified for this Mars trip—but unprepared for the five men she was going with!

MORRIE GROVER
This pink cheeked kid was too busy looking at a gorgeous dame to be interested in what was going on in space.

THE MARTIANS
They were half animal, half vegetable. They had acid for blood and radar for sight. They were also cunning little devils…

THE RED PLANET

By
RUSS WINTERBOTHAM

ARMCHAIR FICTION
PO Box 4369, Medford, Oregon 97504

*For more information about Armchair Books and products, visit our
website at...*

www.armchairfiction.com

Or email us at...

armchairfiction@yahoo.com

CHAPTER ONE

I GOT NO SLEEP that Thursday night. I tossed and dozed and tossed again. Operation Jehad and Willy Zinder were on my mind. Operation Jehad was the designation given to the proposed first manned flight to Mars, and Willy was our last chance to fill the six-man crew.

If Willy didn't make it, Doc Spartan would be fit to be tied in a hangman's knot. More than anything else, he had insisted on a six-man crew and, if he couldn't get six qualified astronauts, including himself, on the Jehad ship, he was as likely as not to postpone the voyage for 26 months, when Mars would be in the right spot again and by which time more men could be trained.

While I rolled and tossed in my bed sheets, Willy Zinder was playing carousel in his Jupiter capsule three hundred miles above old Momma Earth. And I hated to speculate about what had happened to him. When I'd watched him get into the cherry-picker Thursday morning, he'd been a poor, frightened kid. He'd probably been suffering ever since. And now, after this dreadful night, re-entry was staring him in the face.

Feeling scared was natural and nothing to be ashamed of, because we all got butterflies on our first solo orbit. But when I took my ASD tests, I'd managed to keep my teeth from chattering. Willy hadn't and somehow I got the feeling that he was suffering as much as all the rest of us combined. He looked so ready to collapse that I wondered what was holding him up.

Finally I gave up trying to sleep. It was daylight anyhow and I dressed, hurried to a restaurant and had scrambled eggs and coffee. Then I went over to the reservation to see how things were going. Dr. Spartan probably had spent the night there, but the rest of us had knocked off when the midnight operations shift came on duty. If they'd all spent a night like I had, the other members of the Jehad crew would be on hand almost as soon as me.

Besides Spartan, the others were Axel Ludson, the big Swede from Minnesota; Dr. Warner Joel, who probably would hide his feelings by slapping people on the back and trying to joke about inconsequential things; and Morrie Grover, who was a pink-cheeked kid. We, plus Dr. Lewis Spartan, had already qualified for the first manned trip to Mars.

But plans had been made for six and Willy Zinder was our last candidate. To say we were scraping the bottom of the barrel would be selling Willy short. He was Number 12 out of 100 fine physical and mental specimens who had been selected for astronaut training three years before. Eighty-eight others had been washed out, one way or another, before twelve were fingered for Operation Jehad—so named because Jehad means holy war to Moslems. We were going to Mars, which was named after the Roman war god, so that accounted for the war part of the name, but I don't know what was holy about it except that going to Mars would materialize an ancient dream of man to travel through space to another world.

Willy was as healthy as a mountain and even if he looked scared I could tell he had guts. By the time the lift-off date of the operation got a few months away, Willy had climbed to position Number Six. Two higher numbers had flunked the ASD—Aeronautical Systems Division—tests. Dr. Spartan had said two others wouldn't do—the space boys in Washington took Doc's word as gospel. One had been banged up in a car wreck and was still in the hospital, and the sixth man had undergone an emergency appendectomy, which left him too weak to lift off for Mars at the scheduled time.

There wasn't time now to train more men for the job, which meant that Willy *had* to pass and Doc Spartan was enough of a perfectionist to insist that Willy get as thorough a testing as the others of the crew.

Sure, there were other astronauts. There were ten or twelve working on other projects, but the plasma space engine isn't an ordinary spaceship that anybody can take on a 150,000,000-mile round trip without rigorous training.

I reached the gate that separated spacemen from mere Earthlings and flashed my badge on the security guard.

"William Drake," he said, grinning. "Sure hope you have luck today, Mr. Drake."

"Thanks," I said. "How's Zinder doing?"

"Very well, the last I heard. The boys coming off the last Operations shift said he'd handled everything pretty well."

I went through the gate. Almost anybody can get through this one, but there are other security officers, at other gates further on down, to keep the place from being overrun by tourists, newspaper guys and people looking for rest rooms. How far you got depended on the color of your badge. Mine was blue, for the wild blue yonder, and I could walk right into Dr. Spartan's office with it, provided I had business there. And I wouldn't dare call on Dr. Spartan unless I did have it. He could eat a man out better than acid.

Finally I reached the bunker. I glanced into the room filled with the Operations staff which was keeping track of Willy—communicating with him, tabulating his heartbeats, respiration and maybe his thoughts—and checking the behavior of his capsule. I wasn't interested in them. I went to the end of the hall, flashed my badge again, and entered the room reserved for the panel that was going to pass or flunk Willy Zinder.

Doc Spartan was the man in charge. He was the leader of our little group, but that was no break for Willy Zinder. Doc Spartan was an old space hand. He'd been to the moon and he had conducted the trial flight of the plasma engine. First, last and middle, he was a perfectionist. I hated him, so did everyone else, but there was one thing that we all could say: if Doc stamped you okay, you were as good as he expected to find. And there was another thing that could be said: Doc Spartan made a top sergeant of the Marine Corps look like Peter Pan.

He was there, along with three other men who looked as if they'd been without sleep for a week. Maybe they'd taken a few naps during the twenty-four hours, but it didn't show. They were red-eyed, their hair was uncombed and they each showed a day's growth of beard. Although the room was air-conditioned, they looked sweaty and hot. Mugs full of black coffee were on their desks and there were bread crusts and half-eaten sandwiches on trays nearby.

Axel Ludson stood back against the rear wall. Like me, he had nothing to do but watch and he had probably hurried over after eating breakfast, just as I had, in order to be on hand when Willy made his re-entry.

Axel was a big, raw-boned Swede, which is a description you could give of a large portion of the male population of his hometown in Minnesota. He had light brown hair, blue eyes and a long straight nose. His jaw looked big and solid enough to crush concrete. He winked at me and I walked over to him.

"Willy is doing fine," he said, which was an accolade. Axel made his words count. "Doc has thrown everything at him but a flock of asteroids and Willy hasn't missed a pitch."

"Good!" I said. "Where is Willy now?"

Axel nodded toward a screen on the left wall. On it was projected a portion of a globe showing Northern Siberia. A little spot of light showed up in the middle of it.

"In thirty minutes he'll begin his last orbit."

"How did he do on the emergencies?" I asked.

Axel grinned. "He acted like they were the real thing."

The space capsule carrying Willy was the old-fashioned type, with room enough for only one man. However, it had special controls, which made its manual operation similar to that used on the plasma craft. Throughout the flight, Willy was in charge of the operation. Without warning, certain simulated emergencies were signaled to instruments aboard the capsule and Willy was expected to meet them.

Although space flight sounds dangerous, most of it isn't because space is more empty than anything most of us ever saw. The only critical times are usually at the lift-off, the re-entry and the landing. However, other emergencies can arise. The worst would be the sudden appearance of a large meteor, meaning a pebble a quarter of an inch in diameter or bigger. Since about 95 per cent of the meteors in space are less than that size, chances of meeting one, even on a trip lasting two-and-a-half years, are remote. But it could happen.

The plasma ship was equipped with meteor bumpers, which would vaporize anything smaller than a quarter of an inch. Larger ones might puncture the sides, but even then there was patching fluid in the walls of the craft which would prevent too much air loss. A tremendously large meteor can be detected by radar and avoided. Willy'd had to make the right maneuver to avoid such a meteor.

Radiation in space also poses some problems. Space travel requires high speed, and astronauts can pass through a radiation belt in so short a time that the exposure isn't harmful. But a very large cloud might pose problems and Willy would have to meet such an emergency by determining the size of the cloud and the best way to pierce it.

Another hazard could be faulty astrogation. On a 75,000,000-mile trip—the distance we were to travel to reach Mars—a small error at the start might put the ship too far from Mars to be caught by the planet's gravity at the end of the voyage. Willy had to make observations throughout the test flight and go through operations necessary to correct his trajectory. There might be other minor emergencies, such as failure of equipment and instruments, but Willy had demonstrated his ability to cope with them in tests conducted on the ground.

Dr. Warner Joel entered the room. A few months ago he had been overweight, but stringent diet had cut his weight down enough to allow him to qualify for our crew. He was a short, stocky man, with a smooth face and nervous manner. However, his knowledge of geology had made him almost indispensable. Rarely do you find a man with his experience in this particular field who can also qualify for the stringencies of space flight.

There was one thing against Joel that I was determined to overlook and this was his rather ingratiating manner, his eagerness to appear to be more than he was, and his intense desire to win favor from Dr. Spartan.

As he entered he hailed everyone in a loud voice, speaking to no one in particular. And no one in particular answered. Ignoring the rebuff, and with a strict eye to protocol, he walked over to the control board where Dr. Spartan was seated.

"Great show, Doctor! Brilliant show!" Joel exclaimed, extending his hand as if he were congratulating a playwright on opening night.

Spartan, his dark eyes glued to the instruments in front of him, ignored Joel.

"Yes, sir!" the geologist continued, putting his hand in his coat pocket, probably to give it warmth after Spartan's coolness. "We've got a good man in Willy Zinder. I always did say this boy was a sleeper. Better than a lot of men in our group, in fact."

Axel nudged me in the ribs and, as I turned, he winked one of his ice-blue eyes. "Meaning me or you, Bill?"

"You, you big Swede," I said, winking back. "But my opinion puts Willy several notches above Joel, too."

Axel chuckled softly.

"I won't worry with Willy Zinder on the crew," Joel was saying loudly. "No, sir—"

"Why don't you sit down?" snarled Spartan, still not turning his head. "You drive me crazy."

"Uh—ah—why yes, of course! I didn't realize—"

"Then do it!" snapped Spartan.

Joel almost stumbled as he backed away. Now, as he spotted Axel and me, he decided we were appropriate sympathizers. He walked over to us and said, "He's understandably touchy."

"I never pet rattlesnakes," said Axel.

Willy's voice, surprisingly cheerful, came over the loudspeaker. He was A-okay and was passing over the North Pole for the fifteenth time.

Communications responded and wished him good luck.

Dr. Spartan nodded. Then he turned his head and called out: "Miss Loring!"

I turned my head. I hadn't seen Gail Loring when I entered the room. She must have been in Operations and had entered through the door in the other end of the room. Now I saw her fine-featured face as she replied, "Yes, Dr. Spartan?"

"Come here!"

She came over to his control board briskly, holding her head high, paying no attention to anyone but Dr. Spartan. She was all business.

It was a pitiful waste, because she was an attractive girl and so untouchable. She wasn't beautiful in the sense that a stage or screen star is. She was good-looking, the kind of girl who wore well. Without lace or fancy trimmings, she was solid, durable, functional—and feminine, in spite of herself. She'd made a successful landing on the moon and had accompanied Dr. Spartan on the trial flight of the plasma ship. Now she was preparing for some other project—only the NASA knew what it was.

Surprisingly enough, I'd found out in the three or four times we'd met that she had a pleasant disposition, in spite of her businesslike manner. She liked to laugh and she was intelligent, which of course she'd have to be as a woman astronaut. Up to the time I'd met her informally, I'd classified her as a female Dr. Spartan.

"Please take over the control panel for a few minutes," Spartan said. "I'm going to get some breakfast before the re-entry."

"Certainly, Doctor," she said. "Any special orders?"

"None," he said. "Operations has alerted the Navy carrier and it is in position to pick up Zinder after the re-entry, on his next orbit. All you have to do is be ready to switch over to ground control in the event of an emergency."

I felt Axel's elbow shudder against my arm. Resorting to ground control would wash Willy Zinder off the project because it was his job to handle the capsule from beginning to end of his flight. Only during the lift-off and re-entry was there automatic operation—Willy had to take over again after re-entry.

Dr. Spartan rose and Gail took his seat. She glued her eyes on the instruments with all the instinct of a good pointer flushing a covey of quail.

I watched her. Even in slacks she looked good; a statement I could make about no other women I've ever seen. She wore no make-up, except lipstick, and that didn't hurt her. She had brown hair cut close, almost mannish style, and still she looked like a woman.

The disappointing thing about her was that she would not allow a man to become part of her life. Not that she was cold. No one could tell me that a woman who tried so hard to forget she was feminine had nothing to forget. It was simply that men were "out" until she'd got enough of her career.

I turned my head and noticed that young Morrie Grover had come in and was too busy watching Gail Loring to take much interest in what was going on in space.

Morrie was the fifth man in our crew—Willy was qualifying as sixth. Morrie was the youngest of our group, being a couple of years my junior by the calendar. Actually I felt at least ten years older because Morrie was one of those eager young lads who keep too busy learning about the universe to understand what is going on in this world. No doubt he'd grow up a lot on the Martian adventure. The fact that he was looking hungrily at Gail didn't mean his thoughts were grown up. High school boys have the same thoughts.

He watched her until he decided, apparently, that she was less likely to move than the faces on Mt. Rushmore, then he took off his glasses, began rubbing them with a clean white handkerchief and squinted at me.

"Hello, Bill," he said condescendingly. "Is Willy on his last lap yet?"

"He will be in about two minutes," I said, glancing at the clock on the wall. I could have told him about the map and explained that he could see for himself, but that would have been rude. I would have to live with this guy for thirty months and it was best that I learn to get along with him.

Dr. Spartan came in again, carrying a bacon-and-egg sandwich in his left hand.

"Hello, Doctor Spartan," said Morrie.

"Wmpf!" replied Spartan, chomping on the sandwich. He didn't even give Morrie a glance.

Morrie looked shook up.

"Don't mind him, kid," said Axel. "He hates everybody. Especially today."

Morrie did not reply. He blew heavily on his glasses, wiped off the moisture with his handkerchief and held them up to the light. He squinted, nodded with satisfaction and put them on his nose. Then he turned to resume watching Gail Loring.

Though Dr. Spartan had taken a position behind Gail so that he blocked the view, Morrie wasn't going to miss the pleasure of ogling the prettiest girl astronaut in the world. He moved over to the left for an unobstructed view. Realizing there would be about ninety idle minutes to kill, I moved to the right, deciding that I could get even more pleasure out of watching her than Morrie could.

Axel and Dr. Joel remained where they were, Axel watching the little light on the screen map and Dr. Joel bobbing his head, smiling and waving at everyone who looked in his direction.

Gail turned her head and looked up at Dr. Spartan. "You want to take over now, Dr. Spartan?" she asked.

"Go ahead," said Spartan. "I haven't finished breakfast, my dear."

She turned her head in a businesslike manner and glanced at the clock, then at the instrument panel. Finally she picked up the microphone and held it to her lips. She waited a moment, still watching the instrument panel.

"Last orbit!" she said. Her words were echoed by the speaker in the room. "We'll start our countdown for reentry five minutes before you've completed the turn, Zinder. At zero, set the automatic control to take over."

"A-okay," said Willy's voice. He spoke calmly. Apparently he was no longer frightened.

"Remember," she said, "precisely at zero."

"A-okay."

Gail put the microphone back on its hook. She watched the instruments. Suddenly she tensed. Her voice rose as she spoke to Dr. Spartan.

"Doctor, look!"

She gestured excitedly at the panel.

"Good God in heaven!" Spartan reached out, snatched up the microphone. "Zinder! Zinder, you fool! What have you done? Are you crazy?"

"Hey!" Willy's cry was full of fear, but he was not speaking to Dr. Spartan. He was yelling to no one. "Help me! I'm accelerating—decelerating! Something's gone haywire! I'm starting to re-enter—"

The voice broke off as a crash came from the speaker.

"He hit something!" somebody yelled.

"Hell, he probably fell to the floor," said Axel. "He wouldn't have his harness on now."

"He cut in the automatic," Spartan said. "Did you tell him this was the last lap, Miss Loring?"

"Oh, no, Doctor! I told him it was the next to last!"

"He must have misunderstood."

I squirmed to catch a glimpse of the instrument panel, but Spartan's bulk hid it from my eyes. Willy should have known he had another lap to go. There was a clock in front of him. I shifted my position. I could see Gail's hands flying to this button and that as if she were trying desperately to check the fall with the ground controls. But she must have known it was useless to try. Once the reentry cycle is started, nothing can shut it off till the parachute opens in the Earth's atmosphere. Willy Zinder was being returned to a world unready for his arrival.

"Willy! Willy! Please answer!" Gail screamed above the excited voices in the room.

No reply came from the speaker.

Then the intercom from Operations cut in. "The medical section says Zinder may have been injured by sudden deceleration," said the voice. "His heart action is very weak."

"Oh, dear God!" moaned Gail Loring. "It's all my fault!"

CHAPTER TWO

ORDINARY HUMAN REFLEXES, which respond to tangible, near-at-hand crises, were woefully inadequate for the dozen or so men and women in that room. What could anyone do to save Willy Zinder, so far away that he could only be detected by instruments, and whose future and very existence depended upon electronic gadgets which went about their task more cold-bloodedly even than Dr. Spartan?

In fact, Spartan himself seemed to lose his poise for a moment. He appeared to freeze as he stood directly behind Gail, staring at the dials that told what was happening to Willy. At last he seemed to see her hands, fluttering aimlessly from button to switch. He reached out, swept them away.

"Stop it!" he said hoarsely. "Nothing you can do will stop the automatic action of the capsule now!"

Gail seemed to wilt. Spartan released her hands and she sat there helplessly. Behind her Spartan looked like some kind of understudy of Satan, his black beard, dark eyes and sharp features blending into the illusion. He was tall and gaunt to begin with—now he looked taller and more gaunt. Was it a suspicion of a smile that I saw on his face for a brief, fleeting instant? But surely he didn't want Willy to fail. He had a greater stake in this operation than any of us. For him it would mean immortality as the leader of the first manned flight to Mars.

Again the fleeting smile. I tried to tell myself that it was the result of nervousness. I'd often seen men under stress grinning like fools, because laughter is an emotional reflex. But I'd never suspected Spartan of having emotions before. He'd had a wealth of experience and had seen men die in space.

For ten years he'd been one of the top astronauts of the nation—ever since he had risen to fame as the genius who had developed a certain method of converting nuclear energy directly into electricity. In those days he'd been a poorly paid instructor at some obscure mid-western college. Now he was famous as a spaceman, and wealthy from his discoveries.

His apparent nervousness lasted only an instant. Then he became his cold self again. Not that it served to reassure anybody—we all knew that northeast of where we stood, far out over the Atlantic, Willy's capsule was screaming into the atmosphere. It mattered little that the parachutes were open, since the men who had been watching the instruments recording Willy's heartbeat said he had been hurt badly.

There was no button to push, no knob to turn, no switch to flip which would make everything A-okay. And there certainly was no magic wand to break the evil enchantment of the moment.

The loudspeaker squawked out a report from the Navy carrier. Its helicopters were airborne, attempting to reach the place where Willy would come down, but they were hundreds of miles west—at the place where Willy would have come down after his next lap, not this one.

Then there was an awful silence, broken only by a sob from Gail. Spartan looked down at her, his lips curling with displeasure.

She clasped her hands to her face and swayed in her chair. Spartan growled with annoyance, then turned his head and saw me.

"Drake!" he bellowed. He gestured a slim finger toward Gail. "Get that hysterical woman out of here!"

I didn't like the way he gave the order, but it made sense and I started forward to obey. Gail jerked her hands away from her face and turned toward him. She stopped her swaying, turned her eyes on Dr. Spartan and tilted her chin upward with indignation.

"I'm *not* hysterical! I've never been hysterical!"

"Take her outside, Drake," said Dr. Spartan, as if she'd never spoken.

It did seem like the best idea. Every dial in front of her was an instrument of torture. Whatever happened to Willy Zinder, she believed it to be her fault.

I stepped forward and took Gail by the arm. "Please come," I said. "There's nothing you can do."

She jerked her arm out of my grip, then got up by herself. "Willy must have misunderstood me," she said. Suddenly her shoulders sagged. "Yes, Bill Drake, I'll go. You're right. There's nothing I can do."

Her eyes were moist but her voice was firm. She was not crying like a hysterical woman. I believe that, at that moment, if there were anything she could have done, she would have done it as efficiently as anyone in that room, including Dr. Spartan.

She let me take her arm again as I guided her through the door, out of the bunker and into the refreshing warmth of the outside air.

"I told him to switch on the automatic controls precisely at zero," she said. "Those were my words: 'Precisely at zero!' He must have misunderstood. He thought I said it was precisely zero at that moment. He lost track of time."

"Don't think about it," I said. "It wasn't your fault."

"It *was* my fault. People under tension are in a highly suggestible state. I should have chosen my words more carefully, so that he could not possibly misunderstand—"

"If Willy was capable of such confusion, it's best that we know about it now. In space that kind of a misunderstanding could cost lives."

"Willy may be dying," she said. "Even if he isn't, the Mars project is down the drain for twenty-six months."

"Maybe," I said, "and maybe not. Spartan says he's gotta have a six-man crew, but I don't follow him. It's better to try it short-handed than to get there after the Commies."

"But I've heard him say a dozen times that there must be six men," she said. "Dr. Spartan doesn't change his plans once he makes up his mind."

Certainly that was true, but Dr. Spartan was too intelligent to insist on the impossible. Six men could operate the plasma ship efficiently: two could be on watch, two could rest, two could care for the needs of the others—prepare the meals, do cleaning, and operate the water and air regeneration machinery, check the course and so on. But a system could be worked out for five, four, three—even two or one. The fewer the number, the greater the risk, but the important thing was to achieve a successful mission. The risks could never deter him from trying for a first landing on Mars.

We reached the pad, which the big Jupiter rocket had carried Willy Zinder into space twenty-four hours before. Gail stood there looking at it, choking back a sob, and then turned around and started back toward the bunker.

"I could take Willy's place, if he's—he's hurt," she said softly. She probably had been thinking about this while we stood at the launching pad.

I tried to smile at her. "That would cause complications."

"Why? I'm as qualified as you, Bill Drake. I made a test flight in the plasma ship along with Dr. Spartan and Mr. Ludson. I've passed every test you and the others passed and I've made a flight to the moon."

"You've already been assigned to a project," I told her, hoping it would end the talk.

"That can wait," she insisted. "Besides, there are others who could be trained for my job and there's time to train them, whereas Operation Jehad begins its final phase in five days."

"I wasn't selling your qualifications short," I said. "What I meant was—you're a woman."

"Good Lord! Would Dr. Spartan discriminate against me because I'm not a man?"

"Dr. Spartan wouldn't care if you were an ape. But a lot of people would wonder what one pretty girl was doing up in space with five men."

"Not really! You mean they'd think my honor and virtue would be—lost?" For an instant there was the faintest trace of a smile on her face.

"Exactly," I said. "This world has some queer standards of propriety—especially the good old U.S.A. with its puritan traditions. A lot of people would take the stand that an unmarried young woman could hardly expect to spend two-and-one-half years in close quarters with five unmarried men and expect to come back chaste."

She laughed and I joined her.

"Ridiculous."

"Yes, but that's what they'd think," I insisted.

"Do you imagine I give a hoot about what people think?" she asked. "And what does Victorian decorum have to do with going to Mars?"

"Nothing at all, but there are bureaucrats and politicians who could spike Project Jehad on moral grounds. These hypocrites wouldn't give you credit for being a virtuous young woman, nor us credit for being gentlemen with restraint. No doubt they'd judge us all by their own past behavior."

There were no objections when I went on a test flight with *two* men."

"You weren't gone overnight. At least, it wasn't night on the puritan side of the Earth," I explained. "These people think all sins occur at night. Besides, you were in communication with the Earth the whole time. You had a radio chaperon."

"Holy cow!" she said. "Can't we make people see that it doesn't matter if the world thinks I'm a fallen woman? The success of the project is more important than my reputation, my morals, or even my life. I'm going to offer to go in Willy's place."

"Good luck," I said, quite certain she wouldn't have any.

Axel Ludson was waiting for us outside the bunker with the bad news.

Although the Navy had been alert and had done everything possible to reach the scene of the capsule's landing, it had been too far away to arrive in time. Helicopters had been sent aloft immediately, but they arrived at the capsule just in time to see it sink into the ocean, a mile and a half deep at that point.

"How horrible!" said Gail.

"We're not sure he could have survived his injuries," said Axel. "The medical observers believe his neck was broken and that he was dying as his capsule floated down to the sea."

Gail shuddered. "It was my fault."

"You mustn't say that, Miss Loring," said Axel. "The only way it could have been your fault was if you had touched the automatic control button yourself. Did you? Even by accident?"

"No. No, of course not," she said. "My hands were in my lap. I was talking into the mike just a moment before. There was no reason to take over control of the capsule."

Axel nodded. "I was watching you," he said. "That is my recollection. That leaves only two ways for the accident to have happened. Either Willy put the ship into automatic himself or there was a malfunctioning that set it off spontaneously."

Neither theory seemed to fit. In the first place, Willy had been drilled on what to do before re-entering. One of the first things— something even a novice would realize—would have been to get into his harness. Furthermore, Willy had instruments, including a chronometer, in front of him and he should have known he had to spend ninety more minutes in space.

Faulty mechanism might have accounted for the accident, but everything had been tested, checked and double-checked. Dr. Spartan himself had gone over everything. "Dr. Spartan would like to talk to you, Miss Loring," Axel went on. "There will be an inquiry, but he wants to hear your story as soon as you feel up to it."

Gail moistened her lips. "I'd like to get it over with now," she said. "Thanks for telling me—everything." She turned back to me. "And thanks to you, Bill Drake. I feel much better after talking to you."

I remained outside the bunker while Axel took her in.

Later I made a statement, along with everyone else who had had an official part in the test. Dr. Spartan announced that the fate of the Martian expedition would be decided within a few days and if it was decided to go ahead with a short crew, the lift-off would take place on schedule.

I was not surprised, therefore, when I was called into his office the next morning. Dr. Joel was there and so were Morrie Grover and Axel. We sat down in straight-backed chairs opposite his desk to wait. About five minutes later Dr. Spartan accompanied by Gail, came into the room.

My first thought was that he was extending the investigation of the accident, and then I recalled Gail's decision to volunteer for the Mars expedition in Willy's place. Dr. Spartan was as dedicated as Gail and the idea of flaunting convention and risking a lot of condemnation wouldn't have bothered him. But there were powers higher than Dr. Spartan who would step in and halt the project if public pressure were applied.

We greeted him formally. No one ever became informal with Dr. Spartan in his office. In fact, I couldn't remember anyone but Axel who had ever tried to kid Spartan. But Axel was a special case. Even Dr. Spartan secretly admitted that Axel was the most reliable astronaut on the project.

"Thanks for being here punctually, gentlemen," said Dr. Spartan, sitting down behind his desk. Again he looked like the Devil himself, just as he had yesterday when Willy's capsule went out of control. "As you know, the fate of the Martian operation is uncertain because of yesterday's unfortunate accident. But there is an outside chance we can go ahead with it, if an obstacle or two are removed."

He paused, letting his cold black eyes sweep our group, finally resting on Gail Loring who was seated facing us in a chair at the end of Dr. Spartan's desk. She smiled, showing her pretty dimples.

"Miss Loring is willing to fill the vacancy in our crew," Spartan said quietly.

No one spoke. We all looked at Gail, every last man of us thinking what a wonderful trip it would be with her aboard. And every last man realized that with a woman aboard there would be complications.

"She's a fully qualified astronaut," Spartan went on. "No further tests would be needed to prove that she could step into the vacant spot in our crew and hold up as well as any of us during the long, tedious trip through space. However, she is a woman."

"I guess we can all see that," said Dr. Joel, in a feeble attempt to be funny. No one laughed but Joel. Spartan's hard eyes cut him short.

"I wasn't so sure you could, Warner," said Spartan, his voice full of sarcasm. "But your half-witted wisecrack brings the big objection into full focus. A woman, especially an attractive woman—" Spartan bowed toward Gail and permitted himself to smile with all the graciousness he could muster. "—well, it complicates matters."

Again we held our silence. Joel choked back whatever comment he'd been about to make as Spartan glanced at him again.

"A woman, alone with a large group of men, would bring dissension and emotional factors into the situation which would not arise if all our crew were men. Besides, there is convention to worry about. Certain prudish individuals, of which there are far too many on Earth, would accuse us of promoting some sort of Saturnalia in space—free love, even licentiousness."

"It would be a lie," said Gail. "I have nothing to fear from any of you in that respect."

"Not here and now, perhaps," Spartan replied, "but two-and-one-half years in space might have a cumulative effect. None of us are properly called *old* men, my dear. Besides, we'll be making history, and we'll have to *appear* to be, as well as be, above reproach."

"Oh, come on," said Gail, resenting the trend of the conversation. "History has never been that pure—"

Spartan scowled. He resented her remark. "I know that, Miss Loring," he replied. "But the fact that we are making history will cause politicians and bureaucrats, who have the power to call off the project, to fear the loss of public support. Votes are what they want, more than scientific achievement. All of you know our plans call for a six-man crew. Fewer than six would require a revision of plans, redistribution of duties, and a slighting of many important aims. In order to justify the expenditure of billions or dollars of taxpayer money we must show results."

"That's the first time I ever heard of a taxpayer being considered in a space operation," said Joel, once more trying to be funny.

"But it's a point," said Axel, nodding his head and glancing around first at me and then at Morrie Grover; who had sat through the session watching Gail as if he; were hypnotized.

"Does anyone have a constructive idea?" Spartan asked coldly. He was trying to keep the discussion from getting out of hand and, from this, I suspected he had his own plans fully worked out.

"It's your show," I said. "What's your idea?"

Spartan did not like to have anyone reading his mind and he honored me with one of his stern glances. "In the interest of science," he said, "I'm proposing marriage to Miss Loring."

I expected almost anything but that. My mouth flew open.

"In the interest of science? Good Lord!" said Morrie Grover.

Gail half rose from her seat, then settled down. "Doctor!" she exclaimed. "Why didn't you discuss this with me beforehand? That's the least I would expect—"

"This, as I said, is a proposal made purely in the interest of our mission," Spartan said.

"Well, I resent it," she said. I rather guessed that she was showing a natural, female resistance to so cold and unfeeling a proposition.

"You shouldn't," said Spartan. "There's nothing wrong with the idea. I have much to offer you—or any other woman. I have substantial wealth. I have a long list of accomplishments. I am famous and will be even more so at the end of this trip. And certainly I'm not repulsive."

His chin tilted upward slightly as he displayed his profile I'm sure he didn't pose intentionally; his conceit was sub conscious, but nevertheless amazing.

Gail pressed her lips tightly together. For an instant I had a terrible fear that she was going to laugh. Then I was even more frightened at the thought that she might possibly accept this proposal. It would be a waste of such a beautiful, attractive young woman.

"Actually, Doctor," she said after some deliberation, "you're suggesting I prostitute myself for science. If I ever decide to do that, I'll do it on my own terms."

Spartan seemed to stagger mentally, as if she'd landed an uppercut on his subconscious conceit. "But, Miss Loring," he said, "if you were married to me, it would erase whatever objections there'd be to the idea of a woman going to Mars with five men. The unconventionality would become respectability. The puritans would have no reason to object to the space trip and the men in Washington wouldn't need to fear the loss of votes."

"Couldn't we make the trip with a five-man crew?" I asked.

Spartan glared at me as if I'd suggested we organize a Communist cell.

"I told you I want to get maximum results from our trip," he said. "I won't be satisfied with less." He turned to the others to amplify his statement. "There must be a full crew and Miss Loring is the only qualified astronaut available. And the only way she can go with us is as a married woman." Now he turned to Miss Loring. "Certainly you'll not refuse?" he demanded.

"I understand the problem thoroughly, Dr. Spartan," Gail told him. "But I won't consider marriage in the generally accepted sense. If we must conform to convention, we can have a ceremony; everything and anything that may follow a normal wedding will be of my own choosing."

"I'm not sure I understand," said Spartan.

"I mean it will be a marriage in name only, I won't even share quarters with my husband. I've been aboard the plasma ship. As spaceships go, it's a palace. There's room for six men, provisions and equipment for two-and-a-half years. At each end there are observation cabins used in getting the parallax in astrogation. I'll use one of them for living quarters. The rest of you will bunk in the main cabin of the ship. Furthermore, the marriage will end when we return to the Earth. A quiet divorce or, possibly, annulment will be arranged. Do you object to divorce, Dr. Spartan?"

"No," said Spartan with ill-concealed temper.

"Does anyone else object to divorce on religious or other grounds?"

She paused, awaiting an answer. Axel finally spoke. "I do not object to divorce," he said. "However, I do not believe in this kind of marriage, either."

"What about you, Bill Drake?"

"Anything for science," I said. But deep in my heart I knew that if I was ever fortunate enough to go through a marriage ceremony with Gail, I'd move heaven and Earth, and all the planets between, to make the union a permanent one.

"And you, Dr. Joel?"

Joel cleared his throat. "I'd take you under any conditions, Miss Loring."

"Morris Grover?"

"I have no objections." He looked at her hungrily.

"Am I to understand that you intend to pick one of the others?" asked Dr. Spartan. "I've already asked you to be my bride. I suppose your conditions are reasonable. I will accept them."

"That's very generous of you, Doctor," said Gail. "And my reason for turning you down is not to be taken as a criticism of you as a man or as a lover-in-name-only. It's simply that as leader of the expedition you must have disciplinary control over all members of the crew. As your wife, I'd be tempted to ask for privileges, even though I am not a believer in favoritism—especially in space where the line between life and death is as thin as a quarter-inch meteor. It would not be to the best interests of this expedition for you to have a wife. However, I have proposals for marriage from Bill Drake, Dr. Joel and Morris Grover. Am I right? Any of you is free to back out."

"I won't back out," said Morrie breathlessly.

"I won't either," I said quickly.

Joel cleared his throat. "I said I'd take you under any conditions."

"I feel honored, gentlemen." Gail smiled at us, showing her dimples. I decided that, under different circumstances, I could have proposed to her on my own initiative and been as conventional as hell about it. But this like a political convention.

"Which?" asked Morrie.

"Not you," she said. "You're younger than I am. And not Dr. Joel—he's at least ten years older. She paused, stared at me and then went on. "Because this marriage is one of convenience—a propaganda wedding to satisfy propriety—we ought to be convincing. Bill Drake is the pin-up boy to millions of panting secretaries and shopgirls who see his picture in newspapers and on television. Would this public believe in a marriage between us? I think so. For no one could possibly imagine I could resist such a prize."

She paused and waited for comments. None came. Five astronauts, including Dr. Spartan, sat tensely waiting for her inevitable decision.

"Believe me," Gail went on, "I could resist this handsome young astronaut very well. He's somewhat conceited, you know, and he is too much aware that he's the answer to a maiden's prayer. But millions of man-hungry women wouldn't see it that way. I'm not panting over Bill Drake, and that's why he's the logical choice. It'll look like a love match and who'll know the difference?"

She paused once more, then turned to me. "Forgive the insults, Bill. Will you marry me? Or do you want to back out?"

It was the first time she had ever called me Bill without adding my last name. I sat there for a moment, somewhat dazed by the outcome. Should I take her in my arms and kiss her tenderly, passionately? Hardly. My ears still burned from her statement that I considered myself the answer to a maiden's prayer, and that I was a conceited pin-up boy. Considering her attitude, should I back out? Or should I cold-bloodedly allow her the use of my last name for the sake of science? My male ego told me she cared a little, secretly, or at the very least, would learn to care before Operation Jehad ended. I began to feel happy about the whole deal.

Dr. Spartan's voice came through my thoughts. "You're not acting very enthusiastic, Drake."

"I was thinking of the conditions," I said.

"I won't sue for breach of promise if you want to back out," said Gail.

That decided me. "When's the wedding?" I asked.

As I spoke, Joel and Morrie looked at me with ill-concealed disappointment. They'd hoped, down to the wire, that something would happen which would turn the scales in their favor. Even now, I noticed that Morrie hadn't quite given up. He turned his eyes toward Gail. You could practically see him hoping that, in reality, it would turn out to be a marriage in name only that he'd have a chance to win her before we returned.

"Just before the lift-off," said Gail.

"Humph," said Dr. Spartan. "That settles it, I suppose." He didn't like it, but he couldn't back out now.

He turned his eyes toward me.

They were full of hatred.

CHAPTER THREE

SOME UNSCRUPULOUS PUBLIC relations genius attached to Operation Jehad was informed of Gail Loring's betrothal and, in the remaining four days before the lift-off, the entire world was told the most romantic story since Romeo and Juliet—and it was lies, mostly.

Only the marriage was a fact. But the world was informed that William Drake and Gail Loring, high-ranking astronauts, had fallen deeply in love some months before. They had secretly agreed to be married after the completion of Operation Jehad. Drake, brave man that he was, and Gail, self-sacrificing young woman that she was, had pushed their personal desires into the background for science; the cruel, tragic death of Willy Zinder had left a vacancy in the Jehad crew and Gail and Bill had agreed to marry immediately so that both could further this important expedition into the unknown. The fact that inadvertently the trip would also serve as a honeymoon cruise, put the whole project on a more romantic note.

Space officials in Washington, fully apprised of the reasons for the wedding, and sold on the idea by Dr. Spartan, were not only gratified by the world-wide acceptance of these lies, but they announced that the ceremony would be included as part of the countdown proceedings prior to the launching of the big Saturn that would carry us all to the plasma ship, already in orbit around the Earth.

The bride and groom and all of the members of the wedding party, with the exception of a federal judge who was to perform the rites, would be wearing spacesuits. The only charitable thing the officials did was to forbid interviews with either the bride-to-be or her intended. There just wasn't time, they said. Actually they didn't trust us to conceal the real reason behind the marriage. The project's publicity team, however, issued handouts of purported interviews, a fictional history of our love affair, and pictures.

On the day before the launching, I received two mail sacks full of letters from the panting shopgirls mentioned by Gail and a United States post-office truck delivered a full cargo of gifts to Gail. I didn't read the mail, and the gifts were stored in a government warehouse, pending our return from Mars. I don't know how much mail and parcel post came the fourth day. We were too busy to find out.

I developed a monumental guilty feeling when I realized the magnitude of our deception. I was sick of the whole business. There had been many marriages of convenience, of course, and some had turned out better than marriages for love, but this was pure fraud. The only consolation was that through it we had acquired a full crew. Still, I couldn't help feeling that a quiet, secret ceremony would have accomplished the same purpose. Why compound a fraud with a spectacle?

Twelve precious minutes were squeezed out of the countdown for the ceremony. We marched in spacesuits, sans helmets, to the launching pad—five male astronauts and one female, accompanied by a federal judge named Lockhart who had no part in the conspiracy but who had been asked to perform the rites because he was a friend of some governor.

No ring was used, since it would have been impossible to slip it over the spacesuit glove Gail wore. We joined hands while the judge spoke into a microphone and the words were carried, via radio and television, to the far reaches of our planet, even to the fur-clad outposts at Thule and Antarctica.

Nearby were photographers to record the lie for posterity.

A conventional bridegroom is in a state of shock and he scarcely realizes what is going on. I heard everything, realizing I was perjuring myself every step of the way. I accepted Gail as my lawful, wedded wife, knowing we would not really be married. She accepted me as her lawful, wedded husband, knowing it was all a lie.

Finally it ended. Judge Lockhart said, "You may kiss the bride." This I could do without faking. I took her in my arms and drew her close. As she turned her face to mine, I thought for a moment that this, at least, would be real. But when I started to meet her lips with mine, she quickly turned her cheek.

The kiss, too, turned out to be a fraud.

My four companions also kissed her on the cheek. Then we stepped into the cherry-picker, which would lift us to the nose capsule of the Saturn.

Two technicians rode with us to help adjust our harnesses and to make sure we were snug in our seats before the lift-off.

The seats were backed against the wall in a hexagonal arrangement, with a small instrument panel directly in front of Spartan's position.

"Sit on my left, Ludson," said Spartan. "Joel, you sit on my right. I think we can allow the bride and groom to sit side-by-side, since this is to be their honeymoon ride."

Morrie Grover snickered.

"There's no cause for mirth," said Spartan sharply. "There's going to be nothing funny about this trip."

Morrie sobered and grew red-faced. I felt sorry for the kid. The laugh had been caused by nervousness. All of us had been in space, of course, but this trip was anything but routine. The lift-off and the re-entry are the most dangerous phases of space flight, any way you look at it.

We put on our helmets and the technicians adjusted them. There was a microphone in each so that we could communicate, but no one, not even Spartan, said anything.

"Sixty minutes!" came the voice from the countdown.

Sixty long minutes of sitting. I wondered how I could stand the strain. Turning my head, I looked at Gail Loring beside me. She stared straight ahead, her lips pressed tight and her eyes glistening. She must have seen my head move, for she turned and looked at me.

"Good luck, Mrs. Drake," I said.

"The name is Gail Loring, and don't forget that, Bill Drake," she said.

I could have slapped her.

But after a time I was glad she had said it. My angry thoughts kept me occupied and that helped pass the time. Almost before I knew it, I heard the voice outside say:

"Fifteen minutes!"

I am a congenital heathen. This is not to say that I'm an atheist or anything of the sort. It's simply that I've never accepted religion the way most people do. In a way, I think I've missed something and I envy those who can accept their faiths without question or doubt, and mold their lives accordingly. For the first time, I wished I knew how to pray.

"Ten minutes!" said the voice of doom.

It seemed as if the words were still echoing in my ears when I heard: "Five minutes—four—three—two—sixty seconds—"

And then came the final ten seconds, ticked off one by one, ending in:

"*Zero!*"

The huge Saturn shuddered as the fuel ignited. It seemed to hesitate, as if unwilling to leave the Earth. I held my breath. Then I felt the seat pressing against my buttocks and I knew we were on our way.

With each second the acceleration increased, the pressure grew greater.

I heard Morrie groan, but I knew he was all right. He was merely expressing his reaction to the tension. Out of the corner of my eye I saw Gail, her face contorted, her jaw firmly set. Spartan's eyes were on the instruments, although his face revealed that he, too, was under strain. Axel Ludson seemed to bear up best, probably because his body was the strongest of all and his rugged frame could absorb the shock. Dr. Warner Joel looked the most frightened and his eyes were fixed on Dr. Spartan as if that man represented all of the security in the universe at that instant.

Although the long wait before the lift-off had seemed unbelievably short—just as the last hour would seem to a condemned criminal in his death cell—the flight to the plasma ship, which had been nicknamed the Jehad, after our own code name, was interminably long. We felt the momentary halt and resurgence of acceleration as each successive stage of the rocket was dropped. Then, after the third stage had burned out, Spartan's hands grasped the controls, his eyes on a small television screen in front of him.

"Right on the nose," he said, as if talking to himself. "At least, Operations has done one thing right."

It was a typical remark, because as a perfectionist, Dr. Spartan was aware of and magnified each minor imperfection in everyone else. So far as I knew the entire operation had gone smoothly and without a hitch.

Spartan continued to operate the controls. I felt slight pressures as the ship adjusted its orbit. We were moving alongside and close to the plasma ship.

Six years, and as many billions of dollars, had been spent to build the Jehad, which was the most revolutionary space craft ever to be put in orbit.

To be accurate, the Jehad never had been put in orbit in one piece. Each part, and all of the equipment needed to put those parts together, had been rocketed into orbit from the ground. A team of highly skilled scientists and construction workers had pieced it together, an amazing job considering they had done this in a state of weightlessness. Eight men had lost their lives as a result of punctured spacesuits.

The strange thing about the Jehad was that it could never have lifted off the Earth under its own power. Although the twelve generators which would drive the Jehad to Mars produced fantastic voltage, their force would not have knocked down a child—in fact, the push from a single motor was about equal to the power exerted by a pigeon in flight.

However, it was the most efficient and most economical, motor man could use to travel ninety million miles to Mars—which is not the shortest route, but the most practical since it makes use of the Earth's motion and the sun's gravitational power.

The plasma motor, more correctly the traveling-wave plasma motor, was developed after several years of research at the NASA laboratories near Cleveland, expressly for space propulsion. The first big breakthroughs, which led to the eventual perfection of the machine, were made in 1961. Because the machine was so complicated, involving principles laymen found hard to understand, it had received very little publicity.

In the simplest terms, the plasma engine, like the rocket, makes use of Newton's law on the conservation of energy—for every action there is a corresponding and opposite reaction. But here the similarity with rockets ends.

In effect, it means that if you throw a ball, as much pressure and force is backward thrust on the hand as forward thrust on the ball. Since the ball has smaller mass, it sails through the air while your hand and body stay put because you are anchored by your weight and gravity. But in space you would go back in proportion to your mass, just as the ball goes forward. And if you continued to throw balls you would accelerate with each toss.

The plasma motor is an electric generator, "spread out." That is, the rotor—the part that revolves—is removed, the motor opened up and flattened. Then it is coiled into a tube so that the field travels at right angles to its normal direction. This makes the electrical field run down the tube in waves, instead of in a circular motion.

Instead of a rotor, some lightweight element is ionized—heated and vaporized until the electrons and protons of the atoms are torn apart—and the resulting plasma rides down the tube on the waves as circulating systems of positive (protons) and negative (electrons) charges. When they are expelled there is a good-sized kick— kinetic energy. In space, any kick, no matter how small, results in motion, which will continue unless another force is applied to stop it. But in this case the only applied force is more kicks forward, thus there is acceleration.

The chief advantage of the plasma motor is that it can give a very good thrust with a very small amount of fuel. Even the earliest calculations disclosed that the amount of fuel needed to accelerate and decelerate the ship amounted to practically nothing compared to the payload it could push through space. A one-hundred-pound thrust would suffice to drive a 150-ton spaceship to Mars. Compare this with the one thousand pounds of thrust necessary to lift one pound of payload by rocket from the surface of the Earth.

The fuel used on the Jehad was lithium, the third-lightest element. It had been used in the first experiments with the plasma engine but, since it had to be heated to 2500 degrees in order to vaporize it, argon—which was a gas to begin with—was experimented with. However, it had been decided to use lithium, for two reasons: one, heat to vaporize it could easily be obtained through high frequency heaters powered by solar batteries; two, lithium is lighter than argon. Thus was gained double advantage.

In theory, the Jehad could travel five-ninth's the speed of light, or about one hundred thousand miles *per second*. As yet the Jehad had never attained this velocity, because building up to that speed would take months. In the 12-hour test flight, Spartan, Ludson and Gail Loring reported that the craft behaved according to expectations and there was reason to believe that, in practice, it would not fall short of its theoretical speed.

However, speed was not important, since a good part of the time on the trip would be spent in waiting for the Earth and Mars to get into proper positions. It was necessary only to be fairly close to schedule in arriving on Mars.

I had been trained in the operation of the plasma ship and to me it represented the summit of safety in space. That's why the trip to the Jehad seemed so long. I didn't feel secure in the Saturn capsule and I knew I'd be much safer on the Jehad.

We were weightless now as we orbited close to the plasma-powered ship. Spartan, Joel and Ludson could see the craft on a small television screen near the control panel. I couldn't see it from where I sat, but I was familiar with its appearance. It looked something like an elongated sausage with a small glass knob on each end. It was 185 meters long from the center of its forward cabin—an astrogation observatory—to the center of the rear. This baseline had been measured to compute distances by parallax during the flight to Mars.

The center section was partitioned to contain motors, control and communications room, storage and living quarters for the crew. There was a difference, however, inasmuch as the entire interior could be utilized as floor. Small rockets in the side would start the cylinder spinning to give a weak but effective artificial gravity so that we could walk, rather than float, during our weightless voyage. This pressure would be equal on all walls, so it was possible for us to be suspended from what Earthbound people call the "ceiling," or to stand out at right angles from the walls, without fear of falling. No matter where we stood, the centrifugal force would always be outward.

"We're less than fifty yards from the Jehad," Dr. Spartan announced. "This is about as close as I dare bring us. Drake, you'll carry a line to the Jehad—make it fast to the door of the locks. We'll follow you across."

"Yes, sir," I said.

I unbuckled the straps to my harness, taking a great deal of care with my movements. I was weightless, and the slightest exertion might send me spinning away in another demonstration of Newton's law on the conservation of energy.

Grasping a grab rail, I pulled myself upward to the escape hatch. In a rack were six aluminum tanks filled with oxygen. I slipped the straps over my shoulders, tightened them, brought the flexible tube around to my chest and fastened it into the fitting. Then I disconnected the long air hose that fed oxygen to my helmet from the Saturn's supply and opened the hatch. A gentle push of my toes on the grab rail sent me floating into the air lock.

A reel of thin, stout copper wire was fastened to the wall near the outside hatch. I slipped the end of this through a ring on my spacesuit and ran out about a dozen feet, leaving a loose end, twice my height, trailing.

Then I opened the hatch. A small amount of air in the locks escaped, sucking me with it into outer space. For the first time I had a glimpse of the universe, unshielded by atmosphere or clouds.

At my feet lay the Earth, looking up with a bluish-white countenance. To my left was the half moon, peeking over the dark blue horizon, its craters plainly visible. Above was the sun, too dazzling to look at, and all around were brilliant stars and planets, although I had no time to pick them out, much as I would have liked to spot Mars, our destination.

I was aimed toward the long sausage-shaped Jehad, but my trajectory would take me above it and I had to make immediate adjustment. To do this, I used a petcock on the belt of my spacesuit, which released a very tiny jet of oxygen from the tank on my back. I twisted my body so the force would send me in the right direction.

One little push was all I needed and now I had to somersault quickly, and, at the same time, push out the long loose end of copper wire so that it would strike the side of the Jehad before I did. This was very important, for the electrical potential of the Jehad must be adjusted to that of the Saturn capsule to guard against being struck by a bolt of lightning as I contacted the sides of the craft. Apparently there was not much of a differential for I saw no sparks against the black sky.

My feet struck the sides of the Jehad gently, and magnetic strips in my boots held me fast.

Walking with soft footfalls, because even a slightly heavy push might tear me loose and send me out into space, making it necessary for me to maneuver my way back to ship again, I approached the locks. I opened the outer door and then made my line of copper wire fast to an eye just above the opening.

"A-okay, Dr. Spartan!" I announced into my helmet microphone. "The line's fast. I'll stand by to assist you folks aboard."

"Roger!" Spartan's voice echoed in my ears.

They came one by one, hand over hand, with safety hasps fastened over the wire. First Morrie, then Gail, then Axel, Joel and Dr. Spartan, playing his role of captain to the hilt, being the last to leave the ship.

I pulled them into the locks. There had been a little danger from meteors, of course, but the experts had figured that the chance of a meteor large enough to penetrate a spacesuit hitting an individual was one in 241 years. So far the estimate had been holding up. The nineteen men who built the Jehad had worked six years in space—a total of 114 man years. We had yet to experience a meteor casualty.

None of my companions seemed afraid. All were a little glad to be aboard the Jehad.

As Spartan came into the locks, he unfastened the wire line that held us to the Saturn capsule. Then he closed the door. He turned a valve, filling the chamber with air, and after a few seconds he opened the inside locks and we all walked into the large, roomy interior of the little planet of our own.

CHAPTER FOUR

YOU COULD CALL THOSE FIVE DAYS aboard the Jehad a honeymoon, although the usual definition did not apply to Mr. and Mrs. William Drake. Not only had I promised to keep the marriage on a purely platonic level, but Gail, by her actions and formality, gave me to understand that I was not expected to even go through the motions of playing the newlywed husband.

However, it was a happy time for all of us, and I include Dr. Spartan, even though he might never again be described as being in sympathetic rapport with the rest of us.

As soon as we had cut loose from the capsule and filled the plasma craft with air, we got the artificial gravity in operation by starting some auxiliary rockets, which made the ship, rotate slowly. The gravity was only ten percent, but it was sufficient to keep us from floating around the room. We took off our spacesuits and laughed uproariously at our costumes—shorts, T-shirts and lightweight sandals that had magnetic strips in the soles to assist the artificial gravity in holding us to the floor.

Axel relayed our messages back to the Earth, telling of our safe arrival, and Dr. Spartan and Warner Joel got the plasma motors going. There were four banks of three motors each encircling the ship. Although we had twelve engines, we planned to use only eight at a time. Four were for emergencies and extra power, when needed.

There were no portholes except in the control room and even here the outside view was partially blocked by a huge nuclear reactor, well shielded and stuck out in front of the ship. This supplied all our electrical power. However, there were video cameras on the outside—in the front and rear of the craft—so that we could always see the heavens about us on the monitor screens. There were four of these in the control room and four more in the main cabin, which was the middle segment of the ship. There were six sections, not counting the rear cupola where Gail was quartered.

The control dome was in front. Dr. Spartan's private cabin, which was partitioned for sleeping and working, was second.

The large main cabin was where we did most of our living, if you can call it that. Directly behind it was a small galley and storeroom for our food supplies. Next was the lavatory and shower room, and the rear segment was filled with machinery—air and water-cycling equipment, laundry, and some electrical tools for repairing the ship.

There wasn't much to see outside after we got in space but, during those early days when we circled the Earth and gained momentum, we had a beautiful view of our world. There was also a procession of multicolored and unwinking stars. The sun, too, was beautiful because the corona could always be seen.

Probably it was because we were so busy in those first days that we got along so well. Or maybe it was the excitement of finding everything so new and different. From the moment we boarded the ship, we were in another world, an independent planet, no longer associated with the Earth.

We had to learn to walk in diminished gravity; we had to accustom ourselves to looking up and finding a companion sleeping on the ceiling as if he were stuck there. Even the day was changed. Because there were five of us, we had a 25-hour day, each man, with the exception of Dr. Spartan, taking a five-hour control-room shift. The terrestrial day no longer had any meaning, since our little planet rotated once every 30 seconds.

We had a garden—two trays, one above and one below the tube that carried electrical wiring the length of the, ship. We planted hybrid vegetables in the garden-plants using a minimum of water and converting a maximum of carbon dioxide into oxygen. However, the air-cycling machinery was sufficient for most purposes.

Our biggest problem was water. Due to its weight and bulk, we carried as little water as possible, since a great deal of it was already being used to shield the nuclear reactor. For all other purposes—drinking, preparation of dehydrated foods, laundry, sanitation and irrigation of the garden—there was a tank containing 35 gallons. Excess water, removed from the air and extracted from all waste products, was purified and distilled twice, then used again.

At first, Gail Loring made the trip pleasant by her very presence. She was pretty and cheerful, and the fact that she revealed so much in the way of feminine charm in her space clothing caused the usual male response. Not that we were a pack of wolves. There is nothing wrong with looking, or even giving a mental whistle. I think Gail read our minds and I'm sure she enjoyed it.

Axel's face mirrored his thoughts in a slow grin. Dr. Joel, who was acting with the vigor of a sales manager at a customers' convention, treated her to adoring, but not necessarily fatherly, witticisms. Morrie Grover positively drooled when she was around and made a great thing of helping her out with various tasks, even though I think Gail would have preferred not to have the help. Spartan watched her, too, but it was impossible to read his thoughts. As I said, everything was milk and honey in those days.

But after we had the ship functioning, the garden growing, and our schedules perfected, we suddenly found that there was not enough to do. The looks that had been innocently male, began slowly to change to something else.

Gail, who had usually shown me less attention than the others, apparently because I had a greater legal right to claim more attention, spoke of it one day when she came through the machinery room while I was washing out the dirty uniforms.

I'd brought a projector and a microfilm of a book on astrogation and was reading when she paused beside the washer. "Need help, Bill Drake?" she asked in a friendly tone.

I looked up and smiled. "Now that was a nice, wifely thing to say." I told her. "Unfortunately it's my turn to do the laundry so you don't have to help."

"But you wouldn't throw me out if I did?" she asked.

"There's really nothing to do," I said, nodding toward the automatic washer, which was halfway through its cycle. "But if you'd like to join in a little small talk about the universe at large, I'll be thankful for company. You realize, don't you, that this is the first time the bride and groom have really been alone together since they were married?"

She frowned. "Let's not talk about that, Bill Drake," she said.

"Why not? Afraid that if we mention it too often we might suddenly realize we're married?"

She nodded her head slowly. "Something like that."

I shut off the projector. I had no interest in astrogation at the moment. "Is that why you avoid me?"

"I don't avoid you."

"You always find time to horse around with Morrie," I said.

Now she smiled. "Are you by any chance jealous?" she asked. "If you are, you have no right."

"Damnit, I'm not. I just want equal time," I said. "I should have the right to want as much time with my legal wife as those other bums."

"I'm doing the laundry with you," she said teasingly. "That's the first time I've done that with anybody on this ship."

"I'm in your debt, gracious lady," I said. There was a trace of sarcasm, less than I felt, in my voice.

She heard it, too, and gave me a sharp glance. "I do want to talk to you about something, Bill Drake," she said.

"Sure. The laundry doesn't need attention. Let's talk."

"You've noticed that we're not the jolly little group we started out to be when we first boarded the ship, haven't you?"

"Yes, but it's because we're getting bored. We've been going around the Earth in a spiral, like a merry-go-round. We don't seem to be getting anyplace."

"That's not what I mean," she said. "We are getting someplace. The spiral widens a little more each turn. Very soon now—perhaps within hours—we'll break away from the Earth. We all realize it. And the farther away from Earth we go, the less we'll feel bound by standards of the Earth."

I frowned. "I don't see what you're driving at, Gail."

She glanced toward the bulkhead door at the end of the room. It led to the shower room and lavatory. She glided toward it, using the familiar "space walk" we all had learned in order to conform to the very light, artificial gravity. She opened the door, peered in, then closed it and returned. "Just wanted to be sure we really were alone," she said. "What I wanted to talk about was Dr. Spartan. It—it's the way he looks at me."

"We all look at you," I said. "I thought most girls liked it and felt like they were slipping when men stopped looking."

"That's right, when you speak of a normal male look," she said. "But the bearded monster frightens me."

"Relax," I said. "He won't get out of hand. That old boy is no fool and he won't pull any raw deals. The one I'd look out for is Morrie. He acts like a crazy kid sometimes. You can't always figure him."

"Morrie!" she exclaimed. "Bill Drake, you *are* jealous! He's just a kid."

"That's what I said, a crazy kid."

"And I'm two years older than he is." The washer stopped spinning and I went over and began removing the duds and putting them in the dryer.

She started to get up to help me. She'd been sitting cross-legged on the floor, as we all did because we had no chairs aboard. "Don't bother," I told her. "This isn't hard work."

She sat down again. "Do you realize, Bill Drake, that there are no laws here in space excepting those laid down by Spartan?"

"I can think of a few of Newton's laws that he has no control over."

"I'm not talking about physical laws. Spartan is more powerful than any nabob who ever lived on Earth—he is a greater despot than Caesar, than the Pharaohs. That's why he's standoffish with everyone. He has the power of life and death over us all."

I closed the dryer and set the timer. "Forget it, Gail," I told her, dropping down beside her. "Spartan's like a military commander. Not only our lives, but the success of this mission are his responsibility. He can't very well get chummy with buck privates." I didn't particularly love the guy, but I thought—then—that I understood him.

"We're not buck privates," she said, with a woman's logic and hatred of metaphor.

"Okay. We're second looeys. Now, what shall I do? Go to Spartan and say, 'Listen, you old goat, stop looking lecherously at my wife-in-name-only?'"

"This is no joking matter, Bill Drake. I may be your wife-in-name-only but there was a good sound reason for our marriage.

You have to keep me from—uh—well, getting involved. You're a sort of chaperon."

I groaned.

"Let me tell you something," she went on. "During my first trick in the control room—not long after we started our routine on this ship—Spartan came in and spent almost the five hours with me. He talked to me as I'd never been talked to before, Bill Drake. He told me to move my sleeping bag into his compartment and live there. He made it sound as if it were my duty and that I'd be shirking if I didn't."

I gaped at her. "The hell he did!" I just couldn't believe it. "You must have misunderstood him—"

"I most certainly did not!" she said. "Don't you believe me?"

"Well, the guy isn't any tin god," I said. "But he didn't force you to do what he'd suggested."

"Do you know why?" she asked. When I didn't answer she went on. "Because I told him that if he did, he'd have to explain to the whole crew. He'd wind up with a red-hot mutiny on his hands. And when we returned from Mars, I'd nail his hide to the Pentagon, or some other conspicuous place."

I whistled. "And he took it?"

"Not meekly. He said that if he wished, he could "take care" of the whole crew. And if I repeated what he said to me, to anyone, he'd brand it as a pack of lies. He particularly cautioned me against telling you. He said he didn't want to be forced into "taking care" of you."

"But you told me," I said.

"I'm warning you, Bill Drake. Watch out for Spartan. He doesn't intend for you to return alive—or anyone else who opposes him."

I no longer understood Spartan. Would he kill to have his way? I had suspected his hatred since the day the wedding was agreed upon. "He wanted to marry you," I said, "but you changed the plan. Why didn't he object then?"

"Because he couldn't on the Earth. And when I made a point of platonic marriage he thought he could fit it into his plan."

My heart bounded hopefully. "It wasn't a platonic marriage you wanted?" I asked softly. I tried to take her hand but she pulled it away.

"No, Bill!" It was the first time since we'd left the Earth, that she used my first name alone. "I really meant it when I suggested it. I knew Spartan. I'd been in space with him before, but I managed him. This is different. I wanted you to protect me—but not as a husband."

My heart sank and I felt helpless. I walked over to the dryer. "Lots of dirty laundry today," I said.

"You can say that again," she replied.

Spartan's voice came over the intercom as I started to take the laundry from the dryer.

"Attention, please. Just fifteen seconds ago, the Jehad reached the escape velocity for this distance from the Earth. We have broken away from terrestrial gravity. Mr. Ludson and I are now computing the necessary corrections to put us on the proper orbit to reach Mars."

Gail looked at me and I stared back at her. We had gone beyond the point of no return.

CHAPTER FIVE

AFTER THAT TALK WITH GAIL, I had my first thoughts of mutiny. But I'd been raised with a good, healthy respect for authority and, because most persons I'd come in contact with who had it, used judgment in administering it, I had seen no reason for changing my attitude. Even Spartan, when he was drilling us for this trip, had seemed to be right, in spite of his toughness. But as the Earth grew smaller behind us, I began to look for allies, in case we were ever forced into a showdown with Spartan.

I wondered if Gail had been right when she said the others wouldn't stand for any nonsense. I doubted if they would. Not all of them anyhow. Dr. Joel had suddenly seemed to discover that Dr. Spartan was a great man. Spartan fawned on Joel and Joel became Spartan's slave, carrying his meals to him, posting Spartan's orders, and acting as a self-appointed second in command.

Morrie might defend Gail, but he certainly wouldn't raise a hand to keep Spartan from tossing me into the great out-yonder, if it came right down to it. Morrie was in the throes of puppy love for Gail. It showed in every move he made. Besides, the kid was upset. Homesick maybe. Or afraid. Everything was strange here and he longed for something familiar. He turned to Gail for comfort. And if Morrie were told of Spartan's actions toward Gail, the, young fellow was hotheaded enough to march into Spartan's cabin and get himself—and me—in a jam.

Axel was steady, staunch and levelheaded. But I hesitated about confiding in him. Like me, Axel had a respect for authority. He couldn't take my unsupported word that Spartan meant to kill me and take Gail. Furthermore, I remembered that Axel had refused to accept Gail because he did not believe in the kind of marriage she proposed. Was that the real reason? Or did he know Spartan's plans? Perhaps Axel was Spartan's real second-in-command, ready to do the muscle work when the time came.

We were still in radio communication with the Earth and I considered sending a message back. But what could I say? Spartan would claim I was space crazy. And the next message would tell the Earth that in a fit of madness I'd jumped overboard. What proof could I offer in a message that Spartan had ever made his proposition to her? He'd just say she'd dreamed it. It was his word against hers.

Gail agreed when I told her this. "Perhaps he didn't mean it the way it sounded," she said.

"How else could he mean it?" I asked.

"Well, maybe he intended for me to take his cabin and he'd sleep somewhere else."

"What about the bit where he said he had the power of life and death over us?"

"Well, he did mention that, but he might not have been serious. I don't know what to think any more." She sighed heavily. "And he does have the power of life and death, you know."

We'd been talking together in the galley, alone over cups of instant coffee. Now the door opened and Morrie Grover came in. He gave Gail one of his looks, then turned to me.

"Pretty soft," he said. "You got the only girl in umpteen million miles."

I thought he was kidding and I replied in kind. "Yeah. We're honeymooners. Can't you leave us alone?"

"That wasn't in the agreement," he snapped. I knew then he wasn't kidding.

Come to think of it, we'd all been a little edgy lately—ever since the Earth had lost its grip on us. The pleasant feeling within our little group was no more. The honeymoon of the adventurers in space was just as phony as the honeymoon of Gail and me.

"What's the matter, Morrie?" I asked. "Got an upset stomach, or do you just need a cup of coffee? We've got the coffee. Help yourself."

"You're a jerk," said Morrie.

There was no doubt that I was as edgy as anyone. Otherwise, Morrie's attitude would not have set me off. "You're a punk," I replied.

"Come off it, you two," said Gail. "You're acting like a couple of schoolboys."

Morrie turned on Gail. "Are you in love with him?"

"Why—"

"What I mean is, why did you marry him?"

I grabbed him by the arm and swung him around. "It's none of your business," I said. "Now, do you layoff and behave like a grown-up man or do I belt you all the way through the main cabin?"

He swung at me. I ducked but, before I could do anything about it, Gail stepped between us. "Get out, Morrie!" she said, and then turned to me. "Bill Drake, you go back to the machinery room and find something to do there. We can't afford a fight right now."

As usual she was right. We calmed down and, out of respect for her, followed her advice.

As I said, I'd noticed that we all were edgy. Joel had sort of pulled his head into his shell like a turtle, and was having nothing to do with any of us, except Dr. Spartan, whom he followed around like a hound.

And Axel seemed preoccupied. I couldn't put my finger on what had happened to him. I thought it was the same sort of space madness that was gripping us all.

"What we ought to do, Axel," I said one day, in an effort to draw him out, "is to tell each other what's bugging us, rather than to bottle it up inside."

"Meaning me?" he asked.

"Meaning you," I said. "You've been acting like the ghost at the banquet. I don't even know whether I can call you a friend any more. What's the trouble?"

Axel shook his head. "I'm not sure," he said.

"Psychological? Depression?"

He gave me a crooked grin. "I wish it were something like that," he replied. "Trouble is, I know what does it, but I'm damned if I know what it is."

"Animal, vegetable or mineral?" I asked.

He started to get halfway cheerful. "I tried to tell Spartan about it and he accused me of imagining things," he said. "I guess it won't hurt to tell you. I'm getting some stuff on the radio I can't explain."

"Signals? From the Earth?"

"Not from the Earth. From the general direction of Mars."

The way he said it, it sent chills up my spine and down again. "Somebody's trying to signal us?"

"Sometimes I think so, sometimes not," he replied with a heavy sigh. "The signals—if that's what they are—are still very weak."

"Damn it, Axel," I said, "it's ridiculous. If anybody were trying to signal us from Mars, it would mean *they* knew we were on our way."

"Maybe they do," he said tersely.

It was so damned fantastic, I hardly knew what to say. "But how?" I asked.

"I don't know," he said, "but they could have radio, even radar—and they could be a million times better than ours."

We talked about it for about an hour and Axel couldn't add anything to what he'd already told me, which wasn't much.

During the next few days Gail exerted herself trying to restore a friendly relationship between Morrie and me. I think it was more because Morrie wanted to win her approval than for any other reason that she succeeded, partially.

When we were off duty at the same time, she'd bring us together and try to engage us in conversation. The only trouble was, we'd run out of anything to talk about.

"If we could only invent a game!" she exclaimed in one of her desperate moods.

"Charades?" I asked.

"They make me sick," said Morrie in his usual disagreeable manner.

"We don't even have extra paper and pencil," she went on. "All writing materials are under lock and key, being conserved for taking notes when we reach Mars."

Suddenly Morrie smiled. "You know, I'm a little stupid," he said. "I brought along a deck of cards."

"You what?" Gail exclaimed.

And I gave him a look of surprise. Regulations had forbidden us to bring anything aboard—not even a toothbrush—because all personal items, excepting the one uniform we wore at the time, had already been stored on the Jehad. Spartan had announced, with his usual correctness, that every ounce we carried would require extra fuel to lift us off the Earth.

Morrie got up and shuffled over to his locker at the end of the cabin. He opened it, unzipped the pocket of his spacesuit hanging there, and brought out a brand-new pack of cards.

"Morrie! You darling!" said Gail.

"Forgot I had 'em," Morrie said, flushing with pleasure at Gail's words. "I figured things were apt to get boring up here and Doc had mentioned we'd have very little to do. So I stuck them in my pocket when I came down to the pad and, when Doc wasn't looking, put them in the pocket of my spacesuit."

I glanced nervously toward the front of the ship. Spartan probably was in his cabin, or making sure Warner Joel was awake in the control room. Axel was directly above us, snoring gently in his sleeping bag.

"Anyone for gin rummy?" I asked.

Morrie sat down and broke the seal on the deck. At that instant Axel's buzzer went off. The chronometer in the control room was attached to the buzzer, which notified us five minutes before the end of each watch. Axel, who was to relieve Joel, stirred in his sleeping bag as he stopped snoring.

"Darn!" said Gail. "I'm next, and if I don't get a little rest, I'll go to sleep on duty and Doc Spartan will shoot me at sunrise." Naturally, Spartan had made no such threat, but he did make sure no one slept on duty by bobbing in and out of the control room at irregular intervals. No one knew when he slept, but I supposed he took many short naps instead of a single, long sleep.

"Good morning, folks," said Axel from the ceiling.

"You're the only person who thinks it's morning," I said.

"Any time I wake up, it's morning," said Axel. "Miss Loring, do you mind getting out of here? I have to get into my clothes."

Axel, like all of us, slept barefooted up to the ears and his clothing was in his locker at the end of the cabin.

"Next time think of the cards sooner, Morrie," said Gail. "I guess there'll be no gin rummy for me today." She got up, went to the rear of the cabin and out the door toward her own quarters.

Axel wriggled out of his sleeping bag, put on his sandals and went to his locker. He noticed the cards Morrie was shuffling. "Where in hell did you find those?" he asked.

"It doesn't matter," said Morrie. "We got 'em. Two-handed, Bill?"

"Sure. Deal 'em."

Morrie and I were seated lengthwise with the ship, and the first card he dealt sailed clear to the partition at the far end. The artificial gravity didn't pull the card to the deck as it would on Earth. "Guess we'd better sit crosswise," he said, retrieving the card.

We shifted so that no matter which way Morrie sailed the card it would be "down." Axel dressed and then went into the control room. A few minutes later Dr. Joel came in. He saw us playing gin rummy.

"Good Lord! Interplanetary Las Vegas?"

"Want to join us, Warner?" I asked.

"Not for all the gold dust on the moon," he said. "If Spartan ever sees you playing cards, he'll hang you to an asteroid."

He watched us play, glancing apprehensively toward the forward bulkhead as if he expected Spartan to burst in on us at any moment. Then, at last, he got up and went through the door. I was facing the bulkhead but I didn't notice him leaving because I was trying to decide whether to gin or not. It was Morrie who heard the door open, whirling his head so suddenly it almost displaced him from his sitting position. "Hey!" he exclaimed, "Joel's gone. Do you suppose he intends to rat on us?"

"Let him," I said. "These cards are worth the powder it took to shoot 'em into space. They probably will preserve our sanity. That's why Spartan can't object."

Morrie looked at me as if he didn't know what to believe. I shrugged off his doubt, certain that Spartan was intelligent enough to see the cards weren't hurting anything, even though they'd been brought aboard illegally.

I ginned and won. Morrie was reshuffling the cards to deal again when the door opened and Dr. Spartan, followed by Warner Joel, came into the cabin.

"Stop this immediately!" Spartan barked.

We turned our heads and looked at Spartan's angry face. Then I noticed that he was wearing something new—a holster, holding a nickel-plated air pistol. A kid's toy.

"Stand up!" Spartan said, his hand on the pistol butt.

For a moment I wondered if Gail had been right, that Spartan was capable of going in for a little capital punishment to pass the boring hours in space. Morrie and I got to our feet.

"Those things—" Spartan nodded his head toward the cards, "—are strictly against regulations. If you have time on your hands, you should use the projector and study the scientific works aboard. We can't allow foolishness."

"Damnit, Doctor," I said, "all work and no play is going to turn this crew into a dull bunch of astronauts."

"Nonsense," said Spartan. "I forbid card playing. We're not on the Earth any more. We're in space. Beyond terrestrial law. Beyond any standards and regulations that exist on our planet. We are, in effect, another world—and I rule this world. What I say is law and must be obeyed."

Morrie stared at him, open-mouthed. But I had been warned about what to expect from Spartan. After all, he'd said about the same thing to Gail. "We're not questioning your authority, sir," I said. "And what we were doing was very innocent."

"I'm the best judge of that. Give me the cards, Grover."

Morrie hesitated, his face registering uncertainty.

Spartan drew the gun. "This is an air pistol," he said, his manner imperious, his tone hard and relentless. "You understand the danger of a pistol aboard this craft. A bullet might puncture the walls or damage machinery. So I shoot a small dart, which is impregnated with mild, but very effective, poison. It will paralyze a man in a few seconds. Even a scratch on the skin will make you harmless. I can quell any sort of mutiny."

"This isn't mutiny!" I said, speaking with all the deference I could muster. "Sure, I'll admit the cards aren't supposed to be here, but they are. And they're causing no harm. The capsule was lifted into orbit and the flight of this ship has been A-okay from the beginning. Now these cards are helping our morale, which needs a hell of a lot of help right now."

Spartan pointed the gun at me. His jaw was set; his eyes were lifeless marble. "I have the power of life and death over every living thing on this ship," he said.

When a man is threatened with a weapon, he sometimes gives up, but this puny little air gun pointed at me seemed harmless. Besides, I was angry. I took a step toward Spartan. I don't believe I would have touched him. The step was just to prove I wasn't afraid of him or the gun and I thought he was making too big an issue out of something very small.

Ping.

The gun went off and I felt a stinging sensation in my left arm. I raised it, plucked a tiny dart from the flesh. Suddenly my knees buckled and I collapsed on the deck.

I was not unconscious. I could hear Spartan telling Morrie to give him the cards. Morrie was too frightened to disobey.

"Put the cards in the waste disposal, Dr. Joel," said Spartan.

"Yes, sir." Warner Joel's voice had a tremor in it.

I tried to call him a stool pigeon, but my vocal chords wouldn't work.

"For this disobedience, Bill Drake will have twenty extra tours of duty in the next twenty days," said Spartan. "For wasting time, Morrie Grover will have ten extra tours. We need two men in the control room now, so each of you will take his extra turns in company with another member of the crew."

Five hours later, when Gail came through the cabin to relieve Axel at the controls, I was just regaining use of my muscles. Morrie explained to her what had happened.

"Get some antiseptic," she said, examining my wound.

"No need," I said hoarsely. "Ship's been sterilized. No germs aboard."

She examined the wound. "It's sort of deep," she said. "The beast! He just wanted to throw his weight around."

"He'll be tough to get along with from now on, Gail," I said. "Mind if I take my extra duty with you?"

Morrie scowled and said nothing.

"No, Bill. Some of the time anyhow. Part of the watch I'll share with Morrie." I heard him release his breath. "Now listen, Bill. I know you're angry with Spartan, but you've got to be careful. I think you understand why. We've got to keep him from doing anything more rash than this."

I was able to nod my head. I had to get along with the bastard. Not only my life, but her safety depended on it.

CHAPTER SIX

IN THE END, Spartan himself arranged a schedule for Morrie and me, so we had no choice when we would serve our extra shifts. However, I spent equal time with Gail, Axel and Joel, as did Morrie.

Gail and I had no opportunity to talk over our personal problems—concerning, mainly, Dr. Spartan—because he was always joining us in the control cabin. Axel was always engaged in radio astronomy, or trying to intercept terrestrial broadcasts, which were growing more feeble each day. Joel was uneasy in my presence.

"I'm sorry about causing you all this trouble," he said. "But if I hadn't reported that infraction of rules to Dr. Spartan, he might have punished me."

"Axel didn't report it and he wasn't punished," I said.

"Dr. Spartan didn't suspect that Axel knew anything about it." Joel sighed. "I'm afraid my act has made me very unpopular with the rest of you."

"Forget it," I said, "a trip to Mars isn't a popularity contest. If we return with good results, it won't matter. We'll all be fair-haired boys."

But the incident had helped me decide that Joel would not be trustworthy if it came to a showdown against Spartan. On the other hand, it also helped prove that Axel was not a confidential aide to our chief.

On the fourth extra tour of duty, I was in the control room with Axel. He was concentrating on the sounds he was picking up with our ultrahigh frequency receiver. Finally he ran the sounds he was getting through an oscilloscope.

"Look at that, Bill!" he exclaimed, pointing to the strange wave pattern.

"Pretty," I commented. All I saw was that it was something different.

"That signal," said Axel, "was made by intelligent beings. It's not a natural radio pattern—the kind you'd get from a star or a nebula."

I took my eyes off the instruments and looked at the pattern again. "Are you trying to tell me the Russians have invented a new kind of radio?"

"The signal's coming from Mars," said Axel.

"You're space crazy," I said. "There's nothing intelligent on Mars. Just a few plants."

"We don't really know," said Axel. "I've been picking up these signals for several days. They're traveling twice the distance of the terrestrial signals. And the volume is greater. That would mean at least four or more times the power."

"You've reported it to Spartan?" I asked.

"I've entered it in the log book," said Axel. "I've also made a recording. It's not a voice signal, but it has an artificial wave pattern. It's some kind of radar wave—"

"The Martians have spotted us?" I couldn't quite believe it. "They're gonna send out a fleet of spaceships and blast us before we land."

"If they had spaceships they would have visited the Earth," said Axel.

"Then we're more advanced than they are. And if they're intelligent, we've nothing to fear. We'll probably get the keys to all the Martian cities."

"We may not be ahead of them," said Axel. "And even if they're intelligent, we might have things to fear. How would we receive Martians if they landed on the Earth?"

"We'd probably give 'em television contracts," I said.

"Not at first," said Axel. "We'd take pains to contain them somehow—prevent them from causing us any harm. We'd make sure they had come to the Earth with peaceful intent. And we'd be pretty slow to trust them even if they came unarmed."

"Martians may be different," I said. "Why don't you tell Spartan? You know how he is. If he thought we held out anything on him, he might use his popgun on us."

"That's what I've been going to do," said Axel. "But I wanted to make sure these signals came from Mars. Now I'm positive." He touched the buzzer signal on the big globe in the center of the room where all the ship's controls were located.

Spartan's voice came over the intercom. "What's the matter now?"

"We've picked up signals from Mars, sir," said Axel. "Nonsense." There was a click. A moment later Spartan came in through the bulkhead door. His eyes darted about suspiciously, as if expecting some trick.

"It's sort of a carrier wave," said Axel as Spartan anchored himself on the floor. "Seems to be a kind of radar—as if we're being watched." It was obvious that Axel was awed by the new phenomenon.

"It's utterly ridiculous," said Spartan. "Radar would indicate intelligent life. Mars is a dying world. The age of intelligent life ended there long ago." There was still that wary look about him and his lips curled into a sneer.

"Perhaps it's a different kind of intelligence," I suggested.

"What other kinds are there?" Spartan snorted. "Intelligence is knowing what is true and what isn't. A thing can either be true or false. There's not much difference between intelligences."

I'd learned you couldn't argue with Spartan, who refused to recognize that truth is relative and that there are at least two sides to any question; that, more often, there are an infinite number of points of view, all true in a sense, none altogether false.

"Anyhow, we've got signals," I said meekly, seeing the utter futility of arguing.

"Signals. Bah!" He was almost snarling now, unwilling to admit any possibility which might interfere with his preconceived notions.

"Doc, there are millions of stars and even if only a fraction of one per cent of them has conditions suitable to life, we might find intelligent beings there."

"Granted. But Mars isn't a planet with the right conditions. Why, you're even inferring that these Martians might be more intelligent than we are. We on Earth couldn't pick out an object the size of this ship so far away from our planet. Let me check these signals—"

Spartan began twisting the dials controlling the directional antennae at the front and rear of the craft. "Might be something else; different from radar—"

Axel's voice cut in. "Doctor! Look at *our* radarscope!"

I turned my head quickly toward the screen. There was just the flimsy outline of something there; something barely perceptible to the waves that scanned the path ahead of the ship. But whatever it was, it was in our path and it was very large. A cloud, maybe— only clouds don't show on radar.

"Meteors!" screamed Spartan. "Heaven help us! It's a meteor cloud!"

He pushed me aside and sprang to the controls. At the same time, he touched the emergency button, setting off a shrieking siren alarm.

CHAPTER SEVEN

EXCEPT FOR TWO OR THREE METEOR CLOUDS, which the Earth plows through on its annual turn around the sun, the number and location of these in the solar system are unknown. They are not clouds in the sense that they hang like a heavy mist and obscure objects behind them. They are so thin and tenuous that if thousands of meteors did not shower on the Earth when it goes through their midst, we would be unaware of their presence in space.

The cloud ahead of us was, possibly, half a million miles in diameter, making it rather small. The Perseids and Leonids, for example, may extend completely around the sun in the orbit of a disintegrated comet. Very few of the meteors are larger than a grain of sand and they are so widely scattered that all of the meteors in a cubic mile of space might be packed into a teacup. However, a few of them might be as large as a teacup and, very rarely, one might be as big as a house.

For a planet like the Earth to plow through a cloud of meteors, there is little danger. For one thing, most of the meteors are vaporized as they strike the upper atmosphere. Only a few ever reach the Earth and there have been only a couple of cases on record where a human being has been harmed by a meteorite.

But the Jehad had no atmosphere to shield it from meteors. True, we were equipped with double walls capable of vaporizing a meteor up to a quarter of an inch in diameter. And we had methods of minimizing the danger of larger meteors—leakproof fluid in the walls, airtight bulkheads dividing the ship into segments, spacesuits, and a reserve supply of oxygen. But there was always that extreme chance of striking a big fellow, which would cancel out all our defenses. This cloud ahead of us certainly held a few that size.

Had Axel and I not been so interested in the signals from Mars, we might have spotted the meteors several minutes sooner. Our ship was now traveling close to 30,000 miles an hour, however, and those minutes had eaten up precious distance in which we might have maneuvered the craft out of danger.

We were less than an hour's run from the fringe of the cloud. The Jehad, using a very small amount of power to accelerate its huge mass, could not be turned in time to avoid it.

As Spartan sounded the alarm, he spoke tersely into the intercom mike, warning of the danger ahead and telling the crew to scatter to separate compartments, to minimize the loss in the event that a large meteor crashed into one segment of the ship. We had all been drilled on this procedure, which included the donning of spacesuits.

While Spartan remained in the control room, Axel and I put on our suits, zipped them, and then I carried one to Spartan, who put it on while Axel continued to manipulate the controls. The manipulation simply included increasing the power of the plasma motors.

All twelve were now operating, and auxiliary jets on the sides of the ship were being fired in order to curve the ship from its trajectory so that it would pass as near the extreme rear fringe of the cloud as possible. Here the meteors would be the smallest, driven back from the central mass by the pressure of sunlight, which would have less effect on the larger masses.

Wearing a space helmet aboard ship had one major disadvantage. In order to talk, it was necessary to use the radio transmitters located in the helmets. All were on the same wavelength and since all of us were talking at the same time, there was a babble of voices in our ears.

"Silence!" Spartan's voice rose above the others. "Keep quiet! You distract me!"

The sounds subsided. Spartan took over the controls from Axel and continued to increase the power of the ship. Suddenly he seemed to be aware that Axel and I were still in the control room. "Go back to my compartment! Both of you! You know the regulations for an emergency like this."

Dr. Spartan's compartment, like the shower room and lavatory farther to the rear of the ship, was divided in half by a corridor. On one side was his living quarters and on the other was the chartroom, which contained a small but adequate electronic computer, astronomic tables on microfilm, a projector for the film, and our entire supply of writing materials.

Axel stationed himself in the chartroom, and I went to Spartan's sleeping quarters. I felt helpless and trapped. The room, for a captain's quarters, was bleak. His sleeping bag was lashed to the bulkhead and there was a private lavatory and shaving mirror, for he did not share the one the rest of us used. A small chest, like the ones the rest of us had for our personal belongings—was near the bedroll.

I remembered suddenly that the male members of the crew had been clean-shaven and had sported butch haircuts when they'd come aboard. Even Gail wore a mannish bob. But Dr. Spartan had kept his beard. If, in order to cut down on weight, we'd been ordered to trim our hair, why hadn't Spartan made a sacrifice in that direction?

I thought about these things, perhaps, to turn my mind away from the approaching danger. This was also the reason I gave myself for looking into his space chest. I'm not naturally a snooper. Was he the kind of man who would murder me in order to possess Gail? Would a clue be in his chest? I looked inside.

I found a toothbrush, soap, extra clothing and shoes, electric razor for trimming his beard. There was also a locked box, which probably contained poisoned darts. I had an urge to steal it, but I knew his gun was loaded and I'd never get away with the theft.

Next I found a small square of paper on which were written the names of the crew. Morrie Grover's name was first. Mine was second. Joel's had been third, but now it was crossed out and written below Axel's. Gail's name was followed by a question mark. There was no notation to indicate the reason for the names. He did not need a roster of the crew—that was in the logbook.

I replaced the paper and closed the chest. I waited for meteors to strike, and wondered if any would damage the ship. But I knew the only sound I would hear would be when one struck the ship. The greater the sound, the larger the meteor.

I put my head to the floor. I was wearing my helmet, of course, but the vibrations of striking meteors would be transmitted to the helmet and I would hear them. We had often talked to each other this way without using our helmet radios.

For several minutes I waited and heard nothing. Then came a sound.

Ping.

It was faint, but I knew a meteor had made that sound as it hit the craft.

Then *ping, ping, crump!*

Two small, one much larger. But there had been no holes made in the ship. At least, there was no alarm from Dr. Spartan who would know from the air gauges if any compartment had been punctured.

The ringing sounds, singly and in twos and threes, continued. This was a dense cloud, although we were striking them only a dozen or so to a minute. That is density in space. Then I heard a loud *thud.* A tiny bump raised itself in the metal floor not two feet from my helmet. A large meteor had pierced the outer hide of our ship and dented the inside wall before vaporizing. But the fluid in the walls was now closing the hole and we had lost no air.

Another thud. I didn't know where this one had hit. The ship's acceleration, which had increased when Dr. Spartan started the emergency motors, suddenly seemed to decrease. Spartan's gruff voice came through my helmet radio. "A motor has been hit."

He had cut down the power, of course. A single motor conking out would put more thrust on the other three sides of the ship, resulting in a curved trajectory for the craft. Therefore three other motors would have to be cut in order to keep the ship in a straight line.

There were more pings and thumps in my ears as I continued to press my helmet to the floor. An hour passed. Then another. Two hours of terror. Then the noise stopped.

"I think we're out of danger," Spartan's voice came through my helmet radio. "We penetrated a thin segment of the cloud."

"Any leaks, Doctor?" Axel asked.

"The air pressure gauges show no loss. But the motor will have to be repaired. Who's on duty now?"

"Miss Loring follows me into the control room," said Axel, "but this has been a tough experience for her. I won't mind working overtime."

"I can't permit it," said Spartan. "Everyone must do his share. Fetch her, Drake."

"Yes, sir," I said.

I went back to the main cabin where I found Joel slipping out of his spacesuit. I removed mine.

"Where's Gail?" I asked him.

He nodded to the rear of the ship. "She went to the machinery room," he said. "Morrie's in the kitchen."

I shuffled back to the kitchen. Morrie's spacesuit lay in a heap on the floor, but there was no sign of him.

He wasn't in the lavatory, either. I pushed open the door to the machinery room just in time to hear Gail scream.

I stood there a moment, hardly believing what I saw.

Morrie had forced her to the floor. He had almost torn her uniform from her body. She was trying to fight him off, but his arms held her tight.

I pushed myself away from the bulkhead. In the center of the ship there is very little centrifugal force and I literally sailed across the room to drop lightly on my feet beside the struggling pair.

I reached down, caught Morrie savagely around the neck with my arm, and pulled him back, away from Gail.

He squirmed out of my grasp and threw a savage punch, which struck me in the shoulder. But he hadn't been set to deliver the blow and I hardly felt it. I was angry now and I lunged forward, grabbing his arm with both hands. His feet left the floor and I literally hurled him across the cabin into the water purifier on the far side of the room.

He lit with a crash.

I turned to Gail. "Are you all right?"

"I—I'm—fine," she choked. Then her eyes focused on Morrie across the room. "Look out, Bill!" she screamed.

I turned. Morrie had wrenched a pipe from the water purifier and was getting set to dive at me.

CHAPTER EIGHT

CROUCHING, I AWAITED Morrie's onslaught. He held the aluminum pipe—about a three-foot length—biding his time, his mouth twisting in bitter frustration. I remember thinking how lucky I was that the improved weapon was aluminum and not heavy iron. *Small consolation,* I thought. *He can certainly knock me out with it.*

But Morrie's angry face showed more than a desire to make me unconscious. He had the wild eyes of a madman, and there was murder in his movements.

He swung the pipe. I ducked and it passed so close to my skull that I could feel it brush through my hair. The force of the blow tore his feet from the floor and he sailed upward, glancing off the garden trays so that he turned a somersault and came down on his feet above my head.

I sprang at him. He stepped aside and swung the pipe, catching me a glancing blow on the shoulder and knocking me across the ship and against the water purifier. The machine was already a shambles, both of us having hit it. The steam spurted into the room—water dripped on the floor.

Bruised and cautious, I shuffled around the ship toward him. He stood waving the pipe like a batter in a baseball game, determined not to miss again. I could see it in his eyes.

I moved within reach and he struck. But this time I didn't dodge. I caught the blow on my arm. Pain shot through it, but I'd caught the blow soon enough to prevent the full force from breaking the bone. As it hit, I seized the pipe with my other hand and twisted it sharply. It came out of Morrie's grasp.

He lunged toward me. I threw him back with a punch aimed at his chin, landing on his chest instead. He crouched to attack and I threw the pipe at him. Once more I didn't figure on the ten per cent gravity. The pipe went over his head and crashed into the bulkhead at the other end of the ship.

He sprang and I caught him. We stood with our magnetized shoes anchored to the floor, swinging, ducking, punching, each now angry enough to kill. We were about evenly matched as far as muscles and weight were concerned, but Morrie was showing the strength of a maniac. My punch staggered him but did no real damage. He came back and feinted. I suckered and he brought two punches against my chin and belly that sent me to the floor. Only the fact that I rolled with the punches kept me from being kayoed. He tried to dive on me, but I scrambled out of the way. We were both beginning to show some signs of damage. I had a soreness in the belly where he'd landed his blow, and his cheek had been cut by my knuckles. He dived at me again. I scored on his chin but he managed to get me in a clinch.

We wrestled, partly on the floor, partly floating near the garden trays and the cable housing in the center of the compartment. Suddenly he grasped my shoulders and brought up his knee.

It caught me in the groin and I screamed with pain.

Somehow I caught one of the trays and hurled myself out of reach, but as I hit the floor I could hardly move. All the fight left me with that blow. Somewhere, I heard Gail calling: "Bill! Get up!"

It was no use. I couldn't move my arms or legs. Morrie hesitated a moment. Then, deciding that I was helpless, he pushed himself to the bulkhead where the length of pipe lay. He meant to use it in an attempt to beat me to death. He reached the weapon, picked it up and held it a moment in his hand as he turned a savage look toward me.

He came toward me, certain that I was no longer able to defend myself. I rolled away, the pain nearly killing me. Then I wrapped my legs around his and tripped him, in spite of the pain in my groin. He dropped the pipe as he fell.

Holding him tightly with a scissors grip, I lay there, inhaling deeply, trying to rid my body of pain. Morrie turned and twisted, trying to break free. With each movement he was sliding, until finally he was free.

I rolled over and got to my knees, waiting for his next rush. I needed all the time I could get to regain my strength. Knowing this, Morrie wasted no time. He got ready to leap again.

Then I saw Gail. She had picked up the pipe Morrie had dropped. She moved toward him, holding it high, ready to strike. My eyes, watching her, gave her away. Morrie saw my glance and turned just as she was ready to strike. He warded off the blow with his left arm, just as I'd done early in the fight, then he swung hard with his right. The punch landed solidly on Gail's jaw. She gave a startled moan of pain as she went down to the floor.

That did more than all the resting in the world for me. The pain seemed to leave my body for a moment. At least I didn't feel it any more. All that was left was a desire to pound Morrie Grover into a shapeless pulp because he had struck Gail with his fist. I hit him like a truck.

He went down and I fell on top of him. Holding him with my knees on his stomach I punched his face, his nose, his mouth, his jaw. Left, right. Left, right. One, two and again one, two. Morrie's head lolled with the punches and he was out. And then my strength left me. I fell over his unconscious body in a faint.

The darkness seemed to float away as I felt a cooling moisture on my face. I opened my eyes and saw Gail bending over me. Her clothing was in so many rags she looked naked. She had taken a strip of torn cloth, moistened it under the leaking water purifier, and was bathing my battered face.

I turned my head and saw Axel and Dr. Spartan coming through the bulkhead door.

"What in the devil happened here?" Spartan snarled.

"Grover," said Gail, nodding toward Morrie, who was trying to lift himself off the floor.

"He's hurt!" said Axel.

"Attend to him," said Spartan. Then he turned to Gail. "And Drake? Were they fighting? Over you?"

Gail stopped bathing my face. She began to sob. I sat up straight now.

"Stop tormenting her!" I said, my anger rising to choke me.

"Sir!" said Spartan. He always insisted we call him *sir.* Now that bit of rank pulling seemed more important to him than ever. His eyes showed steel-hard determination to force me into submission; his lips were tight with hatred.

"I said 'Stop tormenting her!' and I didn't say *sir!*" I shouted. "Morrie tried to rape her. Can't you figure that out?"

"Sir!" Spartan snapped. "And how do I know you weren't the one who tried it?"

"Because, damn you, *SIR,* I'm her husband!"

Spartan's face flushed angrily. "That's no way to talk to your superior officer!" he snapped. "For this impertinence-"

He stopped in the middle of pronouncing sentence as his eyes fell on the water-purifying apparatus.

"You've wrecked it!" he shouted and sprang to examine it.

Axel was holding Morrie upright now and Gail resumed bathing my bruised face with refreshing water. "Let me have some of that water," said Axel, ripping out a torn piece of Morrie's T-shirt.

Spartan swung around. "Stop wasting that water!" he roared. "Do you realize we're dangerously short of water as a result of this foolishness?"

Gail continued to bathe my face with the damp cloth.

"Stop it!" thundered Spartan.

"Bill's hurt," she replied calmly.

"By his own idiocy."

"Idiocy!" Gail stood up and faced Spartan. "If there's an idiot aboard this ship, it's you—you interplanetary Captain Bligh!"

Spartan didn't move a muscle. His face was frozen into a mask of contempt and resentment. "Miss Loring," he said, "just because you are a woman gives you no special privileges. I'm the captain of this ship, and I *must* be treated with respect."

"Why don't you do something to earn respect then?" she demanded, looking as though she might burst into tears at any moment.

"Ten days extra duty for you, Miss Loring," he said. He turned and went to the bulkhead door. When he reached it, he turned to Axel. "As soon as these men are able, bring them into the main cabin. We'll hold the court-martial there."

He disappeared through the door. Axel got up and went over to the water purifier. He spent three or four minutes examining it. When he finished he looked very grim.

"Two of the four units are wrecked," he said. "We may be on half rations of water for the next two years."

When Morrie and I were able to get on our feet, we went into the main cabin, where Spartan was arranging Morrie's spacesuit beside his sleeping bag. He gave us a frowning glance and beckoned to Axel, who went to where he was standing. They talked for a few minutes, discussing the damage to our water system. Only Joel was absent, being in the control room.

Finally Spartan turned to the rest of us. "Sit down," he said.

He waited until we had arranged ourselves in front of him, Axel, Gail and I sitting cross-legged on the floor behind Morrie, who reclined on his elbows facing Spartan.

"Mr. Ludson has just told me that our water-cycling equipment is badly damaged," Spartan said, seating himself. "Therefore, we will have to use less water, unless we can make repairs. The present outlook is very bad. The cycling units can now distill only half the amount we have been using.

"We can't cut down on the amount of water we use to irrigate our garden. And we can't prepare meals without water because we have to depend on dehydrated food. So we'll have to use less water for drinking, washing and laundry."

"Good heavens, Dr. Spartan! We can't live in filth!" said Gail.

"Perhaps not," said Spartan, "but when we wash, or do laundry, that water must come from our drinking supply. That will force us to hold unnecessary cleanliness to a minimum."

It was obvious that we would be the dirtiest group of spacemen who ever made an interplanetary voyage.

"In addition," Spartan went on, "No. Five motor is not functioning because it was hit by a meteor. We have yet to determine how badly it is damaged, but since it is important that we have that extra margin of safety, we must make every attempt to repair it. And if that isn't enough trouble for us, two of our crew have engaged in a disgraceful brawl."

"It was *not* a brawl," said Gail.

"Miss Loring, I've warned you. I will increase your punishment if you continue with these remarks. I've called you together here to hold a court-martial to decide where to fix the blame for the damage to the water machinery. Now, Miss Loring, if you want to talk, you can tell me what happened."

Gail, who had found time to put on another uniform, bowed her head.

"It is very embarrassing, Dr. Spartan—"

"It is necessary," said Spartan.

Gail hesitated, collecting her thoughts. "When the meteor alarm was given I went to my station in the machinery room, which is nearest my quarters in the rear cupola of the ship—"

"We all know that. It is unnecessary to give these details," said Spartan.

"After you gave the all-clear signal, Morrie—Mr. Grover—who had been in the kitchen, came in through the bulkhead and asked me if I was all right. After I told him I was, he broke down and began to cry. I felt sorry for him and went over and put my arm on his shoulders to cheer him up."

"Are you sure, Miss Loring, that was the only reason you put your arm around him?" Spartan asked.

"I did *not* put my arm around him, Doctor," Gail said succinctly. "Mr. Grover apparently had been under tremendous strain. As you know, he's the youngest member of the crew."

"He's old enough to have mature emotions."

"He has shown that his emotions are definitely *not* mature," Gail replied. "As I said before, I tried to cheer him up, but he—like other people I could name—put a different interpretation on an innocent gesture. He threw his arms around me and kissed me. He said some wild things about being in love with me. I tried to push him away, explaining that I was a married woman—"

"We all understand about that marriage," Morrie broke in.

"Nevertheless, I made promises at that ceremony and I intend to keep them until Bill Drake is no longer my husband," she replied. "I thought Morrie was out of his head. Then, before I knew it, he began to tear off my clothing. I tried to struggle but he held me so tightly I couldn't. Then Bill Drake appeared. He threw Mr. Grover across the room, and Morrie tore a piece of pipe from the condenser and they—they fought."

"Then it was Drake who threw Grover into the machinery?" Spartan asked.

"Yes," replied Gail. "But it wasn't intentional."

"It may not have been intentional," Spartan snarled, "but it has endangered the success of this expedition."

"Morrie also knocked Bill Drake into the machinery," she said. She was calling Morrie by a single name and me by my full name. Suddenly I sensed that in using my complete name she was not being formal. On the contrary, she had turned it into a term of endearment. It was as if she savored the full name, rather than any kind of abbreviation.

"Humph! And are you sure you never, at any time, encouraged Mr. Grover to make these—uh—advances?"

"Of course not!"

Spartan turned to Morrie. "What do you have to say?" It was obvious that he hoped Morrie could successfully refute the story told by Gail.

Morrie shrugged, his whole manner noncommittal.

"I want an answer," said Spartan. "Is she telling the truth?" He was driving for the answer he wanted.

Morrie breathed deeply. "What is the truth, Dr. Spartan?" he asked.

"Surely you know the truth." An incredulous look sprang to his face.

"Don't act so damned dogmatic. The truth can be a dozen different things. Right now I don't know what's real and what isn't. Nothing is the same out here as it was on the Earth. Everything familiar is millions of miles away. Even the Earth looks like a star in the sky and it takes a telescope to see the moon. Stars whirl like a merry-go-round and the sun is smaller and has a corona, which we never see at home except during an eclipse. We travel in something different from any vehicle ever dreamed of, powered by something nothing else runs by. We don't wear clothes, we wear gym suits. Our meals are dehydrated food and hybrid vegetables. And our drinking water is distilled from urine! We have centrifugal force for gravity and we even have a marriage that isn't real."

"The rest of us have adjusted ourselves to these conditions," said Spartan sternly, obviously disappointed at the turn the conversation had taken.

"Do you really think so?" Morrie asked. "I'm not so sure. We're living under conditions that are decidedly upsetting. It wouldn't take much to push any of us over the edge into a psychosis. Nothing is real, not even our thoughts, because our world is totally different."

Spartan's lips pressed together. Then he asked: "Is this your excuse?"

"Gail Loring is the only real thing aboard. That's because she's a woman and I'm a man. The only thing traveling with us that we knew on Earth is sex." Having had his say, he took on a hangdog look, as if putting himself on the mercy of the court.

"Bah! A flimsy defense." Spartan's tone was not convincing. He was too much aware of sex himself.

"Then if it's not a defense or an excuse, it's a reason why I went mad for a few minutes," Grover said. "Perhaps I'm not justified by Earth standards, but those standards don't exist here. You said so yourself. All I thought of was that she was a woman. I didn't think of the consequences. I thought of myself."

I was still angry and could never forgive Morrie, but I also felt sorry for him. Out of frustration, I'd nursed some pretty weird thoughts myself. Fortunately, I'd been able to control them.

Spartan seemed immune to understanding. "I take it that you plead guilty."

Gail cleared her throat. "There are extenuating circumstances, Doctor," she said. "As the injured party, I ask you not to be too hard on Mr. Grover."

Spartan turned cold, hard eyes on her. "Is this an admission that *you* may be more guilty than you admit?"

Gail flushed. "All I asked was a little human understanding for Mr. Grover."

"Humph." Spartan bit his lip beneath his beard. "It is necessary to make Mr. Grover understand that he must control himself in the future. He is not well adjusted. Certainly our examiners are at fault. They were supposed to perceive signs of instability and weakness. If they failed in this case, how do we know they did a better job of judging the rest of you?"

"And *you*, Doctor?" Gail asked.

He ignored her. "We can't send Grover to prison. There is none. But he is unstable," he mused, almost as if he were talking to himself. "The simplest way out would be to execute him—"

"Doctor!" exclaimed Gail.

"What in the hell, sir?" Axel said. "Don't be as crazy as Grover."

For a moment Spartan's eyes flared with indignation, then he waved his hand for silence. "I had not finished. I was just pointing out the simple solution. With Grover out of the way, we'd have less of a water problem, which he caused. If he did not exist, we would not have to worry about his psychotic violence, which might recur. On the other hand, the loss of one able-bodied crewman would certainly show itself in the results of our expedition. We must think of the expedition. However, some disciplinary action is needed." He paused.

"I agree with you," said Morrie. "And as for my being crazy, I'm not, really. I was under a strain. I was afraid. I just forgot to be civilized."

"I'm glad you see it in that light," said Spartan, "because I'm assigning you to a task that might be somewhat dangerous. You will make the necessary repairs to engine No. Five."

I felt a sense of relief. I'd been afraid of what Spartan might do, especially when he talked of capital punishment. And even though making the repairs to the plasma motors would be perilous, the danger wasn't excessive and the job was one that someone would have to do anyhow.

"You'll begin at once," said Dr. Spartan.

"Thank you, sir," said Morrie.

He rose, went over to his bedroll and began to put on his spacesuit. Dr. Spartan watched him with a curious glint in his eyes. Then he turned to me. "Stand by the locks till he returns, Drake."

I nodded.

Turning abruptly, Dr. Spartan went back into his ivory tower.

CHAPTER NINE

GAIL AND AXEL WENT AFT to see what could be done about fixing the water-cycling machinery. I helped Morrie adjust his spacesuit in silence.

Although I felt that he had not been sane when he attacked Gail, I couldn't forgive his actions. I don't suppose he felt forgiving toward me. I was sure he hated me for stopping him from taking Gail, even though he appeared to be remorseful over his actions.

Before I put the helmet over his head, he said, "I—I wasn't myself, Bill. I want you to realize that. And try to make Gail see it that way."

"She'll accept your apology later," I said, "but get one thing straight, Grover. If you ever make another pass at her, whether you're sane or not, I'll kill you in spite of hell and Doc Spartan."

He bit his lip. "Can't blame you for feeling that way. You do love her, don't you?"

"You're damn right," I said. "Even before we were married I loved her."

His helmet was fastened and he stepped into the locks. I closed the door, ready to use the walkie-talkie transmitter for any messages. Dr. Spartan reappeared. "Grover will need welding equipment to fix that motor," he said. "Did he take it with him?"

"No, sir," I said.

"Then get it and take it out to him," said Spartan, turning and going back to his cabin.

I shrugged. I hadn't been sentenced to repair the tubes, as Morrie had, but I still had to obey orders. I got the equipment and a tool bag from the storage compartment of the machine room. When I told Gail and Axel I was taking welding equipment out to Morrie, Axel gave me a worried look. "Don't start anything, Bill," he said.

"We have an understanding," I replied.

Returning to the main cabin, I found Dr. Spartan waiting again, an oxygen tank in his hands.

"Here's the tank I want you to use, Drake," he said. "There's just a small amount of oxygen in it, but to use a new tank for such a short errand would be wasteful. We don't know when we might have another accident."

"Okay. I mean—yes, sir," I said.

"I trust you and Grover won't resume—uh—hostilities."

"No, sir. I'm sure he wasn't himself, sir."

While I put on my helmet, Spartan put the tank on my shoulders. I checked the connections, then I went into the locks. I started the pumps to exhaust the air and called to Morrie on my helmet transmitter.

"I'm bringing some welding equipment, Morrie."

He didn't answer.

"Do you read me, Morrie?" I called.

Still no answer. I called a third time and when Morrie didn't seem to hear, I grew apprehensive.

"Morrie!"

I knew something was wrong now. He should have heard me. Sometimes a man will switch off his transmitter, but he always keeps his receiver on. The locks were emptied of air and I swung open the outer door. I fastened a lifeline to my belt and fitted the hasp of the other end to a ring just outside the door.

Then I pivoted around the doorframe and planted my magnetized boots against the metal side of the ship. They stuck, and I started to walk around the craft toward motor No. Five.

I found Morrie Grover beside the engine, standing like a statue, his hands raised—thrown out by centrifugal force—as if some unseen bandit had ordered him to stick 'em up.

His unnatural position and his failure to answer my calls were enough to convince me that something was radically wrong. He was unconscious or—I tried not to think of the alternative.

What was wrong? Only a meteor could have hurt him here and we'd long since passed through that cloud. I knew the chance of being hit by one was so remote that it wasn't likely to occur in a couple of hundred years.

I stepped over the metal housing of the bank of motors between Morrie and myself. His body looked weird in the sunlight, going into phases like a man-shaped moon, with each revolution of the ship. Half his figure was black, half gleaming like a star. And then, as the sun peeped through the glass of his helmet, I saw a contorted face, open mouth, and staring, sightless eyes.

Sure that he was dead, I stepped to his side and peered down at the oxygen gauge on his chest, worn upside down so that it would be visible to Morrie. The tank was nearly full, but the needle didn't wiggle as it would have done if Morrie had been breathing. He was dead, all right.

"Dr. Spartan!" I called.

No answer came through my earphones. I called again. Apparently, Dr. Spartan wasn't listening, nor was anyone else. I felt the urge to walk to the nearest video camera and wave my arms so that Joel would see me in the control room. Instead, I decided to take Morrie's body to the locks—quickly, in case there was still some spark of life in the man.

The tool kit I'd brought topside wasn't magnetized and would be thrown into space by the rotation of the ship. I opened the bag, took the pliers and cut two short lengths from Morrie's lifeline. One I used to lash the tools to the motor housings, and the other I fastened from Morrie's belt to mine, leaving about eight feet of slack between us. Then I replaced the pliers, closed the tool kit and was ready to move.

Dragging Morrie and his magnetized boots back to the locks would be hard work, especially since I'd have to pull myself the same distance. So I lifted him off the deck and then, holding his weightless body over my shoulder, doubled my knees and jumped upward.

I sailed outward—or, if you choose, upward—for the ship, myself and Morrie, and the sun, formed a right angle, if you're interested in the geometry of our positions. The sun was toward the rear of the ship and about thirty degrees to the right, when you looked toward the tail of the craft. This geometry was presently going to become very important to my future existence.

It seemed as if I were sailing a great distance, although distance is difficult to judge in space when there's nothing to mark it. I had perhaps fifty feet of life line and it wasn't until I was certain I'd gone much further that I began to grow worried.

Then I looked down. The thin copper wire, which had secured me to the ship, was no longer fastened to the ring just outside the locks. It was being pulled upward and Morrie and I were swinging around each other like twin stars around a common center of gravity. The centrifugal force of our motion was swinging the wire with it.

I just couldn't explain it. There was a hasp at the end of the line, which shouldn't have come unfastened. The line could hardly have broken. It was meant to stand a great deal of strain and there had been none. Not only were we weightless, but I hadn't to my knowledge, put any strain on the wire during the entire time.

My push outward—or upward—had been translated into a motion away from the ship and I would continue in that direction forever unless some force were applied to stop me. The only force

I was subject to was the gravitational pull of the sun, which meant I'd revolve around the sun forever, never to return to the Jehad.

But there was another motion, too, and this was the velocity of the ship at the moment I had broken away from it. This carried me forward—which to me was in the general direction of the orbit of Mars. However, my relationship to the ship was not permanent. The ship was being constantly accelerated, second by second, by the thrust of the plasma motors. Even as I looked down, my heart freezing with horror at the thought of never being able to return to the Jehad, I could see the ship inching forward. The right triangle had become acute and presently I'd be behind the ship.

Even in this tense moment my mind was demanding explanations, even fantastic ones. What had happened? If the hasp couldn't unfasten itself, if the line couldn't have broken, something must have broken it or unfastened the hasp. What? Morrie's ghost, vowing vengeance for whatever fancied wrong I'd done to him in the machinery cabin? Or Spartan? Or something else?

These thoughts occupied only a second because I had to get busy and, as Morrie and I whirled around in our ghostly dance in space, I reached for the petcock of my oxygen flask. Just as I touched it, a warning shot through my mind: Spartan had given me a tank with only a small amount of oxygen in it, therefore he had to be the one who was trying to get rid of me. He had released my line, knowing I'd take the quickest way back to the locks, rather than to clamber over the sides.

Small comfort, this sudden discovery. I realized that since I had a minimum supply of oxygen to breathe, it would be suicidal to use any part of it for jetting back to the ship, which was pulling farther and farther ahead.

Across from me, sailing round and round like a devil's carousel, Morrie seemed to grin as the sunlight struck his helmet again. He was dead and had plenty of air, he seemed to say. I was alive and hadn't enough. And that grin was what did it. I realized he had enough to get us both back—if I acted quickly.

I pulled him toward me. It was difficult to twist him around, more difficult to turn him toward the ship. Finally I succeeded in pointing him right and I thumbed open the jet petcock at the base of his oxygen equipment.

He shot forward, but the line attached to both our belts made him somersault, and there was a tug on the thin strand that tied us together. He was pulling me *away* from the ship, putting more distance between me and safety. For him, it didn't matter.

Quickly I pulled him back. I grabbed both his legs, like the handles of a wheelbarrow, and pointed him toward the ship, which with each second was getting farther and farther away. How far I had no idea because, as I said, distances are hard to judge in space.

Now the air jet was shoving us forward, accelerating us toward the ship. I hoped it would match the ship's acceleration but I couldn't tell at first. Then I laughed out loud. My voice made a hollow sound in my ears. We *were* gaining. Just a tiny bit, but the ship was getting larger. Now the question was, did I have enough air on Morrie's back to carry us to the ship? The air jet was intended for only short bursts, such as I'd used when I crossed from the Saturn capsule to the Jehad. Now I needed continued acceleration.

The thin vapor stream from the flask continued and now we were above the stern of the ship, where Gail's quarters had been established. Then the rush of air didn't seem quite as strong—we weren't creeping up as fast.

The air locks weren't far ahead, but we were above the ship, maybe two hundred yards away. Morrie's lifeline, the part still attached to the ship after I cut him loose, was whirling around with the ship, thrown out to its full length by the rotation. Whoever had released my line hadn't bothered Morrie's. Maybe the killer knew Morrie was dead—or maybe his object was only to kill *me*.

I steered down, hoping to get close enough to grab the line. Then the oxygen fizzled out. No more vapor came from the tank. It was empty and I couldn't quite reach the line. It was just a foot or two beyond me.

In desperation I gave Morrie a push and then praised God for Isaac Newton's action and reaction. The shove I gave Morrie was sufficient to push me back so that my free hand caught the line. I grabbed it and held on.

A couple of moments later I was pulling myself hand over hand toward the locks.

Just as I reached the locks, they opened. A hand stretched out, grasped my arm and pulled Morrie and me inside. I detached the lifelines.

It was Axel Ludson, standing there in a spacesuit. Instantly, all the suspicions I'd had in space crystallized.

Axel had unfastened the lifeline!

I watched him close the locks and turn the valve that would presently fill the locks with air. "How long have you been here, Axel?" I demanded.

He turned, but didn't answer. His eyes focused, from within the helmet, on Morrie's body, planted to the floor of the locks by magnetic boots, swaying lifelessly as the ship rotated on its axis. "What's wrong with him? Did he pass out?"

"Dead." I said.

Axel gave me the same kind of a look I must have given him when I wondered about the lifeline. He was thinking of the fight between Morrie and me. "How'd it happen?" he asked quietly.

"Your guess is as good as mine," I said. "I found him that way. And somebody tried to kill me, Axel. Didn't you see how my line was loose and how I was drifting in space?"

He shook his head, then reached down and examined my lifeline on the floor. The hasp was on the end. Someone had unfastened it. "I looked out the port and saw you pulling yourself in. I thought it was your life line," he said.

"It was Morrie's. I had to cut it to lash the tools topside."

Axel didn't seem to believe me. Now he examined the section of line I'd used to tie Morrie and me together. Apparently satisfied, he went to look at the air gauge. A breathable amount of air was in the locks—we took off our helmets. Then we worked Morrie's loose. He was dead, all right. Dead and cold.

Axel examined Morrie's helmet. His fingers probed inside where the valve from the air supply enters.

"Stuck valve," he said.

I looked relieved. "I thought somebody had killed him," I said.

"Somebody did," said Axel. He pulled his fingers from the valve. They held a tiny piece of paper.

"But it could have been an accident," I said.

"There could have been enough air in the suit to keep him alive for some minutes," Axel said. "What killed him was stale air—carbon dioxide he'd exhaled. Somebody put that paper there to keep him from getting air. Probably didn't know what was happening till too late."

I was no longer as suspicious of Axel. A murderer wouldn't be likely to explain how he killed his victim but I had to be sure. "You didn't answer me, Axel, when I asked how long you'd been in the locks."

He gave me a strange look. "You think I took your life line off the ring?"

I avoided his eyes.

"Well, I guess I'd feel the same way. But I just came into the locks a few minutes ago. I'd just pumped the air out of the locks and was ready to go topside to help you and Morrie when I saw you outside. I didn't have time to cut your lifeline loose. You ought to know that if I had murder in mind, I could have pushed you back into space again."

"I'm sorry, Axel," I said. "But things get screwed up in my mind. Nothing seems right out here in high space."

"There was nobody around the locks when I entered them," Axel went on. "Gail and I were working in the machinery cabin till she got worried and asked me to check up on you. I figured I'd give you a hand. Joel's in the control cabin."

He paused and I said nothing. We both knew who'd tried to kill me and who probably was responsible for Morrie's death. That piece of paper didn't get in Morrie's helmet by accident. The entire paper supply was in Spartan's chartroom.

"Why?" Axel asked slowly, a trace of accent creeping into his voice. It sounded like *vy*. He stared at me in utter perplexity. "Is Dr. Spartan crazy, too?"

I remembered something that had happened—ages ago, it seemed, although it had been less than two hours before. "I was in Spartan's cabin during the time we went through the meteor cloud, Axel. I found something there."

"Yes?"

"Yes. A piece of paper—with our names on it. Morrie's was at the top of the list. Then mine. Warner Joel's name had been crossed out and written in again after yours. At the bottom there was Gail's name with a question mark after it."

"A roster of the crew?"

"Perhaps. But the question mark puzzled me. Now I believe he had listed us in the order of execution—in the order of expendability, so to speak."

"It is a ridiculous idea," said Axel.

"He killed Morrie and tried to kill me," I said. "We were Numbers One and Two on the list."

Axel blinked his eyes. Then he looked at Morrie swaying upright, held in place by his magnetic boots. "First we must take the dead man into the ship," he said. "Later we talk about it, Bill. Yust you and I."

We dragged Morrie into the main cabin. Gail was still in the machinery room, and we called Spartan on the intercom. When he came through the door and saw Morrie stretched out on his sleeping bag, he glanced at him as he might have at a soiled spot on the rug.

"What happened?" he asked.

I told him just what I'd found, purposely omitting my narrow escape from death. I figured that if he wasn't told about this he might give himself away. But he had shown no surprise at my being alive and he didn't ask how I'd gotten Morrie inside.

Spartan dropped to his knee beside the body. He picked up Morrie's helmet and probed the valve with his fingers as Axel had done. "Stuck valve," he announced. "Inefficiency on the part of the manufacturer. I'll make a full report of this when I get back to the Earth." I noted he said "when *I* get back." I sensed he didn't expect much company on the return trip. Today's events had proved it.

"What do we do now, sir?" Axel asked respectfully.

"Give him a space burial, of course," said Spartan. He turned to me. "Within the next few days, you can make an oral report on the incident and I'll transcribe it on the tape recorder. We'll need it for the officials when we get back to Earth." He paused and looked down at Morrie. "Our young friend has discovered a second great reality in space, I fear. The reality of death."

He turned on his heel and went back to his ivory tower. I reached down and picked up Morrie's helmet. I felt inside the valve. The piece of paper, which Axel had replaced, was gone now. Dr Spartan had removed the evidence of murder.

We put Morrie's helmet on his head and carried his body into the locks. After we put on our own helmets, we emptied the locks of air and pushed the body out into space. Then we went to tell Gail.

CHAPTER TEN

AXEL AND I did not get a chance to have our talk immediately. For one thing, I was completing my disciplinary tours of duty imposed by Dr. Spartan and, for another, I was faced with the extra duties imposed on me by the death of Morrie.

Spartan had not attempted again to take my life, a fact that seemed very strange to me. He continued to thrive on his hatred for all of us, particularly Axel and me. Understandably, he wasn't quite as harsh with Gail. Toward Joel he seemed to have adopted a special manner. On the surface he was as curt toward him as toward the others, but I noticed that Joel was given light duties, while the rest of us got the menial tasks and the tough ones. Not that this mattered, because to be busy was not to be bored. But Joel was Spartan's fair-haired boy, there was no doubt about that. Perhaps Spartan saw need for an ally, or maybe he planned to use him for things that were to come.

Joel was elated because his chief often invited him into the chartroom for a meal, or to discuss adjustments in our orbit. And I am sure Joel reported every slip of the tongue Axel and I made which showed our true feelings toward Spartan.

Before my extra duty—and Gail's—ended, we reached the middle part of our voyage. At this point we had achieved the maximum speed for the trip, which was 40,000 miles per *hour*. This was far short of the ship's theoretical speed of 100,000 miles per *second*, but Mars was too near the Earth for that kind of travel.

Planners of the trip had computed several possible routes to Mars. The shortest, a mere 40 million miles, would be undertaken when our Earth and Mars were nearest each other. Such a route would be like cutting across a vacant lot from one street to the next parallel street. However, there would be fences to climb in the form of the sun's pull of gravity. The ship would have to use power from the first day till the last, and much payload would have to be sacrificed.

The second route would use a minimum of fuel and maximum time. We would accelerate to an orbit intersecting the paths of the Earth and Mars. Then the motors would be cut and we would coast in free flight to our destination, where we would decelerate. But such a trip would take from five to seven years.

Our actual path was a compromise between the two. We would use a minimum of fuel and a minimum of time. It was faster than plan 2, but more economical than plan 1. We would accelerate to a good speed, coast awhile on the planned orbit, then decelerate. Had we enough supplies, we might have remained on Mars about three months. However, every ounce of supplies we would use on Mars had to be shipped separately on conventional, unmanned rocket ships, which were now orbiting Mars. Three ships of this type had been fired from the Earth two years before. One of these would take us from the Jehad and back again, just as we had boarded the Jehad from the Earth. The other two would be left on Mars.

But only three weeks of supplies could be shipped. After our return to the Jehad, we would orbit for about 75 days, when Mars and the Earth would be in position for our return trip.

Even though we had more work than usual, the trip grew boring after Gail and I completed our disciplinary duty. Then we changed our "day" from 25 to 24 hours, replacing the five-hour shifts, which had included a shift for Morrie, to six-hour shifts. Following through on our dull routines, we realized why Morrie had cracked up. But the rest of us showed no signs of this, and even Joel bore up well. Perhaps the headshrinkers who passed on us were entitled to one mistake. We figured *one* despite the fact that Dr. Spartan could not be considered a direct hit on the psychological target. However, Spartan was a good spaceman, just as Nero had been good at his job, though more than slightly cracked.

Then, as we neared the end of the middle stage of the trip, we picked up a new kind of signal from Mars on our electronic equipment. The first, undoubtedly a radar beam, continued as before. But the second was on a longer wavelength and was undoubtedly a radio transmission. It came to us as a deep chirping sound, and Axel suggested the Martians were trying to communicate with us.

"Maybe words of welcome," he said, adding, "or warning against trespassing."

Then the middle portion of our voyage ended. Mars was now a discernible disc and the gyroscope twisted the ship around so that its tail was headed toward our destination. The motors were fired and the long period of deceleration began.

While this was being done by Spartan, with Joel assisting him in the control room, Gail, Axel and I were together in the main cabin, and we had our first full discussion on what might lie ahead.

"Spartan might have had a change of heart," Gail said, always hopeful. "He really hasn't done anything out of line since he tried to take Bill's life."

"At that time," said Axel, "we believed—and he did, too—that there would be suffering from lack of water. However, we have been able to distill water for irrigating the garden by using the vacuum of the air locks. There is plenty to drink—if we're careful not to waste it—and for our dehydrated food. We can even do a washing once in a while." He smiled and rubbed his hands over his dirty T-shirt. "Now it is not necessary to reduce the size of the crew because of lack of water."

"Why didn't he wait before trying it in the first place?" I asked.

"Morrie Grover had to be eliminated," Axel explained. "Spartan gave his reasons. He said there was no prison aboard the ship, hinting that Morrie should be confined. He figured that what had happened once could happen again; that Morrie might very well flip under further pressure."

"And was I dangerous or unstable?" I demanded.

"Neither," Gail broke in to answer for Axel, "but he considered you expendable and in his way."

"You fought for Gail," Axel said. "Spartan wants no interference when he tries to have this way."

"He's as crazy as poor Morrie," said Gail.

"In a different way," said Axel. "I've known Doc a long time. Went to the moon with him. He's pushed by ambition and the dislike of sharing credit for a job well done. He was very disturbed when the newspapers gave a bigger play to the Loring-Drake wedding than to the objectives of the Mars flight. Spartan wanted to be the only hero."

"Isn't that why we're all making this trip? To win credit, fame, glory—or whatever else you want to call it?"

"Partly. There is also something else," said Axel.

"The old college try," I said. "Just what is the reason for going to Mars? It's costing six billion dollars. We couldn't bring back anything worth that much."

"Knowledge," said Gail.

"Is it knowledge that'll do any good?" I asked.

"We don't know," said Gail. "Remember Columbus? He was tossed into prison. People accused him of ruining the Spanish government through his crazy trips to far-off lands. There wasn't much gold, people said, without realizing that wasn't what really mattered; that the value of the discovery of the new world couldn't be figured in terms of dollars and cents. So will it prove to be, I'm sure, with Mars."

"Okay," I said, "suppose the trip is worth it. Why are *we* going? Particularly if there's no real money in it."

"Soldiers don't get rich," said Axel. "And how many of them risk their lives to win wars, or even to save a comrade, or perform other acts of bravery?"

"Couldn't you call that glory seeking? Selfishness, in other words?"

"Do you call martyrs glory seekers because they die for principles and beliefs?"

"Not many men—sane ones, that is—become martyrs intentionally," I said.

"There are two kinds of selfishness that rule our lives, Bill Drake," said Gail. "One is self-preservation, which makes a man kill to defend himself. The other is race preservation, which includes preservation of ideals and beliefs necessary for race progress. Men will die and become martyrs for that."

"One kind of preservation makes you kill, another makes you get killed," I said. "It doesn't make sense."

"No," said Axel. "But Gail is right. That is the way it works out. Would you call Willy Zinder a martyr?"

"No," I told him. "Willy took a chance and got killed. I suppose he was a hero, though."

"Willy Zinder was murdered," Axel said bluntly.

"He was *what?*"

"Murdered, I said. Spartan didn't intend for Willy to be killed. He only wanted Willy washed out, but he planned the accident."

Gail gasped.

"He wanted Gail to go to Mars," Axel added.

"But I thought it was my idea," said Gail. Then she paused. "But he did fall in with the idea rather suddenly when I suggested it. Maybe he did plan it all along. But how—what makes you think it was murder?"

"Spartan was the last man to inspect the controls on Willy's capsule. They had been inspected by others before him and called okay. But it would have been easy for Spartan to gimmick the re-entry controls so that Willy would return to the atmosphere ninety minutes too soon. Such an event would make it appear that Willy had become confused, or had panicked. You remember he put Gail Loring on the control board just before the accident? He wanted her to believe she'd been responsible. And for a time, she felt she had been."

"But you have no real proof, Axel," said Gail.

He shook his head. "I did not suspect it was anything but an accident until I learned that Spartan killed Morrie Grover and then tried to kill Bill. Also, Bill told me of that little death list Spartan had. Only then did I know that Spartan had killed Willy Zinder."

"Just to get me aboard!" Gail said. Her voice was almost a whisper.

"He wanted to marry you, of course, but you changed his plans. His objections to your plans would have looked suspect and he did not have unlimited power on the Earth to force you into marriage against your will. Besides, the platonic marriage finally decided on did not interfere with his plan. He'd decided Bill would die before the return to Earth."

"He'd made such a big thing of a six-man crew so he could take you along," I told Gail. "We're doing okay now with five—" I stopped. Dr. Spartan had entered the room.

He surveyed the group with angry eyes. I wondered how long he had been listening and how much he had heard.

"Relieve Warner Joel in the control room, Ludson," he said.

Joel had another hour to go before his relief was due, but Axel rose. "Yes, sir," he said.

"Miss Loring, it is time you started preparing our next meal, isn't it?"

"It's Bill Drake's turn in the galley, sir," she said.

"You will take it this time. Drake will take over the duty the next time it is yours. I wish to talk to him." He turned to me. "Will you come into my cabin, Drake?"

"Yes, sir," I said.

I followed him through the door and we entered the chartroom. You don't walk into that room, you drop into it. The corridor, which separates the two parts of Spartan's cabin, is equipped with small doors opposite each other and in the approximate center of the craft. You must pull yourself up to the opening and slide through by aid of centrifugal force.

Spartan was standing opposite the door when I came through. I dropped to the floor beside him and he gestured for me to sit down on the floor.

"Drake," he said, "I understand you had some difficulty bringing Grover's body into the ship after you found it."

This was the first time he mentioned what I knew he knew. "A very minor difficulty, sir," I said.

"For your information, Warner Joel saw the entire episode on the television screens in the control room. You were in view most of the time. It looked as if your safety line broke."

"It became disengaged, sir," I replied.

"Disengaged? How did that happen?"

"I don't know," I said. "And, as you recall, I had a short supply of oxygen in my tank. I used Grover's tank to jet to the ship."

He scowled at me in disapproval. "You call that a minor difficulty?" His hand, I noticed, was on the butt of the dart pistol, but he made no move to draw it.

"I survived," I said, keeping my face noncommittal.

"Then you wouldn't consider a difficulty serious unless you did not survive it?" Was it my imagination or was he deliberately toying with me?

"Most serious, sir."

He thought for a moment. "From now on, Drake, you will avoid dangerous tasks. You are slightly accident-prone and you might get into serious difficulties, which would not be in the best interests of our mission. I need a full crew to do our work on Mars."

"Thank you, sir," I said.

"You may go."

I returned to the main cabin, realizing that Spartan had spoken plainly enough. He knew that I knew he'd tried to kill me and he was now granting me a reprieve, probably because he figured he might need an extra pair of hands on Mars. However, he had warned me—if I wasn't a good boy, he might change his mind and decide I was expendable.

CHAPTER ELEVEN

WE WERE a mere million miles from Mars, traveling at the comparatively snail-like speed of 12,000 miles an hour—a shade over the escape velocity on Mars' surface—when Spartan made his next move.

He announced over the intercom that a serious accident had occurred. The air-lock doors had become unfastened in some mysterious fashion and ten previous gallons of waste water, which was being distilled for irrigation purposes for the garden, had escaped as steam.

"It will be absolutely necessary for us to find water on Mars," he added. "Otherwise only half our crew, maybe only two of us, will be able to return to the Earth. That is all."

It was too damned much, if you ask me. Later, when Axel and I were alone, I voiced my concern and suspicions.

"It was no accident," said Axel bluntly.

"Right," I said. No one had been in the main cabin at the time, about an hour before, when the water escaped. Gail had been asleep in her compartment. I'd been in the machinery room checking the air and water-cycling equipment. Axel had been in the control room, and Joel had been in the galley preparing food for the rest of us. "Maybe he thinks we're stupid," I added. "Anybody could figure out he did it."

"On the log it will look just as Spartan says," Axel told us. "You and I may never live to contradict it. For that matter, neither may Joel."

"Murder?"

Axel nodded his head. "I think he has been planning for a long time to return alone."

"But surely—surely not without Gail?"

"If you were Spartan and thought as he did, what would you do? Gail is the one witness who could endanger him by contradicting his story."

"You think even Gail is in danger?"

Axel shrugged again. "As we mentioned once before, Dr. Spartan is not a man who likes to share glory," he said. "Besides there are two murders which would need some explaining."

It seemed incredible, and yet there was a logical order of events that made Axel's theory plausible. First, Spartan wanted Gail. He had arranged an accident for Willy Zinder and this accident became murder. Second, there had been the accidental damaging of the water-cycling equipment, an incident which had served Dr. Spartan's scheme to cut down the crew—assuming of course that Spartan never intended any of us to return, with the possible exception of Gail. This had resulted in the second murder. Thirdly, he had planned to eliminate me but, for good reason, had changed his mind: I would be needed when the base was set up on Mars. Once that was accomplished I could be disposed of. Or, possibly,

Spartan feared hostile creatures on Mars and could not afford to reduce the size of his crew if fighting could be expected. Now he had produced a water shortage.

"Supposing you're right, Axel," I said after these thoughts ran through my mind. "What can we do about it?"

"Nothing—now."

"Later?"

"If we are to live, something must be done," said Axel.

"One thing we must decide, Bill, is just how far we are willing to go."

"What do you mean by that?" I asked. "If it comes to defending my life, I'll go all out—as far as necessary."

"It isn't that simple," said Axel. "As Spartan said, without exaggeration, there is water enough for only two—three at the most. That means two of us, at least, must die—unless we find water on Mars. Suppose we were to make Spartan a prisoner? What then?"

I realized now what the real problem was. Even as a prisoner, we would not have the right to execute Spartan just because there was insufficient water. And how would we choose the other person to be sacrificed?

"It's a terrible problem, Axel," I said. "Must we decide it now?"

"We must decide it before we leave Mars," he replied. And I agreed. But I also agreed that we could do nothing now unless we wanted to scuttle the entire expedition. In spite of Dr. Spartan, in spite of everything, success of the expedition came first. And ahead of us was Mars—which could mean death to some of us.

The planet loomed like a red giant on the television screens. The signals, which we believed to be ominous, were now signals of hope. If there was life on Mars, there might be water. True, scientists had pointed out that life, different from ours, might exist without water, using ammonia, perhaps. For our sakes, we hoped this wasn't so.

We looked thirstily at the polar caps, the northern one diminishing rapidly, because it was nearly summer in that hemisphere. The southern cap was growing as winter set in.

But we were still uncertain of our reception. "They're uneasy about us," Gail told me. "Just think how you'd feel if a fleet of spaceships from Mars was closing in."

"A fleet? This is only one ship."

"Three rocket ships are already circling Mars," she reminded me. "If the inhabitants spotted us when we were less than halfway here, they certainly would know all about those smaller rockets."

"It shouldn't take them long to see we intend no harm," said Joel. "Unless they're the type who shoot first and ask questions afterwards."

"There may be no common ground for communication at all," Gail said. "Martians may not be life as we know it."

We'd all read everything we could about Mars before we left the Earth. The question of life on Mars wasn't debatable. There was life, but whether it amounted to anything more than the vegetation observed by photo and telescope, was another matter. We tried to imagine plants using radar and sending messages—the idea seemed absurd.

The canals—originally named by Schiaparelli, who called them *canali,* the Italian word for *channels,* erroneously translated to read canals—were so geometrically straight that many people thought they could not be natural phenomena and were, actually, man-made canals.

There was some oxygen, but how much was an open question. It was hard to determine because all the tests had to be made through the sea of oxygen that surrounds the Earth. They were not conclusive. There was water, but the amount could not be determined because the Earth's air is full of water vapor. The climate could be studied. Mars was cold, but not too cold. At the equator a very warm day was possible, with, perhaps, temperatures as high as 60 or 70 degrees. Nights could be very cold, below freezing, even in summer. The ice caps were thin because they melted rapidly. Generally they were believed to be ice, but a few scholars thought they might be of carbon dioxide—dry ice. The poles were cold enough to precipitate carbon dioxide in winter.

There were two kinds of clouds on Mars. Fleecy white ones, which probably were, water vapor, and yellowish clouds strongly suggestive of dust clouds, whipped up by violent storms. Although Mars had thin air, it could have strong winds.

We could now see the two Martian moons. The furthermost of the two, Deimos, is only 15,000 miles from the surface of the planet. Its diameter is about 20 miles, and it revolves around Mars once every sixteen hours. Since the Martian day is about the same length as the Earth's, being only 37 minutes longer, Deimos would rise in the west and sink in the east about three days later, being visible and moving slowly eastward through the entire time. The larger moon, Phobos, is about thirty miles in diameter, and only 6,000 miles from the surface of Mars. Even though it is extremely small it would be seen as a tiny, bright disc from the surface of Mars. It's period is six hours, therefore it rises in the west three times every Martian day. It actually circles Mars four times daily but Mars turns once so that Phobos would appear, to Martian eyes, to circle only three times.

Our problem was not to hit Mars, but to score a near miss. We would come close enough to be captured by Martian gravity. Then we would spiral as a satellite, decelerating and tightening our orbit till we were as close as possible to the group of rockets that had been fired from the Earth with our supplies. We would board one of these, and then, using electronic controls, would land the three rockets comparatively close together at a spot in the desert near an oasis that looked fruitful for exploration.

The most interesting of these oasis, of which there were many, were two oval-shaped greenish brown areas marked on Percival Lowell's maps as Solis Lacus Minor and Solis Lacus Major—generally called Solis Lacus. These were about halfway between the equator and the pole in the northern hemisphere. In 1924 Solis Lacus showed a startling expansion, growing to almost twice its size and extending northward. Undoubtedly vegetation existed in profusion in this area. Furthermore, the two areas were connected by a short canal, which frequently doubled, forming two canals. Between the oasis was desert. Thus, by landing, between the two Solis Lacuses we could learn a great deal about the physical characteristics of Mars.

At a distance of one million miles, we had to aim carefully at Mars. The planet was speeding along its orbit at about fifteen miles per second, in comparison with our speed, which was slightly, more than three. If we missed we couldn't catch up because our acceleration was too slow. We'd have to go home empty-handed.

Our electronic computer worked out the corrections to our line of flight so that we would be caught by Mars' gravitational field. We had already located the three unmanned rockets by radar and we had a small telescope in the control room, plus telescopic lens on the video cameras to help us. This was lucky, because as we approached Phobos, Axel called excitedly from the control room.

"We're having trouble with the Martians, Dr. Spartan!"

There was nothing on the television screens to indicate an attack by spaceship, but we did see an unusual amount of "snow," as if there were interference. It wasn't until I took my turn in the control room that I found out the trouble. Axel was there then, having remained to check out what he was certain was the truth.

"They're jamming our radar," he explained. "It's so fogged up we can't locate the unmanned rockets."

"Then they're not friendly," I said. I'd suspected they wouldn't welcome us with open arms, and I think the others had felt the same way.

"Maybe playing safe," he said.

"If we could only find a way to communicate with them," I said. "Maybe we could make them understand that we're friendly."

Axel shook his head. "Would you believe everything a man from outer space told you?" he asked. "With three rocket ships circling their planet, they must expect an invasion, now that a bigger one is approaching."

"At least they don't have missiles," I said. Then a sudden thought struck me. "This fogging of the radar may prove something. Maybe they don't have eyes."

He gave me a blank look. "How do you figure it?"

"They have radar and they must know we'll contact the rest of the 'fleet.' They figure it'll be by radar. Since they don't seem to suspect that we can *see* the rockets, maybe radar is their only method of seeing."

"Even if you brought that in from left field, you're thinking, boy," said Axel.

But the fogged radar had given us a distinct message:

Earthmen, you're not welcome because we don't know your reasons for coming here. We don't want you to land. The message was as plain as if it had been sent in English.

There was no thought of turning back. What the hell? We'd come this far, hadn't we?

We got a good look at Phobos, a jagged, uneven rock. It wasn't even round. It looked like a chunk of basalt, but Dr. Joel, the geologist, pointed out black streaks which, he said, were outcroppings of meteoric iron. It hadn't originally been a part of Mars, as our moon was once a part of the Earth. Phobos was a captured asteroid, and so probably was Deimos.

The unmanned rockets were in a group, all within ten miles of each other. They were circling Mars in two hours, inside the orbit of Phobos. We approached them without radar because they were easily seen as bright moving specks in the sky.

There was nothing to pack, not even instruments, because these unmanned rockets were supposed to contain every item we would need. We just put on our spacesuits, strung a line between the Jehad and the largest of the three rockets—after stopping the Jehad's rotation—and crossed over.

Although I'd been treated to some very pretty sights of the Earth and the moon, Mars was on a par with any of them. It's a small planet, only 4,200 miles in diameter, but it didn't look so small now. It filled half the sky, big, red and angry. In the northern hemisphere, where it was late spring, the polar ice cap had all but disappeared. Brownish green vegetation swept southward. Here and there over the surface was a fleecy cloud and the mysterious canals were as straight as if they'd been drawn by ruler. All those in the north had doubled and looked like parallel lines. There was a suggestion of mountains in the area known as Mare Erithraeum, which was not a sea as the early astronomers thought, but an oasis.

Once aboard the rocket, I took a seat next to Gail. Unlike the Saturn capsule, this one had portholes, to be used for observing Mars once we landed. And through them we could see Mars as we orbited toward our landing site.

We had entered through locks just above the rocket chambers. A large storeroom was packed with equipment, and a ladder ran through it to the nose cone. I noted with a great deal of relief that there was a huge tank marked *WATER*. It contained enough for all uses on Mars. Three weeks of "luxury" as far as water was concerned and if we found drinkable water on Mars, we could replenish our supply on the Jehad.

This, of course, did not take into consideration Dr. Spartan's plans.

Dr. Spartan came aboard last. He sat down.

"Don't remove your helmets," he warned. "I haven't released the oxygen supply yet and it's best that we land in spacesuits. We don't know what kind of terrain we'll strike and it's possible we may wind up with a punctured ship which could cost us our air supply." He paused, then added: "And, of course, we don't know what weapons the Martians have."

There was a sharp intake of breath in my earphones. It was not only Gail but others who made the sound.

"In a short time," Spartan went on, "we'll be the first men to set foot on Martian soil. We've had a long trip, beset by—ah—serious difficulties." He was using my terminology. "Perhaps you have disliked me, or even hated me. However, there is more to be thought of than personalities. The Earth expects us to complete a mission on Mars. I am the leader. I give the orders. And whether you like me or not, you'll obey. We are going into a strange world, where a strange form of life—hostile life—exists.

"The Martians will meet us on their own soil, undoubtedly with superior numbers and, possibly, with weapons we will not comprehend. But on the Earth there are many glorious tales of small, determined groups who have defended themselves against vastly superior forces. In the interest of self-preservation we must stick together. In the interest of the faith of our world in us, the expedition must succeed. We must stick together until our last day on Mars."

Paying close heed to Spartan's words, his phrase, "until our last day on Mars," did not escape me. I was certain he intended no group cohesion after that time.

"Now," he continued after a slight pause, "the planners of this trip had considerable foresight. In spite of the opinions of many men who have studied Mars, that intelligent—and hence, possibly, belligerent—life cannot exist here, the men who selected our equipment saw to it that we could defend ourselves should the need arise."

Dr. Spartan reached up and pulled open the door of a cabinet behind him. There, in racks, were two rifles. Six pistols, in holsters, were on shelves. He pulled out five of the pistols and strapped one on himself before passing out the others.

"We will keep Grover's pistol in reserve," Spartan said, nodding toward the one left. "There are clips in all of them and extra ammunition aboard. We have regular and explosive bullets for the rifles, which are automatic. You'll note that all the trigger guards are large enough to accommodate your space gloves."

As we strapped on the pistols, Spartan reached down and held up one of the rifles. It, too, had a modified trigger guard.

"These are M-14 weapons," he continued. "It's a modern military weapon using a 7.62 mm. slug. It can be fired automatic or semi-automatic and it is simple in its operation. However, besides myself, only William Drake has had experience with these weapons. He was in the army for a short time. Therefore Drake and I will be the riflemen of the group."

At least, I thought, Spartan and I will be armed equally. I looked around at the group. Gail was rubbing her hand gingerly over her weapon. "I don't know how to fire this thing, Dr. Spartan," she said.

"There's nothing to know," said Spartan. "You point the gun and pull the trigger. It's very simple if you aim it accurately."

Axel cleared his throat. "Don't you think it would be wiser, sir, if we made our first appearance on Mars without arms? If we meet the intelligent life of the planet, or if they should detect us through spotting devices, it might convince these creatures that we are not hostile invaders, but peaceful scientists."

"Whoever said we were peaceful?" Spartan asked. "Eventually Mars will become a colony of the Earth."

"That's the same mistake Spain made when Columbus discovered America," said Axel. "A lot of blood could have been spared if the nations of the Earth hadn't thought of land grabbing."

"Idealistic motives become you, Ludson," said Spartan, "but they never got anybody anywhere. Man is the highest form of intelligent life in the solar universe—"

"How do you know?" Gail asked.

"Because I am a man. We will be doing the Martians a favor by giving them the benefits of our civilization. I mean to claim Mars for the Earth. And don't worry about these Martian monsters taking offense at our guns. They may not recognize them as weapons. He paused and then his voice grew harsh. "Wear your guns at all times. Keep them near at hand when you sleep. This is an order."

We knew he was right about guns, as he had been right about many things. No one sold Spartan short on his ability as an astronaut. The Martians would not recognize guns. Anything we carried in our hands, a scientific instrument, even a flag of truce, might be mistaken for a weapon. Just as Mars was new, different and incomprehensible to us, the Earth would be to them, and so would the people of the Earth.

"Fasten your seat belts," Spartan snapped.

As I adjusted my straps, I had the same feeling I'd had the first time I orbited. I was half afraid and half eager. At the time I took my first solo, I'd asked a ground crewman: "What'll I do if something goes wrong?" And he replied: "Just sit there. You won't have time to do anything else."

We'd land on Mars, all right. Chances were good that we'd land alive. Leaving Mars alive would be a different matter. I found myself thinking: *If the Martians don't get me, Dr. Spartan will.*

Spartan touched a switch. A green light flashed on in the control room. Everything was ready for the entry into Mars's atmosphere. The light blinked once. The electronic controls were working. At the proper moment the rockets would slow us down and Mars' gravity would do the rest.

Then the whole ship shook. Our rockets were blasting. I felt pressure in the seat of my spacesuit. After living for eighteen months with gravity so lean that a man could hardly fall down, I had G's in my pants. I felt as if I'd returned to Earth again. I was no longer afraid. We were on our way down to Mars.

The deceleration began to push up the gravity inside the capsule. But it was nothing like the force a man felt when re-entering the Earth's atmosphere. Mars is only one-tenth the mass of the Earth and its gravity is something like forty per cent. We were falling in slow motion, and carefully calculated rocket bursts, all handled by automatic controls, would set us down more gently than a parachute. In fact, a parachute on Mars would only be slightly more effective than on the moon. Mars has some atmosphere, though very thin, while the moon has none at all.

The scenery was beautiful. Perhaps the colors were not as blatant as those seen approaching the Earth. There were no deep blues of the sea, greens of the fields and forests, yellow of deserts and the snow-tipped majesty of great mountain ranges. The Martian polar caps were not the same as ours either, for they were almost perfect circles. The ice, which caps the terrestrial poles, is irregular because of continents and seas.

But Mars was spectacular. Nearly everything had a tint of red. Even the areas the early astronomers called seas, because they had a greenish shade, showed a brownish red base. The mountains, which soon became visible as we approached the planet, were massive but eroded, far less impressive than the Rockies, the Alps, the Andes or Himalayas. We saw nothing that looked like bodies of water.

As we approached the planet, our orbital momentum carried us forward more rapidly than the planet revolved on its axis. Mare Erithraeum swung beneath us and extending eastward was a broad double-canal called Nectar, flowing through a wide expanse of reddish desert.

Then I sensed a trembling in the capsule and I knew we had hit the top of the Martian atmosphere. I could not see anything directly beneath us now, because the capsule base cut off the view, but turning my head I saw the brownish green of the Martian pampas far to the north, desert to the south, Mare Erithraeum to the west, and then two smaller, oval patches of vegetation to the east.

The latter were Solis Lacus Minor and Solis Lacus Major, between which two areas we planned to land.

No friction heat was noticeable in the cabin and it was not unexpected. Although there was air enough to cause some friction on the outside of the ship, our velocity was far less than any we would have encountered on re-entry into the Earth's atmosphere.

I watched the twin ovals that marked our landing site. The larger oasis, Lacus Major, was in full view. In the center was a shiny dark spot, which glinted like polished ebony in the sunlight. And southward, a short distance north of the equator, was another spot just as dark and just as glinting. Cities, perhaps?

"What do you make of those things, Dr. Joel?" I asked, pointing out the spots.

Joel shook his head. "Our astronomers have noticed them," he said. "The one in Lacus Major is called Umbra. The other is Pnyx, at the junction of two canals. Certain people have suggested they are cities."

"Circular cities?" asked Gail, who also watched the screen.

"With a dome over them," I said. For now I saw why they glinted. That shiny surface was some transparent substance, which covered the city like an inverted bowl. Beneath were blackened buildings.

"Since you're so interested in these things, Drake," said Spartan, "you can have the privilege of finding out what they are."

I caught a glimpse of Gail's frightened eyes as she looked toward me, then turned her head so I could not see her fear. But I knew what Dr. Spartan had in mind. He wanted me dead, and by sending me to the very doors of a Martian city, he might save himself the disagreeable task of committing murder.

Very, very slowly we came down toward the Martian desert. Through the windows I saw one of our companion rockets land near the rim of the double canal on our north. The ground was uneven there, being churned by furrows and crevasses, and for an instant the rocket teetered, then fell on its side.

Fortunately all of the fuel had been used up or jettisoned before it touched the ground, consequently there was no fire.

Turning my head I could see the second rocket, standing upright to the west.

Then there was a solid but jarring bump—about what you'd feel if you jumped off a ten-foot wall. Our ship rocked with the impact, but remained upright.

The motors were cut, but the fuel was not jettisoned, because this ship had to take us back to the Jehad.

"We're on Mars," Gail breathed into her microphone. Her hand reached out and grasped my arm with a reassuring squeeze.

"Yes, we made it," I said, and wondered if we would ever leave this planet.

CHAPTER TWELVE

I LONGED for something on Mars that was definitely of the Earth, so I could say, "This is like home." But the similarities, if any, were vague. While the rockets settled down on the desert, I heard faintly the roar of the blasts, like the murmur of a distant waterfall. The air was so thin that sounds were dampened; still, they were sounds, not the deathly silence of outer space.

Now that the rockets were stilled, I was held fast in my seat by gravity—real gravity, not centrifugal force. But it was a very light tug, not at all like Earth's.

"Unfasten your harnesses," said Spartan. "But please remain here in this cabin till I test the atmosphere."

So saying, he unfastened his own belt and climbed down the ladder. As he disappeared through the trap door in the floor I caught a glimpse of his peculiar, pleased smile. Was he responding to the familiarity of gravity, or was he gloating over some particularly satisfying thought of future glory?

I heard him open the doors of the locks. Gail squeezed my arm as a small cloud of dust swept up through the opening to the lower part of the ship. "Air!" she said. Martian air had rushed into the ship.

Looking out of the porthole, I saw Spartan in his spacesuit, standing in the red sand, the first human being to set a booted foot on Mars. He walked gingerly a few paces, then set up a small instrument, pressed buttons and read dials. Then he reached down, picked up a handful of sand and tossed it in the air. A playful gesture for Dr. Spartan. But why shouldn't he be elated? He had led the first voyage from Earth to Mars. The sand he threw seemed to drift down ever so slowly—a little pebble taking fully a second to fall five feet. On Earth it would have fallen 16 feet in that short space of time.

Spartan stood erect and silent, his helmeted eyes fastened on the oasis to the east. For a moment I forgot his arrogance, his murderous heart, and his determination to kill me and to take Gail. He was a representative of the Earth, not an individual now. Then he marched back to the ship, his evil manner suddenly accentuated. Every move, every gesture showed his utter contempt for others. He was the kind of man who was able to make you mad by merely saying, "Good morning."

He entered the ship and closed the locks. Then he came up the ladder to the control room and twisted a valve, which released the air in the ship.

Not until that moment did he address us over his helmet transmitter.

"The Martian atmosphere is much like the Earth's," he said. "It has oxygen, nitrogen, a small amount of carbon dioxide and minute traces of water vapor. Possibly it also contains inert gases—the heavier ones. I doubt if there's much helium here. It is not poisonous, although it does contain a small amount of ammonium vapor. However, it is too thin to breathe. We may be able to pump air into our ship to replenish our air supplies, should they get low, but we can't go out of the ship without spacesuits."

Talk of ammonia in the atmosphere led to new avenues of speculation. Scientists have suspected for many years that a kind of life might exist on compounds of ammonia, instead of water. There are indications that the first life on Earth may have absorbed ammonia from sea water, instead of oxygen, for some such compounds are still present in proteins. As oxygen grew more plentiful on the Earth, life adapted itself to water and oxygen. On Mars this stage may not have been reached, although it seemed rather unlikely. As rare as the oxygen was, Dr. Spartan said, the amount of ammonium vapor in the air was small.

Soon the cabin was filled with air. We descended the ladder and began to unpack the materials.

Axel remained in the control room, alert for Martians, listening to the radio, which now was filled with a variety of weird whistles, chirping noises and rattles.

"They know we've landed," said Axel. "I can't understand these Martians, but I have a feeling a lot of this is about us."

"We can defend ourselves," said Spartan.

"What if they have nuclear weapons?" I asked.

Dr. Spartan shrugged. "It's not impossible," he said.

That first day on Mars was all work. We went to the nearest rocket ship that had landed with us, the one that remained upright, and unpacked its cargo. Since this rocket was not going to leave Mars there was much more gear aboard because no extra fuel had been carried. Most valuable of the equipment were two Mars-cars, self-propelled vehicles, which were similar to those, used in exploring the moon.

They were four-wheeled, with a cabin swung in the middle. Each wheel was equipped with tires sixteen feet in diameter. Although the machine itself was almost as large as a freight car, it was constructed of aluminum and lightweight alloys and even on Earth it would not weigh as much as an ordinary motorcar. The Mars-cars were electrically driven, powered by specially built storage batteries which could be charged from solar cells built into our main rocket.

Also aboard the rocket was ore sampling equipment, which we expected to use in studying the geology of Mars. Dr. Spartan put Warner Joel to work with the digging tools to construct a moat around our headquarters ship. Instead of a drawbridge, a causeway was left to the north of the ship, running diagonally across the moat. Rocks were piled in the middle of the causeway so that two paths were left for the tires of the Mars-cars. A hostile force attempting to cross the causeway could be enfiladed by pistol and rifle fire from behind a small breastworks at the base of the ship, or from the locks of the ship itself.

It was while digging this moat that Dr. Joel found rubies. The soil was full of them. They were more plentiful than pebbles on the Earth.

"Possibly a lot of the color of the Martian sand is due to aluminum oxide tinctured with chromium," Joel explained. He assumed we all knew this was the chemical composition of rubies.

"I suspected the Martians used lidar," said Axel.

And, of course, he assumed we all knew that lidar was light radar, which physicists on the Earth were just learning how to use. It's a method of amplifying light through a special tube of artificial rubies. The light excites the chromium in the rubies and causes the atoms to give off a red glow. The resulting red beam can be focused to pencil thinness and sent vast distances. Scientists believe that some of the nearer stars—meaning stars within the range of ten light years distant from the sun—can be explored by lidar.

We had unpacked most of the gear from the two ships and had assembled the Mars-cars by noon the next day.

"Ludson," said Spartan, "take Drake over to the No. three ship and bring back all the supplies you can carry. The rest of us will make our living quarters habitable."

"Yes, sir," said Axel. He turned to me. "Come on, Bill. Let's get started."

"If you see signs of life," Spartan said, "shoot first."

"But, sir," Axel protested, "wouldn't it be best for us not to do anything unless we're attacked?"

"We must show them that we're more powerful than they are. The best way to defend is to attack," said Spartan.

"They might be better equipped to shoot than we are, sir," said Axel.

"Ludson, whatever gave you the idea that we're inferior to Martians? This is a dying, decadent world. We are young, strong and in our prime—in terms of our planet. Just because the Martians have intelligence, doesn't mean they are superior."

"But—"

"You have your orders," said Spartan. "Carry them out."

We climbed into the car through tiny locks. The interior was pressurized and full of air, so that we were able to take off our helmets. There were large windows on all sides from which we were able to look out on the red sandy plain.

Our ship had landed in the neck of desert between Solis Lacus Major and Solis Lacus Minor, which we now shortened to Major and Minor. We were on a ridge, possibly the highest point between the two oasis, although we could not see Minor to our west, since it was over the horizon.

To the east, the ground sloped downward and on the horizon we could see the dark green of vegetation that marked the edge of Major. To the north was the first of the two canals connecting the double oasis. To the south there was only desert, stretching several hundred miles to the canal junction at Pnyx.

It was about three miles to the fallen spaceship. It had toppled in the soft sand, narrowly missing an outcropping of rock. Perhaps the base of the craft had struck the rock, causing the ship to fall over. I noticed the rocks were highly polished, without any sign of stratification. Probably they were igneous. Sandstorms must have given them that fine polish—there was no water around to erode them and the polar glaciers didn't come this far south.

A little ridge prevented us from looking down into the canal, and we drove over it for our first close glimpse of this Martian phenomenon.

We weren't quite prepared for the grandeur of the view. The canal was at least five miles wide, possibly three miles deep. The walls were sometimes sheer, dropping thousands of feet, leveling off, and then dropping again to form a series of gigantic terraces. In other spots landslides had crumbled the walls and a slope had been formed, rather steep, but not too precipitous for a Mars-car to negotiate.

"Let's go down!" I said.

I wanted to see the bottom of this majestic ditch. It was awe-inspiring, like the Grand Canyon, which it resembled in color, except that the walls were unstratified. These rocks had never been formed at the bottom of the sea, but had been baked by the internal fires of the planet. The last sea had dried before the canals had been cut. Although they were red, the color shaded from a brilliant scarlet to a brownish green at the bottom. There was vegetation down there, and something else, as precious as anything we'd seen thus far—water!

There wasn't too much of it; merely a tiny stream flowing in the center of the canal, its path straight, like the canal itself. "I hope it's fit to drink." I told Axel. "But it's gotta be. This canal wasn't made by forces of nature. Nor could it have been built by hands, beaks or paws. Only tools could have done it. And tools are used only by intelligent life."

Axel knew it. I didn't have to tell him. He was already reaching for the microphone. He snapped on the transmitter. "Dr. Spartan!" he called.

There was no immediate answer. Then Joel's voice came over the radio. "Spartan's not here, Axel. He's checking some of the scientific equipment. Anything important?"

"There's water down here in the canal," Axel said. "Does he want us to bring some?"

"Stand by," said Joel. "I'll ask."

We waited several minutes. Then Spartan's gruff voice came to us. "Of course bring water, you stupid fool. Is it fit to drink?"

"We don't know, sir," Axel said. His face flushed with the anger brought on by Spartans' words. "It's at the bottom of the canal."

"How long will it take to find out?"

"Thirty minutes to an hour," said Axel. "There's a steep incline to the bottom of the canal."

"Drake can do it," said Spartan. "You unload the rocket ship. Both of you can stow it aboard the Mars-car when Drake returns."

"Yes, sir." Axel switched off the radio. He turned to me and shook his head. "That guy doesn't know how to be civil, does he?"

"No," I said, "but what worries me is why he's letting me fetch the water. It must be because he thinks I'm more expendable than you and he figures there's danger down there."

"Martians ?"

"Yes," I said. I checked my pistol. It was loaded.

Axel put on his helmet and got out of the locks. He disappeared into the rocket and presently reappeared with a five-gallon can, which he stowed in the locks. Then I started down one of the less steep inclines toward the canal.

It was rough and bumpy all the way down. Long before I reached the bottom, I noted that the vegetation which had looked so small from the top of the canal, was big and, in some cases, twenty or thirty feet tall.

There was a sort of timberline, about fifty feet above the level of the stream. Beyond that no vegetation grew. Below, the ground was covered with all kinds of plants. That is the best name I could give them. They really were vegetable but, they weren't like any plants I'd ever seen.

Some were tall, like trees. Others were round, hugging the ground and looking like brownish cabbages. There were some that looked like toadstools, except that they were branched and had several caps. Nearly all the plants were branched, and a few had flowers ranging from delicate pink to deep purple. None seemed to have leaves.

The largest looked like the Giant Cactus—the saguaro of Arizona, although it was not spined.

I found a place where none of the plants looked big enough and tough enough to impede the Mars-car and headed for the stream, which now appeared to be about twenty feet wide and very stagnant. I picked up my mike to tell Axel what I saw.

Then my wheels touched the stem of a Martian saguaro shoot. I heard a whiplike crack and the whole car was enveloped in blue flame.

I pressed my foot down on the accelerator and rolled over the plant. Looking back, I saw that it had fallen across another plant, a woody, slender type that was jointed like bamboo. Both of the plants were smoking. Sparks were flying from the saguaro with all the deadliness of a high power line.

"What's the matter, Bill?" Axel called back.

I realized that I must have shouted with surprise at the display.

"These damned plants are charged with electricity, Axel. At least, one of 'em is. It just unloosed a bolt of lightning."

"The hell you say! Are you hurt?"

"No, the car grounded the charge," I said, "but it gave me one big scare."

"Think you can bring in a sample?" he asked.

"What the devil, Axel! Do you want me to be electrocuted?"

"It's just an idea I had. Remember, you'll be safe in your spacesuit. It'll ground the charge, just like the Mars-car did."

"Well, I'll try."

I put on my helmet and got out of the car. First I walked carefully toward the banks of the stream. I avoided the saguaro-type plants, but I noticed that when my boots struck shoots and stalks of some of the other plants, sparks flew. More than half of the plants had the characteristics of an electric eel.

The stream, while stagnant, was steaming. It wasn't hot water, for the temperature must have been in the low forties, but the atmospheric pressure was so light that water was evaporating in great quantities.

It was difficult to see how the stream was supplied with water, since it extended between two oasis, both apparently fed by the same stream. And there didn't seem to be very much flow, although after watching the stream for a few minutes I decided it was moving in the direction of Major.

Then I saw tiny springs along the bank, sending little rivulets of water into the canal. It was so simple that I should have guessed where the water came from. It all came from the polar caps, of course, but the water flowed underground. The Martians had simply cut their canals to feed on the artesian supply from the North Pole.

I took the can Axel had put in the locks and filled it. Then I lugged it back to the Mars-car. After I stowed the water in the locks I walked gingerly back to the saguaro I had knocked down a few minutes before. It was somewhat charred, but the fire had gone out. Apparently the air would not support much combustion. Using my knife I gingerly cut off one of the branches. No sparks flew, but I noticed that instead of sap, there was a thick, pasty pulp inside. It was acid, because before I could wipe my knife on the ground, the substance had etched itself slightly into the surface.

I carried the stalk back to the car and tossed it into the locks. I'd stepped inside myself and had just closed the door when I saw movement to my right—on my side of the canal, in the direction of Solis Lacus Major.

A small creature, a little larger than a St. Bernard, was approaching the Mars-car. It looked like a dwarf camel, except that it was headless. And the hump wasn't a hump, but a shiny bump with a metallic luster.

I said it had no head, but it did have a mouth gaping, grinning and full of pointed teeth. It had four legs and many arms—long, sinuous, many-jointed, with two fingers at the end—growing like a fringe around that bump in the creature's back.

Then I saw that the vegetation in its path was smoldering. The animal had only to move a small black thing that sprouted on a stem from the top of its hump, and whatever lay in front of it started to smoke.

"Axel!" I screamed into my helmet transmitter. "There's a Martian down here!"

No one had told me what it was and none of its acts had shown that it had intelligence, but some instinct told me this creature was the highest form of life on Mars.

CHAPTER THIRTEEN

THE MACHINE in which I traveled made no distinction between forward and reverse. You set a hand throttle in one direction to go forward, and in another to go back. It went just as fast one way as the other and there was no need to turn it around. I started back up the incline without turning anything but my seat, so anxious was I to get away from that Martian.

I'd started up the incline before I glanced back in my rear-vision mirror and saw that this creature had been joined by a companion, identical in every detail to my undiscriminating eyes, although I suppose their mothers could have told them apart.

Axel's voice jabbered in my ears but I wasn't listening. I wanted to get out of this canal and away from these horrible creatures. I didn't like their teeth, I didn't like their black humps or radar antennae, or even their padded feet. That destroying heat ray was radar.

"What's that about radar, Bill?" came Axel's voice. I knew I'd spoken aloud.

"They've got built-in radar instead of eyes!" I said. "It's so powerful it sets fire to things." Radar could do that. Strong stations on Earth could literally cook a man unfortunate enough to get within close range. Even weak stations could set off flashlight bulbs in a photographer's camera. The walls of the car had protected me. Even my spacesuit probably would have been sufficient protection. But I didn't like all this power in a living body.

The Martians, apparently startled as much by me as I had been by them, hesitated before starting in pursuit. I was hitting the steep grade up the wall of the canal before they came after me. But they ran slowly and gracefully, in no hurry to catch me. They kept a reasonable distance.

"Did they do anything to you, Bill?" Axel asked. "Are you all right?" There was a worried note in his voice.

"I'm okay," I assured him, "but these—these monsters are following me. Two of them. They look awful. No eyes, not even a head, just a hump on their backs like a camel and a fringe of arms on each side—" I glanced back. "Eight arms," I told him, counting them. "Stay where you are and I'll pick you up. Main thing is to get back to the ship. They don't run very fast and I think I can outdistance 'em on level ground."

Then Dr. Spartan, who had heard our radio conversation, interrupted. "Why didn't you shoot them, Drake?"

"I was in the car," I told him. "And they're two to one."

He hesitated, then said, "Don't try to outrun them. Lead them slowly. Give me a chance to get there."

"Yes, sir," I said.

You don't argue with Spartan and I was too busy guiding the car over the rocky slope to answer anyhow. I don't think I could have outdistanced the Martians going uphill as I was. On level ground though, it would be different.

My radio suddenly started to chatter with a series of strange noises. The Martians seemed to have discovered my wavelength. It was a sound the like of which I'd never heard before. It's hard to describe it. The nearest comparison would be a cricket singing bass. Or perhaps the *dah* of dit-dah Morse on a code transmitter. But the Martians had demonstrated that they could change frequencies, and vaguely I wondered how they'd do on television and FM channels.

Suddenly they seemed to be trying to imitate my voice.

"Yessir—yessir—yessir—"

They were like talking crows.

Finally I reached the lip of the canal and, rolling over the ridge, saw Axel standing beside a pile of light crates he'd stacked up beside the rocket ship. He waved his hands and I steered toward him.

Beyond him came Spartan, in the other Mars-car, hitting high speed on the sand. I thought of the garrison rushing to rescue the besieged wagon train in the woolly frontier days.

"Bill Drake!" Axel called, his voice wedging into the chattering Martian voices.

"Billdrake—billdrake—" mocked the Martians.

I braked the car and Axel scrambled toward the locks as the Martians appeared on the rim of the canal behind me.

Axel took one apprehensive glance in that direction before he climbed aboard.

"Tain't human!" he gasped, which was the understatement of the solar system.

Dr. Spartan's Mars-car halted about two hundred yards south of us. I saw him climbing out of the locks, his rifle in his hand.

"Tanetooman," chanted the Martians.

"This way, Drake!" Spartan signaled with his arms that I was to pass to his left.

"Thiswaydrake—" screamed my earphones in raucous echo. "Billdrake—tanetooman—yessir—"

"Aw, shuddup," said Axel to the Martians.

"Shuddup—"

Axel looked at me and shook his head at the Martian reply.

I wheeled the Mars-car around behind Spartan's, halting in a position which would allow me to watch.

The Martians were loping casually toward the two cars, seemingly in no rush to get there. And it was then I suddenly realized that their actions weren't hostile. I'd been frightened when they'd set fire to the Martian saguaro in the canal, but I realized that this had been defensive. They had been as afraid of me as I had been of them. Nothing in the world panics a man as does a situation he's never encountered before and does not know how to handle. And I suppose, in this respect, the Martians were human.

In fact, I was soon to learn that although physical bodies were apt to assume strangely different shapes, the psychology of the Martians was as human as intelligence. And it was a logical thing, too. After all, most of life's actions, possibly all, are aimed toward a double purpose—preservation of the individual and of the race. This fact is as basic as Newton's laws governing the physical actions of the universe.

In fact, the two kinds of matter in space, animate and inanimate, may not be so different, after all. The energy that is in all matter, may be seeking to control its destiny, and life may be a basic property of the power that exists in every atom.

But it was no time for philosophy. I didn't think these thoughts then—it was not until long afterwards that they occurred to me.

I was watching the Martians who now had slowed to a lazy canter, focusing their biological radar on the two similar objects parked in the desert.

As they came abreast of the spaceship, they looked at that too. I expected to see the pile of supplies Axel had stacked near the ship to go up in smoke—flames being highly unlikely in thin air like this. But the Martians were no longer frightened. The enemy had fled at their approach. They assumed, no doubt, that we were no match for them. And this is another trait that has proved the undoing of many a human being—to suspect weakness where it does not exist.

Dr. Spartan dropped to a prone position and raised his rifle. Apparently the Martians had not noticed him because they were to busy examining the rocket ship, the supplies and the two Mars-cars. Perhaps they mistook the cars for Earthlings. They'd never seen us before.

As they looked, their chattering ceased, so engrossed had they become in the sights before their antennae.

"Don't shoot, Dr. Spartan," said Axel. "They're not acting hostile."

The Martians picked up the last words, "Nottacking hossile."

"Bah!" said Spartan. And he fired.

An explosive bullet struck the Martian on the right. We didn't hear the crack of the rifle or the blast of the bullet as it struck the poor creature. But we saw the smoke and flying flesh. What remained of the beast collapsed in a heap on the sand.

The second Martian, not having seen Spartan, seemed to freeze in terror for an instant. Possibly there had been some sort of a dying scream from his companion—one that could not be heard on the wavelength of our helmet receivers. At any rate, it took only a split second for Martian No. 2 to realize we were neither weak nor harmless, as we had seemed. He turned and fled toward the canal at full gallop.

His speed was astonishing.

Dr. Spartan fired again. His shot missed and sent a geyser of sand skyward, ahead of the fleet monster. He swore and fired again. But the next shot was not an explosive bullet. It missed, too, and he switched his weapon to automatic and emptied the magazine with rapid fire. I saw the path cut across the sand and intercept the Martian. The creature staggered, then sank to the ground.

"Hah!" Spartan exclaimed triumphantly. "Let's take the dead creature to the ship! I'd like to see how he's constructed."

It was a gruesome business, but we loaded the scaly body into the locks of our car. The one Spartan had shot first was too torn and shattered to be worth transporting. Besides, the fluid that might be called blood, or sap, looked like acid and I was afraid it might damage the floor of the locks. My judgment turned out to be correct, for when Gail, our biologist, examined the beast we brought back, she announced that he was a mass of deadly poison and so were the plant samples I'd brought back from the canals.

"What kind of poison?" Spartan asked.

"I'm not sure, but Bill Drake can tell with a few tests," she said.

Spartan gestured to me. "Go ahead, Drake."

I got chemicals from the supplies Axel brought from the overturned ship and set to work.

It was fortunate that I made these tests. The Martian plants and the dead Martian were very similar chemically; giving rise to speculation that the evolution of life on Mars had taken place about the time the planet had stabilized into its present state. On Earth, life began while the planet was evolving from an earlier form and the changes continued while life developed. The changes probably brought about the division of the animal and vegetable kingdoms and they might have continued until sixty million years ago when the giant reptiles were wiped out, or even later through the glacial ages.

But on Mars there was only one kingdom. It wasn't wholly animal, or wholly vegetable, although it was more the latter than anything else. And the tissues were formed from a very deadly series of molecules, which had cyanide as their base. In other words, Martians were poison to us, and very likely we were poison to the Martians.

Furthermore, the water we had brought from the Martian canal was impregnated with ammonium hydroxide, in large enough quantities to cause serious illness should we be foolish enough to drink it. However, it was very useful for washing the cyanide from our gloves and spacesuits after we performed the autopsy.

And the autopsy, beyond determining that the Martians probably obtained chemicals and oxygen by chewing up the soil, which contained many oxides, was bewildering. Spartan made pictures and microscope slides, which could be studied if, or when we got back on the Earth.

All we know was that on Mars, life was a sort of mobile vegetable, which wasn't really a vegetable; and it was decidedly poisonous. We didn't know how these creatures reproduced, but Gail expressed the opinion that some of the "arms," all of which seemed to have different uses, might be sex organs and that Martians gave birth to their young by a kind of "budding," which exists among lower forms of life on Earth. "Probably every Martian is both male and female," she said, "like some worms."

Like the electric eel, they had organs that produced a strong electric current. But their radar equipment—the metallic hump and the black spot on top of it—baffled us all. Nature had done the job compactly and bewilderingly, with cells.

"Those teeth look vicious," said Gail.

"I wonder if their owners are," said Joel. "They spied on us during the entire trip from Earth. They clouded our scope so we couldn't use radar. They chased Drake. That's an indication that they might be vicious."

Axel shook his head. "They were just cautious," he said. "We'd have been just as cautious if Martians had come to the Earth. And they didn't really seem to be chasing Bill. He was frightened and ran. They saw no reason to fear him, so they followed, possibly trying to establish communication."

"Yes," I said. "They tried to imitate our language. Did a pretty good job, too." There had been nothing vicious or hostile in that.

"But one thing we can be sure of," said Axel, "is that the next time they see us, they will attack us. We have lost our chance to be friends of the Martians. I'm sure the two who saw Bill had been sent to spy on us and they must have notified others, by radio, that they had made contact. Now they are missing. Only one conclusion could be drawn. We killed them. And this is an act they'll demand revenge for."

"Bah!" said Spartan. "There's nothing to worry about. We've shown them we are the ones to fear. We have strength. These lower forms of life understand strength—they'll leave us alone."

"Lower forms of life?" said Axel. "And what makes a creature a higher form? I'd say we're the lower forms on Mars, because we have difficulty living here. We're not successful in this environment. We'd become extinct in a short time if we were transplanted here permanently."

Dr. Spartan's face grew dark inside his helmet. His words were spoken in a manner implying threat.

"You're forgetting, Ludson," he said, "that I'm the commander here. I'm not to be contradicted or spoken to in the way you've just done. I'll do all the thinking for this group."

He rinsed off his gloves with the water from the canal and went into the ship.

CHAPTER FOURTEEN

IF SPARTAN WAS DOING all the thinking, his mental processes were similar to Axel's, or perhaps Axel's stated ideas had taken root. He ordered Joel and me to get the ship ready for a lift-off, in the event of a Martian attack. This would cut down our exploration time on Mars, but we already had made a successful landing, and we had determined a few facts about life on Mars. Naturally, we still would try to push forward with our mission until the Martians drove us off. This would include the exploration of a considerable area of the planet in our vicinity. Later, while the Jehad was circling Mars, we would be able to take pictures of the rest of the surface features. Later expeditions, which would follow someday, could do the rest.

All of our supplies had been piled inside the moat and those we needed were taken into the headquarters rocket. Spartan and Axel dismantled the overturned rocket and obtained enough metal to construct a scaffold and ramp from the ground to the locks, eliminating the necessity of using a ladder to enter and leave the ship.

During the time we prepared our living quarters and defenses, all of us were engaged in the task of learning as much as we could about Mars. We made analysis of the soil and rocks, studied the weather and took countless photographs. Gail made a trip to the canal, unmolested by Martians, and brought back additional samples of Martian vegetation.

The water problem still confronted us. There were many things in the Martian water that could not be removed by distillation. However, the water was an excellent solvent and was used for our cleaning and sanitary purposes.

Spartan and Axel made a short trip to Lacus Minor, which was 150 miles west of our ship. Gail and I were left behind to analyze the plants she had found, while Dr. Joel was picking up rock samples along the rim of the canal.

We finished our analysis and when we'd cleaned up and disposed of the poisonous substances we had examined, I said, "It's time to do something about Spartan, Gail."

She gave me a sharp look. "I thought we decided the expedition came first, Bill Drake."

"It's a matter of survival now," I said. "We all know we're in a worse situation than before as far as the water is concerned. There's only enough for three. Spartan needed a six-man crew mainly to get things organized here on Mars. Now the worst is over. Even if he gets a chance to do some more exploring, four can do it all. There are only two cars anyway. Come to think of, two people would be enough—one to a car. There's no reason for Spartan to delay his plans any longer. He'll start expending the expendables."

"What of the Martians?"

I shrugged. "We've made enemies of the Martians by killing two of them. I doubt if they'll forgive us for that. They've shown too many human qualities—curiosity, fear, bravado, for example. They probably have the ability to be angry and to extract an eye for an eye. So we're fighting a whole planet. Whether there are five of us or three wouldn't make much difference. But Spartan has us prepared for a lift-off and I don't think he intends to wait for an attack to trim down our numbers."

She looked thoughtful, then said, "Bill, are you suggesting we murder Dr. Spartan?"

I hadn't suggested it. All I was thinking of was saving my life and hers. Self-protection. But that included killing in self-defense. Possibly I'd had murder in the back of my mind. But when she said it in so many words, I was revolted.

"Not if we can avoid it," I said.

"But there isn't enough water for five, you said. That means—" She stopped.

"I'm willing to try it on rations," I said. And I was. "Spartan isn't. Spartan planned to get rid of us anyhow."

Slowly she shook her head. "No, I don't believe even Spartan could be like that. I'll admit I did think it once. But he'd have too much to explain when he got home. Still, if he could arrange an accident—"

"He's arranged two of them. Willy and Morrie. What's to stop him from getting rid of Axel and me? Perhaps you, if you were likely to be a witness against him."

"We can't be a party to murder, Bill Drake," she said. She was right. I knew that even if I had carried the idea around in my head, I couldn't kill in cold blood. If Spartan tried to kill me and I had to stop him, it would be a different matter. But even though I knew he had no intention of letting me live, had already tried to kill me once, I couldn't deliberately plan his death.

"But we can restrain him," I said. "Take him prisoner."

"That would be mutiny," she said.

"No. We have evidence that he murdered Morrie Grover," I said. "We'd be putting him under arrest."

"But the mission!"

"The rest of us could do what has to be done. The main thing is to prevent more killings. Arrest would make it unnecessary to kill Spartan."

She sighed and said nothing.

"Axel will help," I said. "Joel won't interfere, either way; there's even a possibility that he might join us once he's made to understand what's been going on."

She sank down on a packing case we'd been using as a chair. "All right, Bill Drake. But please be careful," she said.

That night Spartan called us by radio. He and Axel had run into a terrific storm just as they left Lacus Minor. Red dust had practically overwhelmed them, and winds up to 75 miles an hour had thrown the Mars-car into a marsh. However, there had been no serious damage and they'd return the following day.

When Joel came in, and after we had eaten our evening meal, I told him bluntly what we'd found out about Spartan.

"He murdered Zinder and Morrie Grover," I said in conclusion. "He means to kill two more of our party in order to insure enough water for the return trip. You could easily be a candidate."

Joel listened, bewildered, to all I said, about finding the paper in Morrie's helmet air valve, about Axel knowing he had tampered with the machinery in Willy's capsule, and how Spartan had unfastened my safety line when I brought Morrie's body from the top of the Jehad.

"I—I can't believe it," he said. "You're making it up."

"Why should I?" I asked.

"For the same reasons you're attributing to Dr. Spartan," he said. "You want to kill him so there'll be enough water. Maybe you want to kill me, too."

"Damnit," I said, "we don't want to kill anybody. There may not be enough water to keep us from being thirsty, but there's enough to keep us from dying. I'm willing to suffer to avoid murder. That's why I'm planning to arrest Spartan."

"Arrest! It's mutiny! When you get back to the Earth there'll be a lot to answer for, Drake."

"Then we'll have to arrest you, to," I said. "The rest of us—Axel, Gail and I—know the score, Warner. I've tried to explain it to you. If we can't trust you—"

"Now just a minute! I didn't say that."

"Not in so many words," I told him. I put my hand on the butt of my automatic pistol.

His eyes followed the move. There was fear in his face. "I don't know what to do," he confessed.

"Do nothing," I said. "That's all I ask."

He gulped. He seemed a little relieved. "I don't see how I *can* do anything," he replied.

"Stand up!" I said.

He looked frightened again. "What are you going to do?"

"I'm taking your gun," I said. "Just to make sure you won't try anything."

He stood up and I made him turn around. Then I took his gun. "You'll sleep in the lower cabin tonight," I told him. "Gail and I will take turns doing guard duty."

The next morning, Dr. Joel was a very subdued man. He ate breakfast silently and then volunteered to tidy up the cabin. He went about his tasks eagerly, anxious to please. All of the truckling he had done for Dr. Spartan now seemed to be transferred to Gail and me.

About noon the Mars-car rolled in. I had been waiting for the arrival in my spacesuit and, as soon as it came within view, I slipped my helmet over my shoulders, sealed it and went out to meet them.

The car bumped over the causeway and came to a stop at the base of the ramp. Spartan, holding the rifle in his hand, was standing in the locks. Axel was at the controls, putting on his helmet.

Presently Axel entered the locks. Then both men jumped out to the ground.

"Help Ludson with the samples, Drake," Spartan ordered.

As he turned his head to gesture, I brought my automatic into view.

"You're under arrest, Dr. Spartan," I said.

Axel's mouth, which I could see through the glass of his helmet, gaped with surprise as he heard my words in his earphones.

"What's the meaning of this?" Spartan cried.

"Just what I said, Dr. Spartan," I told him. "You're under arrest for the murder of Morrie Grover. And if that isn't enough, for killing Willy Zinder and trying to kill me."

"You're talking nonsense, Drake. This is mutiny, punishable by death, Axel!"

I don't know what he expected Axel to do. I think he wanted me to turn my head so he could attack, or draw his own pistol, but I refused to be taken in by that old dodge.

"He's right, sir," said Axel. His habit of addressing Spartan by the title "sir" couldn't be shaken in a moment. "I found the paper in the valve of Morrie's helmet before you removed it."

"Lies!" said Spartan. "Now listen. If you put away that gun, Drake, I'll forget this. It's just another case of overwrought nerves—the same thing that affected Grover."

"And cause you to kill him because that was the easiest way to handle him?"

This seemed to hit Spartan because he didn't realize how well we knew his motives. He seemed to quiver. "I'm to be killed so you'll have enough water—"

"That's one reason you would have killed me, probably," I said, "but we're a different sort, Spartan. We're taking you back to the Earth. And you'll share our rationed water all the way. We won't kill you. What happens to you after your trial on Earth is not up to us."

His shoulders seemed to sag. "And I was the first man to walk on Mars!" He seemed to think that ought to atone for everything. "Now you're gutting the whole expedition."

"You're wrong on that score, Spartan," I said. "We'll complete the mission. You'll be under guard, but the rest of us can carry it out. We're doing this now to defend ourselves."

I heard Axel's sigh in my earphones. "I'm glad you said that, Bill," he said. "I didn't quite know what was coming off."

We took Spartan into the ship after disarming him. We removed his helmet and spacesuit and tied his hands. He said nothing, showed no emotion except anger.

Dr. Joel came into the room. He saw Spartan and avoided his eyes. "You're in on this too, Warner?" Spartan asked. "You, the one man I believed was my friend?"

Joel turned to me without answering his former chief.

"There's quite a bit of Martian chatter over the radio, Drake. I got a directional fix. It's coming from the south."

"South?"

"Yes, and it's strange, too. There's nothing but sand in that direction."

"There's Pnyx," said Axel.

"We thought Umbra was the nearest city," I said. "That's east, in Lacus Major."

Joel shook his head. "I tried to pick up the jargon from Major. Not much sound there."

Axel stared at the floor for a moment. "Doc and I saw some things at Minor that may be the answer. There was a big area where the vegetation had been cut away. We decided that the Martians had been there and harvested a crop. If that's true, Umbra might be a farming town and, like most farming communities, a peaceful place. Pnyx, on the other hand, is larger and might be a place where troops could be assembled. A sort of military base. See what it means?"

He didn't have to draw a picture. Mars was mobilizing to defend itself against the invaders from Earth.

"Ah!" said Spartan. "What you need is an astute leader. Release me. I'll take charge in this emergency and we'll forget these silly things you've been saying—"

"Shuddup," said Axel. He turned to me. "What does a good commander do in a case like this, Bill?"

Even though I'd been in the Army, the generals had never confided their methods to me. But you do pick up a few military principles, even as a buck private. "Send out a patrol," I said.

"What good does that do?"

"Well, if we sit here like lame ducks, we won't know when they're coming, how many, and we certainly won't find out what they have in mind," I said. "But if we scout them, and view their potential, maybe we could figure out some way of defending ourselves."

"You don't think we could fight a whole planet? Or even a small company of armed soldiers, do you?" Joel asked nervously.

"If it looks like they're coming to get us real quick, we can lift off," I said. "Maybe they figure they'll need a pretty big force which will take a couple of weeks to organize. If that's the case, we can do a lot of scientific work before we leave."

"Okay, Bill," said Axel. "You're the patrol."

"Now?"

"The sooner the better," said Axel.

I got my helmet. Then I picked up the rifle Spartan had carried on his trip. It was loaded with two rounds of explosive shells and eighteen rounds of ordinary bullets. I slipped a couple of spare clips for my automatic into my pocket. Then I went into the locks.

Axel followed me. "Just a minute before you put on your helmet, Bill," he said.

I gave him a curious look. "Okay. What's on your mind?"

"Take Gail with you," he said.

"But this will be a dangerous mission," I told him.

"Not half as dangerous for all of us if you leave her behind."

"Why?"

"I don't trust Joel," said Axel. "If he turned the tables and got the drop on Gail and me, nothing could keep Spartan from blasting off, leaving you behind and probably me, too, if I lived that long. But Spartan has his plans for Gail. He won't leave without her. If she's with you, he won't do anything till you get back."

"And if he's in control, what chance would we have?"

Axel shrugged. "As long as there's life there's some kind of chance," he replied. "But if Gail were aboard the ship, you wouldn't have any chance. Spartan could go back to Earth, report a mutiny and subsequent casualties that occurred in quelling it. Nobody could prove anything different. But with Gail gone, I think Spartan will postpone any moves he might make until she returns."

I thought it over. Gail, being one of us, would never live to reach the Earth that was certain.

The thought decided me. She would be safer with me, facing all of the Martians on Mars, than in Spartan's hands.

"Tell her she's on this patrol, too," I told Axel. "I'll get some grub and water aboard the Mars-car."

CHAPTER FIFTEEN

OUR CHART, WHICH WAS VERY SPARE of detail since it was made from the maps drawn by Percival Lowell many years ago, showed Pnyx as the junction point of two large canals. One, called Agathedaemon, ran southeast from Oasis Erithraeum to another junction point, Messeis Fons. The other ran southwest from Lacus Major and ended at Pnyx, which seemed to be at the edge of a small oasis.

I set my compass due south, deciding to travel in that direction until I reached the canal from Lacus Major, which Lowell called Chalus.

Gail was happy to be making the extensive land trip over the surface of Mars. Pnyx was at least three times as far as Lacus Minor, but since the Mars-cars could easily maintain a speed of 150 miles an hour over the desert, we expected to reach it in a little over three hours, if nothing interfered.

"If there were only some way of communicating with the Martians," she said. "If we could only explain to them that the man who murdered the other two is in custody and will be punished and that the people of the Earth didn't come to this planet to kill Martians!"

"It would solve everything but I'm afraid it's impossible," I said. "There was a big gulf between Martians and Earthmen to start with. Now this thing has spread them farther apart."

"You mean they're poison to us and all that? We've demonstrated that we have some things in common, psychologically speaking."

"That could turn out to be the main stumbling block," I said. "Remember when you, Axel and I talked about personal selfishness and race selfishness? How a person would kill to save himself and die for an ideal that was important to the race?"

"Yes. Are you suggesting the Martians want to become martyrs?"

"No. Race preservation or race selfishness exhibits itself in other ways besides that of dying for principles. One manifestation is intolerance. There's a hatred for anything that is different or nonconformist. Martians and Earthmen seem to have the same psychology, but we're different in looks so we repel each other, just as do certain elements. Maybe intolerance and hatred have their roots in the chemistry of an atom. Be that as it may, most creatures of the Earth tend to destroy what they don't understand."

"But we don't hate Martians!" Gail insisted.

"Maybe hatred is too strong a word. However, for want of a more accurate one, let's consider the difference between the hatred we feel for, say, a Dr. Spartan, and the kind we feel for Martians. One stems from self-preservation, and one from race preservation. This scouting trip, for example, is hate motivated. We're trying to get the best of the Martians without getting hurt ourselves. And they want to destroy us with a minimum of casualties."

"I suppose, as you've hinted, this hatred of differences is the foundation of racial intolerance?"

"Basically," I said. "Racial differences on Earth—between men, I mean—are so slight they don't actually matter. Some people are a little darker or lighter, with maybe a few differences in features. But the Martians are so different that you can hardly find any resemblance except in psychology. The gulf is just too big to cross."

"Even if we're intelligent?"

"Perhaps intelligence can cross the barrier, but there are bound to be different levels of Martian intelligence. The ignorant Martians would heap indignities on us because we're a *different* minority."

"You have it all figured out, haven't you, Bill Drake?" she asked, leaning back in her seat. We had removed our helmets—they weren't necessary in the car—and her hair, beautiful and now grown out from the mannish bob she'd worn when she left the Earth, fell nearly to her shoulders. "I suppose you are insecure because we're in an environment so utterly strange and unreal that we can hardly convince ourselves we're living in it."

"I'll admit that sometimes I think I'm in a dream world," I said, "and I'd like to be surrounded by things I'm used to. But I have confidence in myself to pull through. I like self-confidence. It's something you can have in yourself, which nobody else may have in you."

"But some things are the same," she said quietly. "The very things I didn't want to bring along with us. And I don't mean self-confidence."

I glanced in her direction. Her eyes were closed, her lips looked soft and her body yielding. "Such as?" I asked.

"Morrie mentioned it," she said.

Now I knew what she was talking about. I took a mental grip on myself. Morrie went off his rocker. I'd stay sane. It'd be a tough fight but—

"Did you say something, Bill?" she said, opening her eyes. I hadn't said anything. She went on:

"Morrie said he was a man and I was a woman. That's something that exists on Earth and it existed in space. You are a man and I am a woman here, Bill."

"Damnit, we agreed—"

"Bill Drake," she said. "Let's just say the agreement was made years ago and the statute of limitations has caught up with it. To hell with the agreement. In those bygone days I thought a trip to Mars was a career. I'm a woman, Bill Drake. That's my real career."

I braked the car, stopping in the middle of the big, red desert. There, millions upon millions of miles from that little planet where we had been married, I took her in my arms. My lips tasted hers and we clung to each other.

The damned spacesuits bothered us. I fumbled with hers and then with my own, and finally we shed them.

A long time later, we remembered we still had a job to do and we went on our way again. We reached Chalus, as deep as the Lacus canal, but containing more water—it was half as wide as the Hudson.

As we paused on the rim, looking toward the deep channel, Gail seized my arm and pointed. I'd seen it, too, about the same time—a long, flat barge, heaped with what looked like hay. It wasn't hay, of course, but Martian vegetation, cut and stacked on the barge. It was being taken by canal in the direction of Pnyx.

And Martians, pulling ropes tied to the barge, were the motive power. There were slaves on Mars.

"Martian commerce," I said.

We rolled on, paralleling the canal until suddenly, ahead of us, lay another deep cut, branching out from Chalus and running almost directly west.

We had no idea how long it was, for there was no sign of it on maps. And when we decided to try to cross it in our machine we saw the reason why. The canal was empty. It was half filled with sand from countless dust storms, and there was not a blade of Martian grass in the bottom.

It was an abandoned canal.

And on the other side was an ancient road.

It was paved with some kind of material that resembled concrete, although it was cracked and looked as if it had not been used for years.

"Do you suppose the Martians had cars?" Gail asked as we stopped on the road.

I shook my head. "I have some ideas about the Martians," I said. "They're probably far ahead of us in some ways—they are built for radar and they may have other senses we know nothing about—but that barge we saw was the first actual tool I've seen. If you can call a boat a tool."

"They must have had machines to build the canals," she said.

"Yes, but not a wheeled machine," I replied. "I don't think they have wheels on Mars. You see, the wheel was an invention man stumbled onto when he noticed that logs roll. The plants, which grow on Mars, unlike our trees, have some sides that are flat. Consequently, Martians never got onto the idea of wheels."

"Then what's this road doing out here?" Gail asked. "The material is pretty smooth, even though it's been etched by sandstorms," I said. "Possibly it was used to drag things over. It would be easier than dragging things over the sand."

The road angled south, in the direction we were going. I hoped that all roads led to Pnyx and followed it, even though it led away from the canal.

Beyond the canal we saw a round, symmetrical mound on the horizon, looking like half an overripe tomato sticking out of the sand.

It was the dome of some Martian city stuck out here by a dry canal. But it wasn't Pnyx and we saw no sign of life around the town.

We approached the city apprehensively. Possibly we would have avoided it altogether had we seen some sign of life, but the city looked as if there was no one at home. And the highway showed no signs of travel. In places where it was covered with sand, there were no tracks of padded Martian feet.

I saw that the road led through a large arched door.

"A ghost town!" Gail whispered. "An ancient, abandoned city!"

"I hope it's abandoned," I said.

We rode on. We had to find out, even at the risk of our lives.

The archway was just wide enough for the car. Still seeing no signs of life, we drove through it. Then we found that it had not been necessary to go through the arch at all. Above us was only half a dome. Beyond the gate we could see where it had been smashed and broken. Overhead, the cover ended with a jagged edge, as if some giant hammer had struck it with a terrific, shattering blow.

Before whatever disaster had struck the city, it had been a thriving community, at least a square mile in area. There were ruins of buildings, columns, monuments and narrow streets. The buildings were not like those on Earth; they had ramps for entering and leaving the upper floors. The structures had no spires or architectural flourishes, but were strictly utilitarian—plain walls, narrow windows, and doors. Whatever had been used for glass was gone now, probably shattered when the city met its fate.

"Wonder how they raised that dome," said Gail.

"It might have been blown, like a bottle," I said.

We crossed the city and resumed our southward trip. Looking back at the dome, I noted that it was constructed of a shiny, glasslike substance, which probably had been transparent at one time. But now it was coated with a fine layer of reddish dust. Centuries had passed since Martians lived here.

At the edge of the city stood a monument—a headless camel, a Martian, with his eight arms raised proudly above his spine.

"Glory wasn't unknown to the Martians, either," I said.

"A trait that springs from the urge to self-preservation," said Gail. "An individual, seeing a glorified image of himself, feels more secure."

We left the city after taking photographs. A minute or two later our Geiger counter began buzzing wildly. I slammed on the brakes just as we approached a terrific crater.

And now I knew why the city was no longer lived in, why there was no water in the canal, and why the road wasn't used.

"The bomb!" I said, almost in a whisper.

Mars had its own nuclear war! How long ago, I didn't know. Had I the time I might have measured the amount of radiation and determined approximately when the explosion had occurred. The radiation was not dangerously strong now and I knew the blast had taken place many, many years ago.

"You know," said Gail quietly, "maybe this is why the Martians were afraid of us."

"They knew we had the bomb and might use it on Mars?" I asked.

She nodded her head soberly. "I think the Martians must know a great deal about the Earth. More than we ever knew about Mars."

"The question is," I told her, "whether they still have the bomb and if they're likely to use it on us."

"Maybe they've outlawed it," she said.

"If so, they're more civilized than we are."

"Maybe the Martians have had more time in which to become civilized," she replied.

"Civilization has a way of turning back," I said. "If they had the bomb once, they can build it again."

As we continued southward, we saw another domed city rise above the horizon. This was no ghost town. The dome was whole, larger than the one we had seen by the dried-up canal. It stretched across the horizon for five miles, at least, for the horizons of Mars seemed to be shorter than those of the Earth.

I flipped the switch of the transmitter and called our base. Axel answered.

"We're not far from Pnyx," I told him.

"Have they spotted you yet?"

"No, but I haven't seen anything to report, either," I said. I squinted toward the city for a couple of minutes before I saw there was movement on what seemed to be an east-west highway running past the dome. A cloud of dust hung there and I thought I saw figures moving.

"It's too far off to see clearly," I said, "but there seems to be a lot of traffic on the main highway."

"Highways yet? You got money for toll?"

"Not funny, Ax," I said. "They got paved roads, but no cars that I've seen. We followed an old road part of the way. It's worn out and unused. I'll tell you about it later."

"See what's going on, if you can, Bill," said Axel. "We're still getting a lot of radio from Pnyx."

"I came here for information and I'll find something to report," I said. "Keep listening."

I slipped on my helmet, picked up my rifle and went through the locks.

I could feel the city as I stepped from the Mars-car. There's a kind of sensation you get when you're approaching a large metropolis, and it holds true on Earth as well as on Mars. It's much different from the way you feel in the wide open spaces—on the prairie or in the mountains. Maybe it's extrasensory perception. Or maybe the soles of our feet transmit seismic vibrations of living people to our nerves. I had the feeling now.

Gripping my rifle I moved toward a little ridge just ahead of where I'd stopped the car. This ridge, I'd hoped, would protect the car from radar detection on the part of the Martians, but I believed I could risk a glance at the highway over the top of it without exposing our location.

I was about a half mile from the road and, from the ridge, I could see it, crowded with Martians, trotting in formation eastward toward the canal. They walked five abreast and there must have been hundreds of them.

I didn't have to be a Martian to recognize that this was a military group. Soldiers. Ants march to war like humans do. It's another fundamental that may have its roots in atomic energy, or in the nuclear intelligence that has formed all life so that atoms can control their destiny.

No local war was to be fought by these troops. They were off to meet the Earthlings, in the first interplanetary war of the solar system.

So interested was I in watching the Martians that I didn't realize I was standing in full view; and I'd been seen, but not by the marching Martians, of which there were at least fifteen hundred.

A small patrol probably had been put out to protect the flanks of the main army, or even to look for us, since my approach probably hadn't been as concealed as I'd thought.

Three Martians of this patrol had started toward me, joining "hands" as they charged. And behind them were a dozen others.

CHAPTER SIXTEEN

THE MARTIANS CAME galloping toward me, each grasping the extended trunk-like appendages of the creatures on either side. I didn't notice now, but when I saw them in this kind of formation later, I noted that it was the second pair of appendages used for this particular business, the reason for which soon was to become apparent.

They were about sixty feet from me when the Martian on the extreme left raised his second appendage, which of course was unattached to any other Martian. From the end flashed long, crackling flame, the nearest thing I'd seen to lightning since my last thunderstorm on the Earth.

It wasn't quite as good as a lightning bolt, however, because it fell short of my position by about six or eight feet.

Now I knew why they grasped "hands." Each Martian was, for all practical purposes, an electrical cell, and the three of them joined together were in series. If one Martian could produce a hundred volts, three Martians could produce three hundred. This voltage is for illustration purposes, of course. I don't know how much they produced and quite probably it was more than one hundred volts, in view of what happened later. It may have been a thousand.

But, although I knew the Martians were trying to electrocute me, I felt safe. My spacesuit had enough metal in it to carry a pretty good size charge to the ground and, since I was inside it, I could suffer no harm.

I raised the rifle to fire and they flashed another jarring charge at me. This time it hit. The blue flame licked down the barrel of my rifle, shot to my suit and, as I expected, grounded itself through my boots. I felt no shock, but I noticed with alarm that my rifle was suddenly so hot that I felt it burn through my gloves. Then I realized the danger. They could, literally, cook me inside my spacesuit by making it red-hot.

Before they could use their bizarre natural weapon again, I fired. The bullet hit the center Martian when he was less than thirty feet from me. He exploded as if he'd had dynamite for lunch and that broke the circuit.

The other two Martians dug their feet into the ground and slid to a stop. As I lifted the gun again, their radar apparently detected the motion. They broke and fled, unashamed, back to their flanking patrol. I didn't shoot after them. I had only one explosive shell left, plus eighteen non-explosive standard rifle shells. I might need 'em, I thought.

And I was thinking right for a change. The two survivors were screaming in *AM* or *FM*, whatever they used for private conversation and cuss words. I could see their antennae waggle, but I wasn't tuned in on their network. The other twelve seemed to understand. They all joined appendages and started toward me.

It looked like the camel corps storming Khartoum, except that these weren't camels and they were slinging enough electricity to light a small city. I hated to think of the heat that would be generated if a bolt hit me. Even if they didn't get enough of a charge into me, my Achilles heel would be obvious once they saw that voltage, continually applied to a resistance unit, will make it rosy red-hot.

On came the Martians. Their soft, padded feet, looking so much like those of camels, sent a dust cloud rolling behind them. I lifted my rifle and aimed carefully at the middle of the line. This was my last explosive bullet and it had to produce spectacular results. I pressed the trigger and a flash of flame marked the spot where one of their number had ended his last charge.

The line was broken, the others hesitated. But six or seven Martians could swing heavy lightning and I had to break the two segments again. Had they attacked in two groups they could have fried me where I stood, but they didn't realize it.

I flipped my gun to automatic while the two groups consolidated. Now I cut loose. I didn't aim. Who knows what's a vital spot on a Martian? I just held down the trigger and swept the line from left to right. Half the Martians fell thrashing to the ground.

But my magazine was empty. I transferred the rifle to my left hand and pawed at the automatic in the holster at my side. The seven or eight uninjured Martians were trying to consolidate, and I wasn't having any of it.

Again I aimed at the center, to cut the voltage in half. The Martians had just managed to form a series again and flame lashed into the ground at my feet, but they were crazy with fear or rage or some Martian version of a terrestrial emotion and they didn't aim true. Then I banged at them until my pistol was empty. The line was chopped in three places but there were still five Martians left.

They were game creatures, for they came on desperately. Self-preservation, race-preservation, all the things we talked about including heroes and martyrs, were in this final charge. My pistol was empty, my rifle was empty and I was a sitting duck with no time to reload.

But I worked at it and as I did I heard a faint puffing sound, like the pop of popcorn. Mars is almost silent, but not quite. There is enough air to transmit the sound of a loud noise near at hand. Even though every split instant was precious, I glanced quickly to my right.

Gail Loring was there, clad in a spacesuit, holding her automatic pistol with both hands. The gun was bucking and kicking and making that puffing noise.

I glanced back. Two of the five Martians were on the ground. It wasn't luck, it wasn't good shooting, it was a goddamn miracle.

Gail broke up the party.

The three surviving Martians had had enough and, as Gail emptied that enormous .45 without hitting anything, they broke and ran in all directions, waving their trunk-like arms in sheer terror. My earphones gave the cricket-burp. Martian cuss words, no doubt.

Still holding my rifle in my left hand and my pistol in my right, I clasped Gail in my arms, yelling things like "sweetheart, darling, angel."

"Sweetheart—darling—angel!" screamed the Martians.

I tried to kiss Gail through my helmet and hers, too. And we laughed and cried as we ran back to the Mars-car. Tears were streaming down her cheeks as I helped her into the locks.

As we entered the car again, we stopped laughing. A half-mile away fifteen hundred Martians were leaving the highway and advancing toward us with joined arms.

My earphones screeched with Mars talk: "Ha-ha! Haha! Sweetheart!"

They'd interpreted our cries of relief as battle cries.

Without removing my helmet, I put the car into high speed, away from the advancing Martians, and headed northward. The desert lay ahead of us, rolling and vacant, its wide expanse broken only by outcroppings of smooth rocks. I advanced the throttle till the car was traveling as fast as it would go. But as I worked up to that speed, the Martians had gained a little. Now they galloped in pursuit like racehorses, except that they were faster than any Derby winner I ever saw. The gravity had something to do with that.

But it wasn't fast enough to catch us, although I knew now that the Martians Spartan had shot hadn't been really pursuing me. They'd been loping along, believing I was frightened and harmless, and they'd assumed they had nothing to fear from me. Possibly, if Spartan had not fired, Mars men and Earthmen might have co-existed, in spite of their basic differences and the fact that they were deadly poison to one another.

Then the radio crackled with Axel's voice. "What's your trouble, Bill?"

Our helmet radios, being short wave, don't carry very far on a spherical planet, the signals tending to shoot over the horizon into space. However, Mars must have some kind of a heavy side that caused freak reception just as the same thing happens on the Earth. Axel had heard the gist of our cries and laughter in the Battle of Pnyx. I switched on our transmitter to reply, since the Mars-car radio was powerful enough to carry quite a distance and, besides, its wavelength was longer.

"We just won the first battle of an interplanetary war, Axel," I said, "but a million Martians are chasing me. They've just begun to fight."

"You must have found a bar at Pnyx. Talk sense, will you?"

"Fifteen hundred Martians, anyway, Axel, and I'm not kidding. They're running, really running, and they've shown no signs of tiring after more than twenty miles of it, even though they're not catching me."

"Where are you headed?"

"North. Toward you."

"Tell me what happened, Bill, and talk sense."

I told him briefly of my encounter with the patrol and how the main body of Martians was on my trail. I was miles ahead of the Martians who were on the horizon back of me. I even explained how the Martians fought, and how I was a nasty little circuit breaker. Axel listened without interrupting. When I finished, he said, "I guess you can beat 'em here. Once you get aboard the ship, we can blast off if we can't handle 'em with guns."

"Good heavens, Axel," I said, "you don't expect to fight 'em, do you? You've no idea how big a wallop these Martians carry. You and Warner Joel couldn't possibly battle fifteen hundred Martians. Even if Gail and I were there to help."

"We've got another rifle, plenty of explosive bullets and pistols to go around," said Axel.

"They might use the bomb," I said.

"What bomb?"

"The atom bomb. Mars had it once," I said. "Gail and I found evidence that it destroyed a city north of Pnyx."

"You don't make an atom bomb like you bake a cake," said Axel. "And I doubt if they've got one. If we can't lick 'em, we'll just leave this stinkin' planet—begging your pardon, Miss Loring." He paused. "And we've got Spartan—he'll fight with us."

"Don't turn him loose, Axel. Don't give him a gun."

"This is us against Mars, Bill. Spartan has to help out. He's got no choice. And if he helps, we'll go less hard on him when we get home."

"We'll talk it over when I see you," I said.

I glanced back. The Martians were not in sight. I slowed and waited. They did not reappear over the horizon. And then I saw the reason. Ahead of us was the bomb crater. These Martians, so sensitive to radiation, could not stand the radioactive ground of the area, even though it was harmless to Gail and me who came from a planet which is continuously bathed in radiation of all kinds, from gamma rays to radio. No Martian would come to the bombed-out city. This explained why it was desolate, why it was a ghost town, and why the canal, which brought water to the place, was dry and half-filled with sand.

I brought the car to a halt and let the motors cool and the batteries charge.

Gail brought out some food and water from the locker and we had a little lunch. In the west, the Martian sun was sinking toward the horizon. Soon it would be night and we would have to make the rest of the trip in darkness. Mars had the blackest nights I'd ever seen. The moons are not large enough to cast much of a glow—in fact Jupiter was brighter than Phobos and Jupiter was millions of miles away. Earth and Saturn were not visible at this season, but I have a hunch that Earth was much brighter to Mars than any other object in the sky. Venus could be seen occasionally, but Mercury was never visible because it is too close to the sun.

We finished our meal and Gail slept while I watched. Then she roused up, told me to get a couple of hours sleep and sat by the radio.

Shortly after midnight I was awakened by Gail.

"I've just been talking to Axel," she said. "He believes there are Martians near the spaceship."

I was wide awake instantly. I turned some switches and checked our power. The sun hadn't been up very long after we stopped for the night, but the solar cells had recharged the battery sufficiently for us to resume our trip, providing we conserved our power.

I took my position at the controls. "Axel," I called. "Have you seen 'em?"

Axel's voice came over the radio. "No but I hear them. They're using some English words. *Thiswaydrake. Tanetooman.* The things you yelled that day when you flushed Martians in the canal. Some of them must have overheard you."

If that was the case, this wasn't the bunch that had been chasing me. Another attacking force must have come down from the north—or possibly from Umbra. They were closing in from two directions and if fifteen hundred were behind me, heaven knows how many were on the other side of the ship.

I started the Mars-car forward. "We're on our way, Axel. It's dark but there shouldn't be any trouble, if we keep from running into a large rock in the desert. If you can't hold 'em, blast off. Forget about us."

"Don't talk like a lunatic, Bill."

"Don't think about me!"

"Hell, I'm not thinking of you. I'm thinking of Gail. And I don't want a year-long ride in space with Doc Spartan and only Joel to help keep him from killing me."

"All right," I said, "I'll try to make it—"

"Tend to your driving," said Axel.

I laughed without humor. It was ironic that after all our talk about cowards, selfish men, heroes and martyrs, not one of us—not even Dr. Spartan—had a choice in the matter now. We all had to be heroes and, perhaps, martyrs. We were going to be attacked by a whole planet and the only course open was to fight for our lives.

The starlight was hardly any help but I was able to make out the vague shapes of rocks in the desert after we had crossed the abandoned canal. I couldn't go fast, but I was making time.

The radio was not silent. There were explosive, bass cricket noises of Martian talk from time to time. Nothing further was heard from Axel, even though his transmitter had been left open. And I had nothing to say—I was too busy driving.

The first streaks of dawn were appearing in the east when at last I heard a shout in the squawk box. It was Dr. Joel yelling at the top of his lungs.

"Ludson! Wake up! Martians are attacking."

I heard a startled grunt. Then Axel's voice came to my ears.

"Untie Dr. Spartan and give him a gun."

It was light enough to see now, and I pushed the Mars-car's throttle to its peak.

CHAPTER SEVENTEEN

I HAD NO IDEA how far we were from the spaceship. But it certainly wasn't more than a ninety-minute run if I held the machine at top speed. But battles can be won or lost in considerably less time, and there was a battle being fought in the Solis Lacus area.

They were outside the ship—Axel, Joel and Spartan. I heard them shouting in their helmet radios. I couldn't hear the sound of firing, but Spartan—unwilling to relinquish his authority even though he was a prisoner—was shouting orders. "Get that group to the left, Axel! About nine o'clock—"

Axel must have the rifle, I thought.

Dr. Warner Joel was hysterical. His voice choked sobs. He prayed. He swore. He moaned.

Axel mumbled incoherently. For all I knew he might have been talking in Swedish. Maybe he was—I don't know. He was born in Minnesota of Swedish parents and might have learned it in his childhood. Ordinarily, he spoke good English, except that occasionally his phrasing took on a foreign flavor, a throwback to something he'd learned from his parents and neighbors.

Joel was sobbing. "My gun's empty! They're still coming."

Then he laughed hysterically.

"Look at them run! The fools didn't know my gun wasn't loaded!"

Apparently the radar eyes of the Martians could distinguish objects as small as a .45 automatic.

Gail sat tense as she listened to the sounds of battle. Her lips pressed tight, her eyes staring straight ahead.

And then we saw the brownish green depression to our right. We had reached Solis Lacus Major, and the spaceship was not far north and only about a dozen miles west.

Even minutes seemed like hours as we sped along. The Martian voices were plain now and we could still hear our three companions talking. At least, none had been baked in his spacesuit yet. As long as they kept the Martians from forming into long lines their spacesuits would protect them.

Then Gail screamed and pointed. To our left we saw the spire of the spaceship.

Swerving, I saw hordes of Martians closing in from the south. To the north were more of them. I was steering the Mars-car into the jaws of a trap that would close on us the minute we entered.

But not to enter the trap meant surer death. There was a chance for us if we could reach the ship.

Those Martians from the south were chanting: "Ha-ha! Ha-ha!"

It was the same group that had pursued me near Pynx. Although they had shied at approaching the ruined city, they apparently had traveled all night, going around it, and now were helping to encircle the spaceship.

I stopped the car and fastened on my helmet. "Put yours on too, Gail," I said.

She did and when she was finished, I said: "Take the controls of the car. Try to break through any Martians that are in your path and reach the causeway. Pay no attention to me." I got out of my seat and went to the locks. My rifle was there and I picked it up. I ejected shells from the magazine and filled it with explosive bullets.

"What are you going to do?" she asked, her eyes wide with fear.

"I'm going topside," I said. "I'll fasten myself to the top of the car with my spacesuit belt. Then I'll raise a little hell with these men from Mars." I tapped the gun for emphasis. She opened her mouth to protest, then closed it. It had to be done. She might hate it, just as I did, but it was the only thing to do. I couldn't shoot Martians from inside this four-wheeled boxcar.

She waited till I called to her that I was securely fastened, then she started forward.

Ahead I could see the Martians. They had encircled the ship at a distance of about a quarter of a mile. I could tell that Axel was on the north side, where the largest group of Martians was assembling for a frontal assault. I could see explosive bullets from his rifle tearing gaping holes in the ranks. But they were preparing to charge onto the causeway.

Joel and Spartan were stationed on either side, the three of them forming a triangle. They had only pistols and were not firing because the range was too great. I couldn't tell which was which, but I saw their figures standing behind heaps of rocks, which they used as breastworks. Apparently the moat, shallow and makeshift as it was, presented an obstacle to the Martians because the sides were difficult for the four-footed creatures to descend and to climb.

The Martians were starting to move toward the causeway when they first perceived our car rolling toward them. The line wavered, hesitated and then started to wheel to face the Earthling reinforcements.

"Drake!" I was startled by Spartan's voice over the helmet radio.

"Yes?" I said, omitting the sir.

"I want you to know that whatever our differences were in the past, they are forgotten for the moment. We are all Earthmen. We are being attacked by an entirely different form of life. I remain your enemy, and you have reason to hate me as much as any human being alive. But what matters is that the Earth and the scientists of our planet are waiting for us to bring back information about Mars. Therefore we must survive. We will fight together now. What happens afterwards is something different."

"That's damned white of you, Spartan," I said. "But I had this all figured out and you have no more choice in the matter than I."

"Dam-white, dam-white. Ha-ha! Ha-ha!" chirped Martian voices in my ear. Looking to the south I saw the plain crowded with the creatures, galloping arm in arm, their trunk-like limbs waving. The group from Pnyx had joined the attack and was assaulting the ship from the rear.

Warner Joel screamed and I knew he was facing them all alone.

The Martian horde was coming at full speed.

Joel stood up, holding an automatic pistol as they came within range. I saw flame jet from the muzzle. A Martian in the middle of the line stumbled and fell. Instantly the men on either side joined arms.

I raised my rifle and leveled it at the attackers. The jouncing of the car made it hard to aim and I held my fire for an instant too long.

A lightning-like bolt swept from the end of the line toward Joel who was firing wildly and hitting nothing. A scream rang out in my helmet.

I watched with horror as his spacesuit turned cherry red and actually melted in front of my eyes.

Then I fired.

The explosive shell blasted two Martians in the line. I fired again, splitting one half of the broken line into quarters. A third shot split the other half. One great thing about these explosive bullets, you didn't have to hit a target dead center. The fourth shot didn't even hit a Martian, but the ground at his feet, and he went the way of all cyanogenic plant men.

The Martians at the causeway were now getting ready to give me some of the medicine that had ended the career of Warner Joel. But I swung my gun in their direction and blasted again.

Before I could fire once more, Axel, who apparently had stopped to reload his rifle, began to bombard them from the rear.

The Martians couldn't stand being blasted from two directions at once. The line broke and they dashed to the north.

My car swept to the entrance of the causeway and across. Axel's helmeted figure rose from behind his barricade of rocks. He didn't even take time to wave, but I saw his eyes, full of deep appreciation because I'd arrived at a most critical time.

Then he dashed to the spot where the remains of Warner Joel lay steaming.

The Martians who had killed Joel were pouring across the moat at the rear of the spaceship.

"Watch the front, Bill!" Axel cried as he leveled his rifle.

There was nothing to watch. The Martians had been routed.

I fumbled with my belt and unfastened myself while Axel aimed his gun at the Pnyx Martians. His semi-automatic fire was sending geysers of poisonous Martian flesh out of the ditch when I jumped off the car.

The bass-chirps of the Martian voices were screaming panic now. It wasn't necessary to know their language to realize all the fight was gone from their hearts—or whatever they used for a heart—as Axel pumped explosive shots into their midst.

Part of them was trying to scale the back wall of the ditch. Others were stampeding, like cattle, in all directions. Those that came my way were halted by the causeway and now I opened fire on these.

Gail had emerged from the car and now she stood without cover at the edge of the moat, shooting at the Martians with her pistol.

"Get back, Gail!" I screamed.

A single Martian sent a flash of flame toward her. It sparked off her helmet. Then she realized she was exposed and jumped behind the barricade Axel had used.

Axel's gun had stopped firing now and he was starting to reload. I shifted my aim, pouring the rest of my magazine into the group nearest him. They had no way of knowing it was not his gun. Even their radar senses could not follow the path of a bullet.

It was a massacre, but the kind of slaughter that saved lives.

The panic of the Martians in the moat communicated itself to those on the desert. Instead of joining hands to try again to overwhelm us, they broke their ranks and fled as the straggling remains of their allies from the south scrambled out of the pit around the spaceship and fled in all directions.

"After them!" cried Spartan, who still believed he was our commander.

But I paid no attention to him. Following a routed and disordered enemy and cutting him to pieces may be a sound military precept, but we were no army and we were outnumbered hundreds to one. It would have been plain stupidity to pursue.

Axel's gun was reloaded now and he emptied it again at the retreating foe. Each bullet, whether it hit a Martian or a rock or the desert sand, increased the terror of the retreating host.

Then his gun was empty.

To my surprise I saw Axel half turn. Then his knees seemed to give way and he fell to the ground, clutching his side.

Turning my head, I saw Spartan with an automatic in his hand, starting to level his gun at me. There was an ugly grin on his lips. He had shot Axel.

As he fired, I dodged behind the barricade, on the opposite side of which Gail crouched. She had not heard the shots, of course, and had not seen Axel fall. I shouted, "Gail! Come here! Around on this side!"

She couldn't understand me. She was puzzled, thought I was crazy, because her side was safe from Martians.

I raised my rifle and aimed at Spartan as he came running toward Gail.

I pulled the trigger, but it didn't fire. The rifle was empty. I'd sent my last bullet after the retreating Martians.

As I tried to jerk my unused pistol from its holster, Spartan reached Gail with a single thirty-foot bound. He swept her from behind the barricade and held her as a shield as he turned the gun on me.

I couldn't use my pistol without hitting Gail.

A bullet struck the ramp to the spaceship, just beside Spartan's head, knocking a piece of metal against his arm. He didn't hear the shot, but he felt the splinter strike. He turned his head. Axel was lying on the ground, still clutching his side with his left hand, but holding his pistol in his right.

Spartan lifted his gun to fire at Axel, and I, taking advantage of the instant in which he turned to defend himself, leaped.

Martian gravity, being what it is, permits a man to make prodigious jumps. I sailed like a man in slow motion over the rocks and I struck Spartan, still clutching Gail, in a football tackle, bowling them over.

I grabbed his gun, twisted it from his hand. Gail struggled and wriggled out of his arms.

But the gravity that had aided me, now worked against me. Somehow Spartan threw himself upward and I was literally bumped into the air. He rolled out and dived for the gun.

I came down, grabbed his foot and pulled him away, but he twisted free.

We were both in spacesuits and it would have taken a battering ram to hurt either of us. Fists were useless, even though Spartan didn't realize this. Nor did I until I felt him hit me. The blow, I scarcely felt, but the force behind it sent me staggering back.

I struck the rocks and bounded, like a boxer off the ropes, back at him. I tried to wrap my arms around him, to hold him securely, but he was a big man, in splendid physical condition, even though he was a few years older than I. We clinched, struggling to throw each other off balance, flailing helplessly with our fists.

Suddenly I stepped back. Spartan, crazy with anger and rage, swung his fist toward me. I didn't try to dodge or block. I knew the fist wouldn't hurt me. As it struck me I grabbed his arm with both hands. I hung on as he tried to wrench free. Then I pulled back and started to turn.

His weight, without the spacesuit, would have been in the neighborhood of 180 pounds, perhaps more. The spacesuit weighed at least twenty pounds. But all two hundred pounds of him was a mere eighty pounds on Mars.

As I swung, his feet left the ground—and on Mars you don't drop very fast. His feet stayed off the ground as I heaved and turned and then let loose.

His body sailed in an are, over the rocks, and thudded in the moat, onto a heap of Martians, not all of them dead. A number of them must have had enough consciousness left to respond to contact with an Earthling's body.

As I sprang to the edge of the moat, I saw Spartan's spacesuit turn a cherry red. Then it glowed white. Little rivulets of metal poured over the Martian bodies, but still that current—it must have been thousands of volts—kept surging through.

I heard a long, drawn-out scream. Then Dr. Spartan was dead.

CHAPTER EIGHTEEN

GAIL SCREAMED as she came running to the edge of the moat. I seized the pistol which she held in her hand—later I learned it was Spartan's own gun that she picked up off the ground. I fired into the mass of bodies.

It was too late. I killed the Martians but there was nothing I could do to save Spartan. Turning, I rushed to Axel's side. He was weak, but still alive. "Punctured spacesuit," he murmured, nodding to his left hand which clutched the garment. I understood. Axel's suit had been punctured by Spartan's bullet, but he had closed the hole with his hand. Fortunately the bullet had lodged in Axel's body and had not pierced the suit on the other side.

"Hang on!" I said.

I picked him up. He groaned as I lifted him and carried him up the ramp and into the ship. Inside, Gail and I stripped the suit away from the wound. The bullet had struck a rib in the suit, glanced to a rib bone and then lodged in the muscles of his shoulders. It was a nasty wound, made by a flattened bullet, but it was not the kind of an injury that would prove to be fatal. We applied antiseptics and removed the bullet.

While Axel rested, I took the digging machinery, which we had used to construct the moat and covered Spartan's and Joel's remains and the bodies of dead Martians. I found many large rubies and sapphires—unusual stones, but not six billion dollars' worth. Whatever profit came from the trip would be in scientific knowledge.

Gail and I erected a small cairn over the spot where Spartan lay. It was not to Spartan alone, but to four men, including Willy Zinder, who had died in order that our trip to Mars might succeed. I objected to Spartan's being listed as a hero, but Gail said, "It's not really him, Bill Drake. It's what he stood for."

"Murder, egotism, selfishness?"

"He was a human being," she replied. "The monument is to humanity. There are good human beings, bad ones and the strong."

"It's hard to swallow," I said. "But including him doesn't detract from the others."

People, I decided, shouldn't be judged by specific, isolated acts, but by the sum of their contributions. Besides, not many folks will go to Mars to see the cairn—at least, not for a long, long time— even if the Martians leave it standing.

We didn't stay long on Mars because we didn't know for sure if we'd put a big enough scare into the Martians to keep them away permanently. Besides, as I told Axel, "They might bring the bomb next time."

We never learned if Mars still had the bomb. They'd had it once, but they were now decadent, far below what they had been in ages probably long before the first ape-man came down from a tree to walk on his hind legs. Those cities were evidence of past glories. But except for the barges on Chalus, we saw no means of locomotion. They must have had tools, but we never saw them. And the only art we saw was a statue in a ruined city. Had man come to Mars a million years ago, who knows what might have been here to greet him?

I found a small animal on Mars before we left. It was hiding in the vegetation on Lacus canal and proved that there were other forms of mobile life besides the Martians. The creature was rabbit-size and had the same general construction as a Martian. The hump was poorly developed, however. The animal died and since it was poisonous, as were all Martian beings, we did not try to bring it back for examination. However, I made a thorough study of the chemical content of its tissues and took several photographs of its dissected organs. Earth scientists can do a lot with very little evidence.

In spite of our harrowing experiences with the Martians we had a treasure of scientific data, material that could never have been obtained by telescope. And we hoped that someday a basis of communication with Mars could be established—after the soreness of the wounds had gone away—and perhaps the two planets could understand their differences.

Getting Axel back aboard the Jehad was not as much of a task as we had expected. After we blasted to the Jehad's orbit, we slid him across space between the rocket and the plasma ship without hurting him. After all, what is there in space to hurt anyone?

Axel computed our route home on the electronic calculator, and we blasted off exactly twenty-one months from the day we left the Earth.

"How about our duty shifts on the way home?" Gail asked as we were at last in space again.

"Whatever you say, my dear," I told her.

"Me? I'm not in charge."

"Axel's injured," I said, "and you're my wife. That makes you top banana."

"You fool!" she laughed. "But it'll be nicer going home than it was going away."

"Yes," said Axel. "There is enough water for all, Miss Loring."

"I wasn't thinking of the water. And you can either call me Gail or Mrs. Drake from now on. I'll never be Miss Loring again."

Axel threw back his head and laughed. "I was sure it would happen this way," he said.

THE END

If you've enjoyed this book, you will not want to miss these terrific titles...

ARMCHAIR SCI-FI & HORROR DOUBLE NOVELS, $12.95 each

D-11   **PERIL OF THE STARMEN** by Kris Neville
THE STRANGE INVASION by Murray Leinster

D-12   **THE STAR LORD** by Boyd Ellanby
CAPTIVES OF THE FLAME by Samuel R. Delaney

D-13   **MEN OF THE MORNING STAR** by Edmund Hamilton
PLANET FOR PLUNDER by Hal Clement and Sam Merwin, Jr.

D-14   **ICE CITY OF THE GORGON** by Chester S. Geier and Richard Shaver
WHEN THE WORLD TOTTERED by Lester Del Rey

D-15   **WORLDS WITHOUT END** by Clifford D. Simak
THE LAVENDER VINE OF DEATH by Don Wilcox

D-16   **SHADOW ON THE MOON** by Joe Gibson
ARMAGEDDON EARTH by Geoff St. Reynard

D-17   **THE GIRL WHO LOVED DEATH** by Paul W. Fairman
SLAVE PLANET by Laurence M. Janifer

D-18   **SECOND CHANCE** by J. F. Bone
MISSION TO A DISTANT STAR by Frank Belknap Long

D-19   **THE SYNDIC** by C. M. Kornbluth
FLIGHT TO FOREVER by Poul Anderson

D-20   **SOMEWHERE I'LL FIND YOU** by Milton Lesser
THE TIME ARMADA by Fox B. Holden

ARMCHAIR SCIENCE FICTION CLASSICS, $12.95 each

C-4   **CORPUS EARTHLING**
by Louis Charbonneau

C-5   **THE TIME DISSOLVER**
by Jerry Sohl

C-6   **WEST OF THE SUN**
by Edgar Pangborn

ARMCHAIR SCIENCE FICTION & HORROR GEMS SERIES, $12.95 each

G-1   **SCIENCE FICTION GEMS, Vol. One**
Isaac Asimov and others

G-2   **HORROR GEMS, Vol. One**
Carl Jacobi and others

If you've enjoyed this book, you will not want to miss these terrific titles...

ARMCHAIR SCI-FI, FANTASY, & HORROR DOUBLE NOVELS, $12.95 each

D-21 **EMPIRE OF EVIL** by Robert Arnette
THE SIGN OF THE TIGER by Alan E. Nourse & J. A. Meyer

D-22 **OPERATION SQUARE PEG** by Frank Belknap Long
ENCHANTRESS OF VENUS by Leigh Brackett

D-23 **THE LIFE WATCH** by Lester Del Rey
CREATURES OF THE ABYSS by Murray Leinster

D-24 **LEGION OF LAZARUS** by Edmond Hamilton
STAR HUNTER by Andre Norton

D-25 **EMPIRE OF WOMEN** by John Fletcher
ONE OF OUR CITIES IS MISSING by Irving Cox

D-26 **THE WRONG SIDE OF PARADISE** by Raymond F. Jones
THE INVOLUNTARY IMMORTALS by Rog Phillips

D-27 **EARTH QUARTER** by Damon Knight
ENVOY TO NEW WORLDS by Keith Laumer

D-28 **SLAVES TO THE METAL HORDE** by Milton Lesser
HUNTERS OUT OF TIME by Joseph E. Kelleam

D-29 **RX JUPITER SAVE US** by Ward Moore
BEWARE THE USURPERS by Geoff St. Reynard

D-30 **SECRET OF THE SERPENT** by Don Wilcox
CRUSADE ACROSS THE VOID by Dwight V. Swain

ARMCHAIR SCIENCE FICTION CLASSICS, $12.95 each

C-7 **THE SHAVER MYSTERY, Book One**
by Richard S. Shaver

C-8 **THE SHAVER MYSTERY, Book Two**
by Richard S. Shaver

C-9 **MURDER IN SPACE** by David V. Reed
by David V. Reed

ARMCHAIR MASTERS OF SCIENCE FICTION SERIES, $16.95 each

M-3 **MASTERS OF SCIENCE FICTION, Vol. Three**
Robert Sheckley, "The Perfect Woman" and other tales

M-4 **MASTERS OF SCIENCE FICTION, Vol. Four**
Mack Reynolds, "Stowaway" and other tales

If you've enjoyed this book, you will not want to miss these terrific titles...

ARMCHAIR SCI-FI & HORROR DOUBLE NOVELS, $12.95 each

D-31   **A HOAX IN TIME** by Keith Laumer
INSIDE EARTH by Poul Anderson

D-32   **TERROR STATION** by Dwight V. Swain
THE WEAPON FROM ETERNITY by Dwight V. Swain

D-33   **THE SHIP FROM INFINITY** by Edmond Hamilton
TAKEOFF by C. M. Kornbluth

D-34   **THE METAL DOOM** by David H. Keller
TWELVE TIMES ZERO by Howard Browne

D-35   **HUNTERS OUT OF SPACE** by Joseph Kelleam
INVASION FROM THE DEEP by Paul W. Fairman,

D-36   **THE BEES OF DEATH** by Robert Moore Williams
A PLAGUE OF PYTHONS by Frederick Pohl

D-37   **THE LORDS OF QUARMALL** by Fritz Leiber and Harry Fischer
BEACON TO ELSEWHERE by James H. Schmitz

D-38   **BEYOND PLUTO** by John S. Campbell
ARTERY OF FIRE by Thomas N. Scortia

D-39   **SPECIAL DELIVERY** by Kris Neville
NO TIME FOR TOFFEE by Charles F. Meyers

D-40   **RECALLED TO LIFE** by Robert Silverberg
JUNGLE IN THE SKY by Milton Lesser

ARMCHAIR SCIENCE FICTION CLASSICS, $12.95 each

C-10   **MARS IS MY DESTINATION**
by Frank Belknap Long

C-11   **SPACE PLAGUE**
by George O. Smith

C-12   **SO SHALL YE REAP**
by Rog Phillips

ARMCHAIR SCIENCE FICTION & HORROR GEMS SERIES, $12.95 each

G-3   **SCIENCE FICTION GEMS, Vol. Two**
James Blish and others

G-4   **HORROR GEMS, Vol. Two**
Joseph Payne Brennan and others

If you've enjoyed this book, you will not want to miss these terrific titles...

ARMCHAIR SCI-FI, FANTASY, & HORROR DOUBLE NOVELS, $12.95 each

D-41   **FULL CYCLE** by Clifford D. Simak
IT WAS THE DAY OF THE ROBOT by Frank Belknap Long

D-42   **THIS CROWDED EARTH** by Robert Bloch
REIGN OF THE TELEPUPPETS by Daniel Galouye

D-43   **THE CRISPIN AFFAIR** by Jack Sharkey
THE RED HELL OF JUPITER by Paul Ernst

D-44   **PLANET OF DREAD** by Dwight V. Swain
WE THE MACHINE by Gerald Vance

D-45   **THE STAR HUNTER** by Edmond Hamilton
THE ALIEN by Raymond F. Jones

D-46   **WORLD OF IF** by Rog Phillips
SLAVE RAIDERS FROM MERCURY by Don Wilcox

D-47   **THE ULTIMATE PERIL** by Robert Abernathy
PLANET OF SHAME by Bruce Elliot

D-48   **THE FLYING EYES** by J. Hunter Holly
SOME FABULOUS YONDER by Phillip Jose Farmer

D-49   **THE COSMIC BUNGLARS** by Geoff St. Reynard
THE BUTTONED SKY by Geoff St. Reynard

D-50   **TYRANTS OF TIME** by Milton Lesser
PARIAH PLANET by Murray Leinster

ARMCHAIR SCIENCE FICTION CLASSICS, $12.95 each

C-13   **SUNKEN WORLD**
by Stanton A. Coblentz

C-14   **THE LAST VIAL**
by Sam McClatchie, M. D.

C-15   **WE WHO SURVIVED (THE FIFTH ICE AGE)**
by Sterling Noel

ARMCHAIR MASTERS OF SCIENCE FICTION SERIES, $16.95 each

MS-5   **MASTERS OF SCIENCE FICTION, Vol. Five**
Winston K. Marks—Test Colony and other tales

MS-6   **MASTERS OF SCIENCE FICTION, Vol. Six**
Fritz Leiber—Deadly Moon and other tales